SITTING MURDER

A Lancashire Detective Mystery

A. J. WRIGHT

ENDEAVOURINK

AN ENDEAVOUR INK PAPERBACK

First published in 2017

This paperback edition published in 2017
by Endeavour Ink
Endeavour Ink is an imprint of Endeavour Press Ltd
Endeavour Press, 85-87 Borough High Street,
London, SE1 1NH

ISBN 978-1-911445-50-0

Typeset in Garamond 11.75/15.5 pt by
Palimpsest Book Production Limited, Falkirk, Stirlingshire

Printed and bound in Great Britain by
Clays Ltd, St Ives plc

www.endeavourpress.com

For Jenny

ACKNOWLEDGEMENTS

Once again I should like to thank my agent, Sara Keane, of the Keane Kataria Literary Agency for her unstinting support and encouragement.

I should also like to express my thanks to Alice Rees and the team at Endeavour Ink. I owe Miranda Summers-Pritchard a particular debt of gratitude for her amazingly meticulous editing of the novel. She made many sensible suggestions that greatly enhanced the quality of the manuscript.

CONTENTS

"Blest is the corpse the rain fell on,
Blest the bride on whom the sun shone"

PROLOGUE

Wigan. 1894.

Alice Goodway sat by her dying husband's bedside for three long days and nights, courtesy of Mr Draper, the colliery owner. He had insisted that the management at Wigan Infirmary provide a private room.

'The least I can do, Mrs Goodway,' he'd said when it became clear that Jack Goodway was the sole survivor from the blast. Mines Rescue had found him beneath a mound of coal, and the only reason he hadn't died instantly, like the twenty-two others down there, was the thick prop that had wedged itself inches from his face and taken much of the weight from the collapsed roof. Nevertheless, the injuries he had sustained, especially to the head, had given the doctors no cause for optimism. Their bland comments containing such phrases as . . . there's always hope . . . never give up . . . we cannot discount the possibility of recovery . . . sounded hollow and formulaic. But

it was from their eyes that Alice got the truth: it was simply a matter of time.

Sometimes he would come round, gaze at the flaked plaster of the ceiling, and say a few words. She leaned forward, clasped his bandaged hand and cherished it like some badly wounded bird as she strained to hear what he was trying to say. Once, he spoke with some clarity, describing a day in the woods, the two of them lying by a rippling brook and smelling the wild roses that grew all around them.

He spoke in hushed tones, as if it had been an almost mystical moment between two people so much in love, and he whispered her name over and over, like some incantation in church.

She had sobbed uncontrollably at that. And she had cursed God.

Sometimes Father Clooney took her place, for Jack had at one time been a great believer in the sanctity of the Holy Church. In his lucid moments, she could see clearly, not just from his words but from the resigned expression on his ravaged face, that he knew that Death was getting ever closer, and when he turned to look at Alice, there were often tears in his eyes. Still, she knew the priest's presence brought him comfort. There were other times when he was drifting so badly in and out of consciousness that it was clear he had no idea to whom he was talking in his ramblings: his confessor or his wife. From time to time he would ask if anyone else could smell the wild roses.

'So strong . . . makes me feel dizzy . . .'

Their final conversation lasted longer, and he spoke with great difficulty, his chest rasping and his words punctured by painful, laboured coughing. Once, he called Alice 'Father' and began the Act of Contrition, but she leaned close to him and told him, between

2

sobs, that she had no power to cleanse his soul. She could feel the heat of his foul breath as he poured forth his passionate feelings, compounded of love, regret, guilt and a desperate plea to her, to God and to the whole world for forgiveness.

'He is cleansing his soul,' Father Clooney had whispered. 'Getting it ready for Heaven.'

She heard it all, and she knew that those final words of Jack's would stay with her until she herself died. Then, in the early evening, his life drew to its dribbling and devastating end. When she heard his last breath – long and rattling – she buried her head, cursing God and all the unfairness of life and refused to pray, even when Father Clooney came down from the ward to comfort her.

Later, after the priest had escorted her home, she spent her first night alone.

She hadn't slept, of course. There were too many memories swarming inside her head like a hive of bees violently shaken, the honey destroyed and the stings many and painful. But in the dull grey of morning, she rose and moved to the window, where a bird was whistling on the window ledge outside. It stood there, its head cocked to one side, and stared at her defiantly, issuing a sharp chirrup but remaining where it was. She turned away, and with the drizzly light fighting its way into the room, she caught a glimpse of herself in the looking glass, where the black crape covering the glass – her final act before climbing into bed – had somehow slipped down to reveal a sliver of reflection in the centre. Nothing but pale, sickly features stared back.

Then she caught her breath. Watched herself slowly bring a hand to her throat as if she were finding it difficult to breathe.

She glanced around the small room, looked up at the half-open curtains that hung limp and undisturbed by any breeze sneaking through the locked frames. She noticed the window sill was empty now. The bird had gone. Then she turned back to the mirror and looked into her wild eyes.

That was when it all began.

Chapter One

There were three people sitting around the small table, their eyes fixed on the bare candle flame that swayed gently to and fro. There was no other light in the room, for the curtains had been drawn and their thickness kept out the dim glare of the gaslight across the street. No fire was lit, thus avoiding the accidental flicker of shadows that might take the group's attention away from the flare of the flame. Thin wisps of smoke drifted upwards, but once they left the wick of the candle, they quickly vanished into the darkness that pressed on them, leaving only the acrid smell and the occasional sizzle from the molten wax.

'I'm bloody freezin'!' said one of them, an old woman whose face, weathered and creased, looked even paler than normal in the feeble glow from the candle's flame. 'Tha'd best be doin' or I'm off.'

The one she addressed her comments to sat as she had

done for the last ten minutes, with her head bowed low, her hands clasped together on the table as if in prayer. She said nothing, but the woman seated to her right, sharp-eyed and with a firm set to her jaw, leaned towards the old woman and hissed, 'She's not a bloody dog in a side show, Peggy. Sometimes nothin' happens. Sometimes our Jack comes. It's not our Alice's fault. Spirits are a law unto themselves.'

Old Peggy Clayforth sniffed. She'd lost her husband, Matthew, two years ago when the black lung took him, and since then she'd become used to the solitude of her tiny terraced house, glad of the company of neighbours when they called round but equally glad when they shut the door on the way out. It took a while for the pungent aroma of his pipe smoke to fade and finally leave the house, even though his memory was brought back on occasion whenever she walked past a pub and caught the whiff of tobacco drifting into the night.

The silence of her house, enhanced by the sizzle and crack of the coals as the flames took hold, the hollow *tock* of the grandfather clock in the corner, the creak of the rafters in the attic: all of these sounds were like the comfort of a blanket to old Peggy, reminders of a solitariness she had become used to and even treasured. Sometimes, she even imagined he was lying beside her in the still of the night and willed herself to hear once more the harsh rasp of his breathing in the darkened room.

But recently, she had noticed that something was wrong. At first, she dismissed it as the onset of a cold, the harsh, racking cough that is soon followed by sniffles and shivers and soreness in the throat. But when she saw flecks of blood in her phlegm, the bright red spots in the handkerchief, then she knew that something was wrong and it would never be right again.

All of which put her in mind of death. She was shocked to discover that since those dark days when Matthew had died and she'd spent some time grieving and wearing the customary black, she hadn't really given death much thought. All she knew was that she had to plough onwards, sit in the same pew each week at Mass and utter the same words of Forgiveness and Salvation so often that they lost any meaning they once had for her and became mere recitations. True, she was always willing to call upon the recently bereaved to offer her condolences and advice borne of her own widowhood, but such visits were prompted by an innate goodness that had little to do with the religion she paid lip service to every week.

Now, though, she realised that her time was fast approaching, and she began to sense the awesomeness of what she would soon face. And so, when she heard from Jack's aunt Doris that young Alice Goodway had suddenly developed the Gift, she wondered if by some miracle it might be possible for her to speak once more with her dear departed Matthew – if there were solace to be had from the other side, then he would bring it to her. He was always good like that. Besides, Matthew and Jack Goodway had worked together down the pit, Matthew having taken young Jack under his wing when he first went down.

'*Happen they've bumped into each other, like,*' Peggy had mused in justification of her visit, '*on t'other side.*'

Her neighbours had sniffed and told her what a waste of time it would be. '*When you're dead you're dead, Peggy, love. Comes to us all in th'end.*'

Still, they'd asked her to call in and tell them how she'd gone on *wi' all that nonsense.*

She was beginning to think they were right, when suddenly, Alice Goodway raised her head, her eyes wide open and catching the sparkle from the candle's flame.

'I can hear you, Jack!' she said with a rise in her voice.

'Is my Matthew with him?' Peggy was now leaning forward, her skeletal hands clasped together.

'Aye,' said Alice. 'Matthew's here all right. He's a bit distant though.'

'Always was a funny bugger if he didn't know you,' said Peggy.

Alice shook her head. 'I mean he's faint. Far off.'

'Tell him it's me. Peggy.'

Alice frowned and said, 'He knows it's you. He can see you.'

Quickly the old woman's eyes flitted around the room. Dark shadows lurked everywhere.

'Do you want to ask him a question?'

Now that the moment was here, Peggy found herself both tongue-tied and embarrassed.

Doris Goodway, Jack's aunt, reached across and touched the old woman on the arm. 'Best get your question in quick-like,' she said in a hoarse whisper, 'in case he buggers off. They don't tend to 'ang around for long.'

Peggy took a deep breath and said in a loud voice, 'How's your chest, Matthew?'

Doris shook her head, but Alice didn't flinch.

'He says he has no need of one now.'

Peggy blinked, gazed down at her claw-like hands. 'Will you be there, Matthew? Waitin'? When I come?'

For a few moments, Alice turned her head, as if straining to hear something. Then she said, 'He says he'll wait. But there's no rush. In your own sweet time. That's what he says. He's . . . he's growing fainter . . .'

Doris put an arm around Alice's shoulder as her head fell forward onto her chest, eyes now tightly closed.

'Is that it?' Peggy asked, disbelief and disappointment in her voice. She'd expected far more for the money.

'When our Alice drops off like this, it means she's lost all contact with the ones on t'other side. Our Jack brings 'em, an' our Jack takes 'em away.'

The old woman pursed her lips.

Suddenly Doris pushed back her chair and stood up. 'We'd best leave her now. Doesn't do to wake her after she's been in touch.' She moved quickly to the dresser and picked up the oil lamp resting there. There was a scratching

9

sound, a match flared briefly, and she lit the wick. Shadows seemed to scurry away now as the room regained its dull normality.

Peggy was about to say something but shook her head instead. She too stood up and turned for the front door.

'You forgettin' summat?' said Doris, a sudden sharpness in her voice.

Puzzlement gave way to understanding when she saw the woman's outstretched palm. She reached into her pocket and pulled out a sixpence, placing it none too gently in Doris's hand. Then she opened the door and was about to step outside when she heard Alice's voice behind her. She stopped and turned. Alice was staring at her.

'What did you say?' Peggy asked.

Doris, standing beside her with one hand on the door-knob, was frowning.

This time, when Alice spoke, her voice was frail, and cracked. 'He forgot summat. Said to tell you where he hid it.'

Now it was Peggy's turn to frown. 'Hid what?'

'His briar.'

All of a sudden, Peggy felt light-headed. 'How . . . ? I've looked high an' low for that bloody thing.'

'It's . . . at the . . . bottom . . . of the . . . clock.' Alice's voice faded and once again her head drooped.

Peggy took a deep breath and swayed a little before speaking. 'Well, by the bloody 'ell!' she said with the beginnings of a smile appearing on her face. 'By the *bloody* 'ell!'

She pulled her shawl tight around her shoulders and almost skipped through the doorway.

Once Peggy had gone, Doris closed the door behind her and sat down facing her niece by marriage.

Alice lifted her head. 'I think I need a lie down.'

'What did you tell the old fool that for?'

'What?'

'About some mouldy old pipe?'

'I thought she might want it. You know, as a reminder.'

'And what if old Matthew had put summat else at the bottom of that clock, eh?'

Alice frowned. 'Such as?'

'I don't bloody know but it's too late anyroad 'cos that old buzzard'll be scratchin' around 'avin' a look. Could've hid summat worth hidin'. Like a gold watch. He was always an old fool, Matthew Clayforth, and not short of a bit of brass either.'

Alice sighed and made to stand up. 'That all you think about, Doris? Is money the be all an' the end all?'

Doris reached out and clutched at her arm, pulling her back down.

'You're a bloody fool, Alice. A bloody fool.'

*

Swann Street, where Peggy Clayforth lived, lay in the shadow of Victoria Cotton Mill, a large and imposing edifice a few minutes' walk from Wallgate and the centre of Wigan. As Peggy made her way home, she passed small groups of mill workers wending their way home for tea, their heads and shoulders draped with shawls and swinging empty snap baskets from side to side, their giggling an audible sign of the sheer relief of being out in the fresh air and away from the musty confines of the weaving rooms.

Peggy allowed herself a wan smile, casting her mind back to a time when she too had been like them – arm in arm, carefree, making some poor chap's working day uncomfortable with their tittering and their mee-mawing. It was a lifetime ago now.

One or two of them gave her a nod as she pushed open her front door. Once she'd closed it again, she heard the chatter and the merriment fade into silence as the girls turned the corner into York Street.

She gave a long, slow sigh and removed her coat, hanging it on the peg behind the door. Then she stood and gazed at the grandfather clock over in the corner of the front room, heard its familiar *tock-tock* and took a deep breath before stooping before it.

'Like bloody prayin',' she said to herself. Her hand was shaking as she reached for the small key in the lock.

She turned the key and swung the oak door open. A musty, metallic odour crept from its innards. The rusted chain was hanging from above, the heavy iron pendulum hanging squat and swinging slowly in the darkness. She leaned forward and tried to peer inside, but the angle and the darkness made it impossible to make out what – if anything – was resting at the bottom of the wooden casing. There was nothing for it but to reach inside and feel around.

At first, all she got for her trouble was a smearing of dust specks and tiny splinters of wood, some of which were sharp and made her wince. But then she pressed her hand against the right-sided wall of the frame and immediately gave a gasp.

It felt like . . .

With great care, she kept her hand pressed against the clock's frame, slowly dragging the object upwards until it came into sight. Gingerly, and with both hands trembling now, she lifted the briar pipe from the inside of the clock and stared at it in wonder. How on earth had young Alice known about this?

Then she blew away the dust, lifted its curved bowl to her nose and took a deep, deep breath.

And prayed for real this time.

*

Word soon began to spread. Alice Goodway could tell you things nobody else knew about. Nobody still living, that is. Peggy Clayforth took the briar pipe with her wherever she went, knowing full well that once the conversation got round to the young widow in Vere Street, she had actual evidence in her possession that would quickly silence the doubters. She merely had to pluck it from her bag and point to it, imbuing the mouldy object with all the sanctity of a saintly relic.

In a real sense, too, the discovery of Matthew's old pipe gave her a new lease of life, or a sense of one, at least. It reinforced her belief in what was to come once she passed away; it gave her something definite to look forward to – a post-mortem reunion with the man she had spent so much of her life with; and it removed at a stroke the lingering terror of the unknown.

Death wasn't an end after all.

For Alice, too, things had changed. The raw feelings of frustration and anger she had suffered after Jack's death in the pit explosion were assuaged to some degree by her new-found popularity. To Doris, her niece seemed remarkably stubborn, for there were those who meekly called to ask for a sitting and were firmly refused by Alice, who merely said that she could feel no connection with them. It was like throwing money into the canal. True, there hadn't been the rush to her door that Doris had predicted – little more than a handful so far – but that was simply because most folk were afraid, and it was one thing spreading word that Alice Goodway had a rare gift, but it was quite another to try things out for yourself.

For Doris Goodway, Alice's constant companion during the *sittings* as they called them, the weeks since old Peggy Clayforth's visit had caused her to rescind her earlier admonition; as a result of the old woman's testimonials, people were now talking, and some were willing to hand over money. Doris had suggested that ninepence was now the going rate for a sitting because of what she termed 'increased administration costs', although she responded vaguely when asked for more details, and, as she saw herself as an indispensable part of the mystic proceedings, she felt justified in retaining fifty per cent of all monies earned.

But it went against the grain to turn folk away.

*

There was a special bond between Alice Goodway and Hazel Aspinall. Their husbands, of course, had worked together in the same pit, drank and got drunk together in the same pubs, and each had acted as best man for the other. Both died in the pit blast three months ago.

Such closeness had prompted Doris to declare, quite unexpectedly, that she didn't think it a good idea for Hazel to attend one of Alice's sittings. The request had come not from Hazel herself but from her mother-in-law, Mabel Aspinall, who firmly believed in the existence of the spirit world and who had taken her son's tragic death very badly. In her desire to make contact with the spirit of her dead son, she had sought comfort from a number of sources, none of them to do with the church, and each time she had come away feeling frustrated but convinced that the next one she consulted would possess the key to unlocking her son's spirit. She had spotted Alice in the street and, after a halting and stilted conversation, the suggestion had been made and the request granted.

But only if Hazel agrees, Alice had insisted. Mabel, a

woman of a strong and persuasive nature, had cajoled Hazel into coming with her, using the simple argument that if Bert were to be present, he'd only become agitated if his wife hadn't bothered to show her face.

When she heard of the proposed visit, Doris had sniffed into her mug of tea. She and Mabel Aspinall did not get along.

'But if I can bring 'em comfort, Aunty Doris, where's the harm?'

'Doesn't seem right. Not with them two – Jack an' Bert – bein' so friendly, like.'

'But that's all the more reason why Hazel should come. If she hears Bert's with Jack an' he's doin' all right, it'll stop her gettin' so upset. She's been down in the dumps an' nothin' I say'll drag her out of it. Happen this is what she needs. Same with Bert's mam.'

Doris took a long sip of her tea. It was clear she had grave reservations about this proposed sitting. Still, faced with Alice's obvious desire to do what she could for her friend, she decided to let the matter rest.

When they arrived, Doris answered the knock. Although she swung the door wide open for them both to enter, the sour expression on her face contained no welcome.

Within minutes, the four of them were sitting around the small kitchen table where a handful of dried rose petals lay scattered around a solitary candle. Its flames seemed to delight in lighting up the colour of the petals making them seem for a few seconds vibrant and fresh.

'I love the scent,' Alice said, indicating the rose petals. 'It helps me relax. Get ready. And roses were Jack's favourite.'

Hazel lowered her head. It was her mother-in-law who said, 'Aye well, my lad never 'ad time for flowers or anythin' like that. Not many blokes do, come to that.'

Alice smiled away the implied insult to her husband.

'He's got all the time in the world now, though, Mabel, eh?' Doris pointed out with a smile as sweet as the scent from the rose petals.

Before Mabel had time to retort, Alice raised both hands in the air. 'It's my Jack! I can feel him.'

The room fell silent.

Alice closed her eyes, a frown of deep concentration creasing her forehead. For a few moments her lips moved, ever so slightly, but no sound emanated from them.

Hazel's eyes remained downcast, but her mother-in-law glanced quickly round the room. The curtains were drawn, and the small kitchen seemed suddenly filled with shadows.

Then Alice gave a slow nod and said, 'Jack says Bert's with him.'

Mabel placed a hand against her mouth, her eyes wide and tearful.

'Is he all right?' she asked.

Alice nodded.

'Tell him his mam's thinkin' about him. Tell him . . .'

But Alice said suddenly, 'What's that?' She was straining to listen. 'Aye. Aye, I'll tell her, but . . . All right, Jack, no need to shout.' She blinked her eyes open and looked at Hazel. 'Bert's got somethin' he wants to tell you . . . He says you'd best tell his mam. It's gone on long enough.'

Hazel went pale and licked her lips.

'Tell me what?' Mabel asked, sitting bolt upright and looking at her daughter-in-law.

Hazel raised her head and said nothing, but tears were beginning to glimmer in her eyes. 'There's nothin' to tell.'

Again, Alice raised her hands and closed her eyes. 'Aye, Jack, they smell lovely. Just like them wild roses from that place in the woods.'

'Will you shut up about them bloody roses! What's our Bert talkin' about?' Mabel said with greater insistence this time.

There was the sound of sobbing now from Hazel.

Mabel tutted. 'Don't waste time talkin' about the bloody roses, woman! Ask my Bert what he means. Tell me what?'

Alice once more strained to listen. Then she nodded and said, 'Bert says he hopes the little bugger looks like him.'

Mabel gasped as Hazel's head drooped once more. She stared at her daughter-in-law with an expression that was a compound of shock and hope.

'What little bugger?'

*

The young man who stood at Alice Goodway's front door was well dressed, his suit dark and sombre. He raised his bowler hat and introduced himself to a suspicious Doris Goodway.

'Lucas Wesley,' he said. His voice was low, respectful.

Doris, standing in the doorway like some terraced Cerberus, eyed him shrewdly. His sharp pointed nose had tiny blue veins on either side, and his narrow cheeks seemed smooth and fresh below eyes that were rimmed with a redness that came from either the growing chill outside or some colder, inner sadness. His hairline was receding, which made him look somewhat older than he was.

'Aye. What do you want?'

'I live in Taylor Street,' he said and paused, as if that were enough to gain her trust.

'So?'

He gave a wan smile. 'In the next street to Mrs Clayforth. Peggy Clayforth.'

'So?' Doris looked beyond him, could see the tiny flecks of snow against the dim glow of the gas lamp.

'I came across Mrs Clayforth in the butcher's. I couldn't help overhearing what she was saying about Alice Goodway. I presume you're her aunt?'

'Her late husband's aunt, matter o' fact.'

'Well, then. Mrs Clayforth told all and sundry how Alice helped her. Concerning her late husband.'

Doris leaned against the door and shook her head. The man's suit, his collar and tie, made her suspicious. She'd had some experience with officialdom, none of it favourable. For a moment she wondered if he were an Inspector of Fraud, if there were such a thing. 'Our Alice isn't feelin' very well.'

'Oh dear.'

'An' she's not doin' any more sittin's. Not for a bit.'

The man looked crestfallen. 'I see. I was hoping . . .'

'Sorry,' said Doris, stepping back to close the front door.

'If it's a matter of money?' There was a pleading note in his voice.

Doris gave him a sharp look. Her interest was piqued.

'I'm sorry,' he said quickly. 'I didn't mean to give offence.'

'Our Alice needs rest,' she explained, but her tone had changed from suspicion to apology.

'Of course. If I came back another time?'

Despite the cold, she took a few steps towards him, causing him to step back in alarm. She pulled 'the door to behind her and leaned towards him. 'I'll 'ave to speak with her.'

'I see.'

'But she's not cheap, y'see? She's 'ad to put her prices up. On account o' demand.'

'I understand. How much?'

Doris took a deep breath, cast a quick glance behind her and said in a whisper, 'A pound.'

Lucas Wesley's eyes widened. He stroked his tie. 'I wasn't expecting to pay so much.'

'Well that's the rate. We've overheads, you see. An' if you want the best . . .'

In spite of the flash of disbelief on his face, it took him only a few seconds to make his decision. 'Agreed.'

'And you pay me. I manage all finances. Alice mustn't be bothered wi' such things.'

'Of course not.'

'Well then,' she said, holding out her hand. 'If you'd like to pay in advance I can arrange for a sittin' tomorrow. Five o'clock?'

He stared down at the upturned palm then reached into his pocket and withdrew his wallet. He took out the agreed sum, paid her then bade her good day.

As she closed the door, she reflected how everything was going very smoothly indeed.

Until two days later, when the first of the letters arrived.

Chapter Two

Constable Jaggery lunged for the woman and managed to grab her by the hair a split second before she could gouge out the magistrate's eye.

Until then, the hearing had passed without incident. Jaggery had given his report, relating how on Saturday night he had occasion to intervene in a scuffle between two women in Hardybutts, Scholes. He had been drawn there by the loud and loathsome language emanating from the mouths of the two women, language that shocked the constable to his very core. Once on the scene, he had managed to negotiate a cessation of hostilities, and even considered letting the two combatants off with a stern warning, when out of the blue – or more accurately out of the nearest house – Bridget Dillon ran into the middle of the road and hammered one of the women with the underside of her clog, screaming, 'That's my sister, you bitch!'

Left with no option but to grab the offensive weapon and arrest the assailant, Jaggery had dragged her down to the station in King Street, submitted the bloodstained clog as evidence to a bewildered desk sergeant and left her to rue her actions in the cells below street level. All that remained was the court appearance and a straightforward statement of the facts, followed later on by a well-earned pint in The Crofter's Arms.

But Bridget Dillon had other ideas. Nursing a sense of injustice at her treatment, that had only festered during her sojourn in the cells, she decided to vent her disgust with the justice system by removing – or attempting to remove – the eye of the chief magistrate who had just fined her ten shillings for assault. Only Constable Jaggery stood between the unfortunate official and blindness.

Once she had been forcibly removed by others and taken back down to the cells while another charge of assault could be prepared, the magistrates were unanimous in their praise for the constable's swift and decisive actions and promised to send a note of commendation to the chief constable, Captain Bell.

Later, in the police canteen, as he regaled a small group of younger constables and reminded them of the importance of remaining vigilant at all times, the door swung open and Detective Sergeant Michael Brennan stood in the doorway.

'When you've a minute, Constable Jaggery,' he said with a frown.

Jaggery mumbled something Brennan couldn't quite catch and left his audience to their mugs of tea.

'Yes, Sergeant?' he said once they were alone in the narrow corridor.

'I hear you've been throwing your weight about in the magistrates' court?'

Jaggery searched his sergeant's face for any trace of irony. He found none.

'I've been doin' me duty, Sergeant, if that's what you mean.'

'Glad to hear it. Now perhaps you'll help me do mine.'

'How d'ye mean?'

'We've had reports of a woman getting some sort of threat.'

'Off her 'usband?'

Brennan gave a cold smile. 'Unlikely, Constable. In fact, I'd say impossible.'

Before Jaggery could question his statement, Brennan had turned on his heel and was marching swiftly down the corridor.

*

Brennan's first impression of Doris Goodway wasn't a favourable one. He knew, from the brief time he'd been speaking with both Alice Goodway and her late husband's aunt, that the young widow was still suffering grievously from her tragic loss of three months ago. Yet her way of coping with such grief was quite a novel one, he thought. She had spent much of the intervening time meeting a number of people in what the aunt referred to as *sittings* and claiming to have been granted the ability to speak with the spirits of the dead.

Bloody nonsense.

It was clear, however, that Doris Goodway had quite an influence over her niece. It wasn't just the way she stood over her at the kitchen table with one hand pressed on her shoulder, the pressure increasing subtly whenever Alice began to falter in her responses; nor the occasional interruption if she thought Alice was giving an ambiguous comment; it was more the way she seemed anxious to make sure that he accepted the genuineness of what they were doing, a service to their fellow neighbours at great emotional expense.

He thought perhaps that the young widow, in her fragile state of mind, had been coerced into such hocus-pocus, although the aunt made it clear that it had been Alice, and not herself, who had the final say in who came for a sitting and who didn't.

He looked at the two women and the contrast between them had nothing to do with age. If there was a hardness bordering on callousness about Doris Goodway's features, there was a softness, almost a gentleness, about Alice. Her cheeks were pale, but the unblemished smoothness of her skin gave an impression of vulnerability matched by the way she returned his gaze.

'There's some she can't do anythin' for,' said Doris. 'They don't like it, but as Alice says, if there's nothin' comin' through there's nothin' comin' through. And that's what I'm allus here for,' said Doris, 'watchin' as nobody takes advantage. She's been through enough, without that.'

'I can see that, Mrs Goodway.'

Constable Jaggery was standing by the doorway that opened onto a small yard, an oval metal tub hanging from a nail behind the door. For several seconds he stared hard at Alice then turned his attention to the aunt and sniffed. It was clear that he too had formed a less than favourable impression of her.

'You sent word to the station that Alice here had been threatened?'

'That's right.' She folded her arms, a gesture of defiance that seemed to dare him to contradict. 'Only she tried to stop me reportin' it.'

Brennan, facing young Alice across the small table in the kitchen, addressed his next remarks to her. 'Who's been threatening you, Alice?'

She looked at him, and he could see her eyes glistening with tears.

'I don't know,' she replied, her voice trembling.

Doris Goodway gave an exasperated grunt. 'Whoever he is, he needs findin' and lockin' up.'

'What exactly did they say?'

Alice dabbed her eyes with a handkerchief. Then she stood up and moved to a small dresser, where a few plates rested on the lower shelf, and a small framed photograph took pride of place in the centre of the uppermost shelf. Brennan noticed the two people's stern expressions: the bride standing with her right hand on her husband's shoulder, while Jack Goodway himself was seated. Despite the dour expression on his face, he was a handsome devil, thought Brennan.

She placed her hand behind the photograph and drew forth an envelope, which she brought back to the table with a trembling hand.

Brennan took it from her. The envelope said simply *The Goodway Woman.* He took out a single sheet of paper, and read the few words it contained:

'*Lying lips are an abomination to the Lord.*'

The handwriting was small and neat.

'Where did you find this?' he asked.

'It were me wot found it,' the aunt snapped. 'Shoved through yon letterbox.'

'You don't recognise the handwriting?'

Doris gave a sharp laugh. 'Who the hell sends letters round here when we all live in the same bloody midden? Besides, I've a bloody good idea who's responsible.'

'And who's that?'

'That toffee-nosed sod Crankshaw.'

The name was familiar.

'Not Mr Ralph Crankshaw? Works for the council?'

'Aye. That's the one. Walks round these streets all high an' bloody mighty. Inspector of Nuisances. That's a laugh when he's nothin' but a bloody nuisance hisself.'

Now he remembered. Mr Crankshaw was a source of annoyance to the local constabulary, carrying out his duties as the council's Inspector of Nuisances with an almost evangelical fervour, reporting all and sundry for the slightest contravention of the local by-laws. For some reason, he was highly regarded by the mayor and the town council.

'What makes you think he sent this?'

She folded her arms. 'Let's just say we've 'ad a few run-ins, me an' his lordship.'

'I'll look into it.' He looked across at Alice, who had resumed her seat opposite. 'I don't suppose you can tell me anything about this? It seems like a quotation from the Bible.'

Before she could respond, Doris Goodway snorted. 'All we know is it's a threat. Bible or no bloody Bible.'

Jaggery gave a sharp cough. *Blasphemy*, said the expression on his face.

Brennan shook his head and put the letter and the envelope into his pocket. 'It's not actually a threat, Mrs Goodway.'

'What the hell is it then? Invitation to a ball?'

Suddenly Alice slammed her fist down hard on the table. Doris bent forward but Alice pushed her away. He could see that, beneath the widow's calm exterior, there was worry beneath the surface.

'No, Sergeant,' she said. '*I* don't know who sent it. Does it matter? It means nothin'. Just some busybody with nothin' better to do.' She took a deep breath, an attempt, thought Brennan, both to rein in her emotions and to gather her thoughts.

She went on, her voice more harnessed now. 'For the last few months I've been speakin' to the dead.' She paused before adding in a low, resigned tone, 'Happen I only think I 'ave.'

'Alice!' Doris's voice was filled with alarm and warning.

'I've 'ad enough, Aunty Doris! Enough!' She calmed herself down, but only with an effort. 'What if it's all up here, eh? What if I'm just hearin' things that's not there? Seein' stuff that can't be? Father Clooney says it's just the grief after what 'appened to my Jack.'

Doris sneered. 'Father Clooney! Just a jealous old buzzard.'

'Jealous?' Brennan repeated. 'Why is that?' Father Clooney was his parish priest, too, a figure venerated throughout the area, and he felt it incumbent on him to give some show of resentment at the aunt's tone.

'Because our Alice can get in touch wi' the dead an' all 'e can do is *pray* for 'em.'

She pronounced the word as if it were an obscenity.

Before he could respond, Alice spoke once more. 'An' there's folk comin' round here desperate to speak with a loved one again. I might've upset someone bad enough for 'em to . . .' She raised a hand and pointed to Brennan's pocket. 'It'd only be natural if they got upset. And if it helps them to call me a liar, well . . .'

Doris flicked a glance at Brennan before speaking. 'That's daft. All these folk who've come an' listened, all the things you've told 'em – they're things they know come from them as has passed away.'

Alice clasped and unclasped her hands. 'When my Jack were alive, he used to tell me things – all sorts o' stuff folk told him in private. He'd come 'ome an' tell me an' all. There were no secrets between me an' my Jack. Happen I just *imagine* I can hear Jack's voice. When all it were was me rememberin' all the things he'd told me.' Then she stabbed a finger against her temple. 'It's just . . . I can *feel* him. Right here wi' me.' She paused for a while then looked at Brennan directly. 'Do you really know what happens after we die?'

'I know exactly what happens, Mrs Goodway.'

She seemed thrown by the note of certainty in Brennan's voice.

'What?' she asked.

'We get buried.'

Jaggery, still by the door, shifted his stance and coughed once more.

Doris folded her arms and made to speak, but Alice went on with a nod of the head.

'Well it might be I just made it seem as if it came from

the spirits. I just remember the stuff he told me. That might be the mystery of it all, Sergeant. A way of makin' folk feel good. Perhaps I have been lyin', eh?'

'Nothin' wrong wi' that I hope, anyroad? Makin' folk feel good,' sniffed the aunt. 'Our Alice has been performin' a service.'

Brennan gave her a cold stare. 'And charging people for the privilege.'

'Aye, well, she has t'live, poor soul.'

'Perhaps somebody didn't like what they'd been told. Perhaps they felt cheated and wanted to get back at your niece.'

'We've 'ad no complaints.'

'Apart from this.' He patted his pocket. 'Well, Alice,' said Brennan with a sigh, 'you might like to write down a list of all the folk you've . . . sat for. Along with their addresses. I can at least have a word with them all, let them see it doesn't sit well with the police when people take to writing anonymous letters.'

Doris gave a disdainful sniff. 'Waste o' time. I've already told you who sent the thing.'

'We'll do it,' Alice piped in with a defiant glance towards her aunt. 'But we'll need to put our heads together. Remember who we can. An' we've an idea where they live. Streets if not numbers.'

Brennan nodded. 'There's no need for haste,' he said in a tone that spoke volumes for the urgency – or lack thereof – with which he viewed the case.

Alice went on, as if she sensed his mood. 'It'll be a waste of your time, Sergeant. That's all. I reckon whoever wrote me that note 'as got whatever it was off his chest.'

He bowed his head, acknowledging privately that she may well be right. He wouldn't even be here at all if there was something more serious to deal with in the borough, like a murder.

Brennan turned to her aunt. 'By the way, do you live here?'

'No. But I've been stayin' here temp'ry like, since our Jack passed away.' She looked down on Alice, whose head was now lowered. 'Gives her some company. And comfort, me bein' here.'

'And where do you live?'

She hesitated for a second before replying. 'Canal Street. Near the tram depot.'

He knew the place. Not the most savoury of areas.

'And you saw no one in the street when the note landed through the letterbox?'

'It's a piece o' paper not a bloody brick! Could've been there hours.'

Brennan caught a smirk creeping its way across Jaggery's face. It quickly scurried away when their eyes met.

Brennan sighed and stood up.

Alice raised her head once more, and her voice was now a barely audible whisper. 'It's me own fault. There's things we shouldn't meddle with. Happen it's best if I put a stop to it all.'

He saw Doris Goodway stop herself from responding just in time. *This woman won't give up her golden eggs so easily*, he thought.

*

As they left Vere Street and began the long walk along Miry Lane towards Wallgate, there was a decided chill in the air. They'd had no snow yet, and the early part of November had been unseasonably mild. But the last few days had seen the temperature drop quite drastically, and, in the weak afternoon sunlight the smooth cobbles in the road had a thin, hazardous coating of frost.

Constable Jaggery had been uncharacteristically silent since they left Alice Goodway's house, trudging along with his hands tucked deep into the greatcoat he wore over his uniform.

'All this talk of ghosts and spirits, eh, Constable?' Brennan said cheerfully enough.

'It's a help to them as lose a loved one. A little 'un, specially.'

Brennan saw a dark shadow pass over his constable's face.

'My dad saw a ghost once,' said Jaggery in a tone perkier than his expression suggested.

Brennan gave him a quick look. He was somewhat surprised to see the large face, with its broken nose, firm jaw and bristling moustache, contorted into an expression of deadly earnest.

'Did he really?' Brennan tried to keep the cynicism from his voice.

'Aye. He weren't a fanciful chap, Sergeant, afore you ask. Far from it. Worked as a navvy on the railways till the cholera took most of his pals.' His voice was gruff, and low.

A rag-and-bone man, wrapped against the elements and perched on his wagon, gave them a cheery wave as he went past. Brennan returned the gesture but Jaggery ignored him.

'He'd been encamped this side o' the Pennines, building the Woodhead Up Tunnel. He were only nineteen – 1849 it were – an' he'd not met me mam then. Bit of a wild bugger, he were, I reckon. Anyroad, his best pal – a lad called Donald – took ill an' died with the cholera, an' that was that for me dad. Told the company what they could do with their job an' left the work camp, came back here.'

There was something in his tone of voice that Brennan hadn't heard before. He'd known Jaggery for several years and had the greatest respect for the man's strength and even his volatile temper, which served him well in the boxing ring and served Brennan well whenever there was a need for more persuasive – or more likely dissuasive – methods of enforcing the law. But as for his patterns of thought or reflectiveness, well, he hadn't seen much evidence. But here, in the dying light, he sensed a rare intimacy between them. So he let Jaggery carry on.

'Anyroad, he'd only been back here a month or so when he gets in bed after a few pints, goes straight to sleep – he were back livin' wi' me grandma then – an' then summat wakes him up. At first, he can't see anythin', then he gets to feelin' warm. Hot, like. An' when he sits up in bed he sees there's a fire lit. Only he had no fire, no grate, nothin' like that, in his room. So it were impossible. Not only that, he sees a figure sat next to t'fire, leanin' into it an' rubbin' his hands.'

He paused, and Brennan sensed he was waiting for some sarcasm, some mockery, but he remained silent and let him continue.

'Me dad swore it were his pal. Donald. Just sat yonder, large as life, warmin' hisself against a fire that weren't there.'

By this time they had reached the busy thoroughfare of Wallgate, where the rattle of carts and cabs and the shuttling and wheezing of a tram heading north into the town centre forced Jaggery to halt his narrative. Only when Brennan urged him to carry on did he speak again, louder this time above the din all around them.

'Me dad said Donald then turned to him an' give him a smile an' said, *I'm awreet, tha knows, I'm awreet.* Me dad thought that were odd.'

'It's certainly an unusual tale.'

But Jaggery shook his head. 'No, I don't mean odd like that, Sergeant. Me dad meant summat else. Said as it were strange, Donald sayin' that to him, on account o' Donald being Scotch.'

Brennan mulled it over. A Scottish ghost communicating in a Wigan accent?

'Perhaps your dad was asleep after all, eh?' he said in a gentler tone than the one he usually addressed his constable with. 'A dream.'

Again Jaggery shook his head. 'Dad said not. Swore not. Said as he could feel the fire, how hot it were. An' he said summat else.' Jaggery stopped and faced Brennan the way a barrister would when about to deliver a telling legal point in court.

'What was that then?'

'Said as how 'e went straight to sleep an' when 'e woke up t'next mornin', first thing he did was get up an' go over to that wall where Donald an' that fire had been. Pressed his hand against the wall – an' guess what?'

'The wall was still warm from the ghostly fire?'

Jaggery shook his head. 'No, Sergeant. It were stone cold. *Stone cold.*'

Brennan tried hard to suppress a sigh, and almost succeeded. 'But it would be cold, Constable, wouldn't it? If the fire hadn't really been there? If your dad had been dreaming after all?'

A look of triumph spread across Jaggery's face. 'Aha! That's just it, see? That wall was always warm, on account of the fact that it was directly above the coal fire in the front room downstairs. A chimney wall. An' me grandma had a blazin' fire goin' an' all. *So why was a wall as is normally warm, cold as stone, eh*? Answer me that!' He paused dramatically before adding pointedly, '*Detective Sergeant?*'

*

Brennan had intended to make a brief note of his visit to Alice Goodway and then finish for the day. He had no time for silly women who dabbled in séances and whatnot – dead was dead and that was the end of it. He'd read about such things and had marvelled at the human capacity for self-deception, for desperately clinging to the hope offered by fake mediums and those who preyed on the gullible and the recently – or not so recently – bereaved. He'd read, too, of the so-called *messages* the so-called *spirits* had sent through some spirit guide, messages of incredible banality: they were content in the spirit world; they sent their love to those they'd left behind; they chalked their names between locked slates like some post-mortem magician, and they made rapping sounds on tables as if they were standing at the bar impatient for a drink.

Rubbish, all of it.

Still, he would go through the motions of an investigation, unless something more interesting turned up.

He was just about to put pen to paper and literally write off the visit to Alice Goodway when the door to his tiny office swung open and the chief constable, Captain Bell, strode majestically in. Brennan stopped himself in time from making the observation that he must have failed to hear the man's knock.

Captain Bell's pale face, gaunt features and stern expression all served to give Brennan an involuntary shudder. The wild thought of his chief constable making some mystic appearance after death at a shadowy séance was a disturbing one – after all, the sudden manifestation of the *living* version was enough to make one reach for the smelling salts.

'Ghosts, Sergeant Brennan?' were his superior's opening words.

'I beg your pardon, sir?'

'I have just spoken to a strangely subdued Constable Jaggery and he has told me the fascinating details of your latest case.'

Brennan held up his hand. 'I see. Please, sir. Sit down.'

Captain Bell gave a sniff but sat facing his detective sergeant.

Briefly, Brennan explained the circumstances of his visit to Alice Goodway. When he told him what was written on the note, Captain Bell held up a hand and closed his eyes.

Then he said, '*Lying lips are an abomination to the Lord.* Proverbs, if I'm not mistaken.'

Brennan acknowledged the depth of the man's biblical mastery.

'And you have no inkling of who sent the note?'

'The aunt seems to think it's from our esteemed Inspector of Nuisances.'

'Crankshaw?' Captain Bell's eyes opened wide. 'Why on earth does she accuse him? Not that I've much time for the man myself. Creates far too much resentment among the shopkeepers for my liking. Remember last year and the miners' strike? He filled his time by reporting tradesmen for neglecting to sweep away the snow in front of their premises while we were up to our necks in serious disorder.'

Not to mention murder, thought Brennan.

'Rather like Bruegel's *Icarus*, eh, Sergeant?'

Brennan blinked. He hadn't the faintest idea what the man was talking about. Instead he said, 'While it could be him, sir – Crankshaw, I mean, not Icarus – it could equally be a resentful neighbour. She's turned her house into a sideshow, after all. And some people naturally find it distasteful to find someone in their street communicating with ghostly spirits.'

'And you see nothing here to cause concern?' Captain Bell asked, his voice neutral.

'Seems a bit of a fuss about nothing, sir.'

If he had expected an endorsement from the chief constable, who normally accused him of wasting his time on trivial matters, he was surprised when it didn't come. Instead, the great man leaned forward and clasped his hands together.

'It ill becomes a man to wallow in cynicism, Sergeant.'

'Yes, sir.' Brennan inwardly sighed. It wasn't Sunday but he was about to get a sermon.

'When I was serving in India,' Captain Bell went on, his voice low and grave, 'a few of us had occasion to visit the monument at Cawnpore. You've heard of the place, I trust?'

'It rings a very distant bell, sir.'

His superior held his gaze for a few seconds, uncertain if his sergeant were attempting some sort of infantile pun on his name. Satisfied by the expression of innocence on his face, Captain Bell explained.

'There was a massacre there, almost forty years ago. In '57. Men, women and children butchered and thrown down a well. A horrific act of evil. The devils paid for it later, of course, but too late to save those two hundred or so innocent souls.'

'A terrible time, sir.' Brennan wondered where the reflection was heading.

'A few of us paid the place a visit. The well was filled in and covered with a memorial. An octagonal Gothic screen of sombre grey stone and an angel standing above the well with folded wings. Gazing sadly down to where the dead and dying had been hurled. We stood there in what was now a beautiful garden in silence and prayed for a long time. But when the light started to fade we turned to go. That's when we heard the sounds.'

In spite of himself, Brennan was interested. 'Sounds, sir?'

'As if they came from afar off. Women screaming and children wailing. We looked around, then at each other . . . We had all heard them. It must have lasted for no longer than a few seconds but to us it seemed much longer. Then the horror faded with the light and there was nothing but shadows and the howling of a wind through the Gothic arches of the walls.'

There was a silence in the room. It was finally broken by a door clattering open somewhere along the corridor beyond the room and a man yelling drunken obscenities as he was frogmarched down to the cells.

Then Captain Bell spoke again. 'So you see, Sergeant, that I am a little more receptive to things we cannot logically explain than you yourself might be. I can never rid myself of those dreadful sounds that day at Cawnpore.'

'It must have been unnerving, sir,' was all that Brennan could think of by way of a non-committal response.

Captain Bell looked at him as if searching for any sign of irony but found only blank obedience on his face.

'My advice, Sergeant, is to tread carefully where such things are mentioned. Tread carefully.'

He then stood up and straightened his uniform before leaving the room.

'Not you as well,' said Brennan, addressing the now closed door. Everybody seems to have a ghost tale to tell, he reflected, while ignoring the evidence of their senses. Hadn't the chief constable inadvertently given a logical explanation of the eerie sounds they all heard and misinterpreted? The wind, carrying with it distant sounds of women chastising their offspring in some village?

Nothing supernatural there.

*

As soon as he set foot through the front door, Ellen Brennan knew her husband had had enough policing for one day. She left her six-year-old son Barry sitting on the rug before the fire, where he was busy playing with the fort and toy soldiers that were his pride and joy, and helped Michael off with his overcoat.

'Your nose is blue!' she said, reaching up to kiss him and feeling his coldness.

'It's freezing out yonder,' he said with a backward nod.

She raised a hand and stroked the creases on his forehead. 'Come and sit down,' she said, 'and we'll see about thawin' out them frowns.'

He laughed and allowed himself to be drawn to the armchair. As soon as he sat down his son yelled, 'Dad!' and launched himself into his lap.

Later, as they sat at the table and spooned away the last of the pea soup, Ellen said, 'Well? What's put them frowns there today then? Don't tell me. Captain Bell.'

He smiled and shook his head. 'No. Not really. I'm just fed up of folk being stupid.'

She adopted a mock serious expression. 'Happen they can't help it.'

He placed his spoon in the now empty bowl and said, 'Do you believe in ghosts?'

The mockery on her face faded. 'Why?'

'Because not only have I wasted an afternoon listening to some crackpot young woman and her even more crackpot aunty by marriage who've been fooling people into believing she can talk to the dead, I then have to listen to Freddie Jaggery tell me *his* ghost story. As if that weren't bad enough I get to the station and lo and be-bloody-hold Captain Bell goes one better!' He paused and smiled again. 'Sorry, love. I just get peeved sometimes when folk should know better.'

Instead of agreeing with him, or offering some soothing advice, Ellen said, 'This crackpot young woman, you say she's been *foolin'* folk. How do you know?'

'She all but admitted it.'

Ellen shook her head, stood up and began to move the bowls to the sink.

'Ellen? What is it?'

She turned to him. 'It's Alice Goodway you're on about, isn't it?'

He frowned. 'It is. How do you know her?'

'I don't *know* her. Not really. But I've heard of her.'

Now his frown grew deeper. 'How?'

'I heard 'em talkin' about her in Yates's. It's murder getting served in that shop when there's a few in. An' all I wanted were some peas.'

He raised an eyebrow. Yates's Grocery Shop beat any council chamber for putting the world – or their small part of the world – to rights. Or perhaps a newspaper office might be a better analogy, he reflected. What they didn't know in that shop wasn't worth knowing anyway.

'Some folk were interested, specially when they found out Len and Ettie Yates had been to see Alice Goodway.'

'Had they now? And why would a grocer who spends his time watering down his milk pay her a visit?'

'He does not water down his milk!' Ellen Brennan scooped some water from the sink and splashed him with it. 'He's as straight as the day's long is Len Yates.'

'If you say so,' he said with a laugh.

'Anyroad, Len wouldn't tell us. Said it was private. An' I got the impression he didn't want Ettie to say anythin' either. Sally was there with me though.'

Brennan gave a little chuckle. Sally Woosey lived just round the corner, and she and Ellen had been close friends since childhood.

'An' Sally was thinkin' of goin' to see Mrs Goodway herself.'

'Now why would she do that?'

''Cos of her brother.'

Brennan nodded. He'd forgotten about the tragedy that Sally spoke of rarely. The poor little soul drowned in the Duggie. He was only ten.

The River Douglas flowed from Winter Hill near the Pennines, through Wigan and on towards the River Ribble. Only two years ago its course had been altered to allow the Central Railway Station in town to be built. Occasionally it burst its banks, and children were always well advised to steer clear. And as so often with children, good advice carried no currency.

'And what possible good could come of Sally going to see Alice Goodway? The boy died a long time ago.'

'She still thinks of him.' There was a slight note of remonstrance in his wife's voice. 'Dead doesn't mean you forget, does it?'

She walked over and playfully stroked his hair with her damp hand. 'Anyway, I think she's a bit scared. She talked about goin' but . . . I don't think she'd go on her own.'

He reached up and clasped her hand. 'If that's your way of suggesting you go with her . . . ?'

''Course not,' she replied, a little too quickly.

'Well I don't think it's a good idea, so put it right out of your head.'

She was about to remonstrate when he raised a hand to forestall her.

'It's a lot of nonsense, Ellen. Pandering to people's grief, opening old wounds. Even Father Clooney's warned her about it. There's something unnatural about all this psychic nonsense. It's not all that far away from devil worship.'

She laughed, but when she saw how serious he was she gave a non-committal shrug and veered the conversation in a slightly different direction. 'It was strange though. You know Len, always got a cheery smile and a cheeky wink. Only when he was tellin' us all he'd been to see her, he was different. And he spoke in such a low voice I had to strain sometimes to catch what he said. But Ettie Yates . . . her eyes were sparklin'. Whatever Alice Goodway told them, I reckon it had a good effect on her. I can tell you, love, a few of us said after how we could feel our hair stand up. Gives you the shivers, stuff like that.'

He noticed her voice too had gone softer, a timbre of nervousness.

Then a small, anxious voice piped up from the front room, 'I don't want a ghost to get me!'

*

It had been a simple matter, sliding the kitchen window high enough to climb through. There was a sudden inrush of ice-cold air and the temperature in the room dropped even lower. Leaving the window open, the dark figure moved silently to the back door, where the key still sat in the lock. This was the most dangerous moment, turning the key so that the door was unlocked. Any metallic click as the bolt slid back might rouse the one sleeping upstairs. But there was only the merest suggestion of a sound, and the house remained silent. Deathly silent.

Now, the dark figure hunched low against the window, although no one would have seen any movement from the backyard beyond, not at three in the morning, in the bitter cold and with the entire house in darkness.

With deliberate slowness, one hand on the banister rail to maintain its balance, the figure began to climb the stairs. From the front bedroom that lay to the left of the landing came a muffled breathing, accompanied by the inarticulate groans of someone disturbed by dreams.

At the top of the stairs, the figure halted.

Listened.

Time for a lesson to be learned.

Make a fool of *me*! My *grief*.

A snarl crept onto the figure's face, which was pale and grey in the dim light cast by the gas lamp down the street. Anyone catching sight of it would have crossed themselves.

But no one saw a thing as the figure moved towards the sounds of troubled sleep.

There was a noise from the house next door, a man's curse and the clatter of a pisspot, then the long gushing flow as he relieved himself before the slither of pot on floorboards and the wheeze of a creaking bed.

Then silence.

The bedroom door was slightly ajar. The faint light from outside created shadows. The figure looked to the bed, to where the one sleeping and mumbling was lying prostrate and ready. Then a glance to the mirror and a vision of how the scene would look to someone watching. God, perhaps.

These are the wages of sin! This is the price paid for pretending to be what you're not.

The one in the bed was stirring, a few mumbles then a long exhalation as if the bad dream had faded away and contentment taken its place. She was lying now on her back, her head resting on a single pillow.

Perfect.

Chapter Three

Although Constable Jaggery, who was standing in the doorway to the bedroom, had said nothing, Brennan could sense what he was thinking. A few days earlier, the two of them had stood downstairs in this very house and listened to the young widow Alice Goodway and her stern-looking Aunt Doris and their fears that someone was threatening Alice.

Now, as he stared down at the lifeless shape on the bed, Brennan felt the sharp sting of guilt, of remonstrance.

He should have taken them more seriously.

There were no wounds, only a blueish colouring to the face and, by contrast, a pallor around the nose and the lips. Her eyes were open and bloodshot. The pillow beneath her head was deeply dented as if a powerful force had been exerted.

'Bit of a bugger, eh, Sergeant?' Jaggery said with a nod in the direction of the bed.

Brennan made no reply. Instead he bent low and peered under the bed.

'What you lookin' for, Sergeant?' Jaggery asked.

'Something that doesn't seem to be here.'

The constable raised an eyebrow but said nothing. He was used to his sergeant's habit of answering a question by not answering it.

Brennan gave a grunt and stood up. He looked round, at the uncarpeted floor around the bed, at the fading wallpaper of the room, at the mirror on the wall and the small wardrobe beside the half-open door that led onto the landing. Moving over to the wardrobe, he opened the door and looked inside. There were a few articles of clothing, and a pair of black shoes lay on the bottom. He shook his head. Finally, he walked from the bed to the door and turned to survey the scene.

'The bedsheets are a mess,' he said. 'Signs of a struggle.'

'Aye, Sergeant.'

Brennan slowly shook his head. It was the sad and grubby ordinariness of the place – a small bedroom over-looking the street below – that struck him. He turned and Jaggery followed. The big constable was surprised when, instead of marching back downstairs, the sergeant moved along the small landing and made straight for the bedroom at the rear of the house. He watched with some feeling

49

of unease as Brennan opened the door, stepped inside and moved to the bed that lay beneath the window. He then lifted the pillow and held it up to the light from outside.

'What's all the interest in pillows, Sergeant?'

Evidently satisfied, Brennan said nothing, just returned the pillow to its original place and looked out of the window to the backyard below.

'This room overlooks the yard,' he said.

'Aye, Sergeant.'

'I wonder why she didn't hear anything last night?'

'Happen she's a sound sleeper. I know my missus wouldn't wake up if the Sally Army were playin' a march on the landin'.'

'The kitchen is directly beneath.'

Jaggery could think of nothing else to say. He wondered where the man's thoughts were leading him. Examining her pillow? Suggesting she heard nothing in the dead of night? Was he thinking she had something to do with the woman's death?

'Well,' Brennan said cheerfully enough. 'Let's get downstairs and see our only witness. We've left her downstairs at the tender mercy of Constable Corns for long enough.' He gave a sharp nod back towards the front bedroom in the direction of the body. 'And she's going nowhere, is she?'

*

It was clear that Alice Goodway had shed further tears since Brennan and Constables Jaggery and Corns had arrived thirty minutes earlier.

Now, Alice was sitting at the kitchen table with Constable Corns, who looked decidedly awkward having been told by his sergeant to sit with her and *make her comfortable*. But how do you make someone comfortable when she'd found her aunt stiff as a frozen rabbit and almost been murdered herself? The best he could think of was a hot mug of tea with plenty sugar – something he'd learned from his mother – and letting the poor woman sit staring into space while Sergeant Brennan and Constable Jaggery made noises upstairs.

Between sobs, she told them how she had woken early that morning and gone straight downstairs to build the fire before Aunt Doris came down. After that, she went into the kitchen and filled a pan with water to place on the range by the hearth in the front room so that they could have a morning cup of tea. Once the fire had got fully going, she stood at the bottom of the stairs and shouted for Doris.

'But there were no answer, an' I thought she's havin' a lie in. She sometimes does, y'see. So I just sat down here an' waited for the water to boil.'

Brennan indicated the back door. 'Did you notice the door had been left unlocked and the window wasn't fully closed?'

She shook her head. 'Not at first. But once I'd poured the tea I got took short so I had to go.' She flushed with shame at such an intimate detail, but Brennan urged her to carry on.

'Well, I went outside an' I were that desperate I didn't take notice. All I wanted to do was get to that petty in the backs.'

Jaggery gave one of his characteristic coughs. He too felt this was unnecessary information.

'Once you'd come back from the toilet in the alleyway and got back to the house . . .'

Alice seemed to be straining to remember. 'I . . . I shut the back door an' then I thought, I don't remember unlocking an' unbarrin' that door. But if Aunty Doris 'ad come down in the middle of the night . . . I know she wouldn't have, 'cos it were that cold last night, but still. I thought nothin' more about it. An' I took no notice of the window.' Her voice now lowered, and it was clear that the tears were once more very close. 'I'd made her a drink so I thought it'd be a nice thing if I took it up to her, let her wake up to a . . .'

She stopped, fumbled with her fingers and pressed both hands together so that her knuckles grew white.

'Go on, Alice. Nearly done.'

She smiled, but it was a sad sort of smile. 'I'm supposed to be psychic, aren't I? But when I walked up them stairs I had no idea . . . I mean, I should've felt *summat*.' She took a deep breath to compose herself. 'Anyroad, I went in with her cup an' saw her lyin' there. And then I saw her eyes. I'll never forget them eyes as long as I live.'

'You heard nothing in the night? No sounds of a struggle, a squeaking floorboard even?'

She shook her head. 'I've been havin' trouble sleepin'. What with Jack an' now the visits an' . . . anyroad, Aunty Doris gave me some of her special stuff to make me sleep. I slept through, Sergeant. I heard nothin'.'

'Special stuff?'

Alice looked down at her hands. 'She has all sorts, Aunty Doris. Should've been a doctor, eh?'

'Did she take any of her "special stuff" last night?'

'Not that I know of. Why?'

'No reason.'

It was a lie, of course. He knew it was hard to suffocate someone – he'd been called to one such suffocation years ago and the victim had fought back hard, scratching the killer on the hands and helping to bring him to justice. Perhaps Doris Goodway's desperate attempts to fend off her attacker had been weakened by something she'd taken. Or been given. He looked at the young widow and wondered if she were capable of drugging then suffocating her husband's aunt.

'Perhaps you could show me where she kept this "stuff"?'

Alice stood up and moved over to the kitchen dresser, stooping to open one of the two doors that lay underneath the row of shelves where the few plates rested. He saw her hesitate slightly as she caught sight of the framed photograph of her and Jack on their wedding day. She reached inside and drew out a small green velvet bag with beadwork along its edges and a handle that was frayed. She handed it to him.

He opened the bag and looked inside. There were several small bottles, each carrying a handwritten label: *Horseradish Syrup, Castor Oil, Pennyroyal, Laudanum.*

'Did she give you laudanum last night?'

Alice nodded. 'Aye. An' it worked. But if I hadn't took it, I might've heard what were goin' on an' stopped it.'

'That's one possibility,' said Brennan. He stopped short of explaining what the other, more murderous, possibility might have been. If Alice had indeed been roused by the commotion, then perhaps they would now be faced with two corpses.

He saw the way her imagination was moving so he changed the subject. 'Can I ask you how many pillows you have? In both bedrooms?'

Alice blinked at him, the question appearing to throw her. 'Just the two. One in the front and one in the back. It used to be Jack's, only . . . Why are you askin' about pillows?'

He hesitated before replying. 'It's just that your aunt seems to have been suffocated. Her head has been forced down hard into the pillow. Something was held there to stop her from breathing. People have been known to use pillows as a murder weapon.'

Jaggery stared at him with the hint of admonition on his face.

'That's horrible!' she said.

'Can you tell me if anything is missing from your house? Any valuables taken?'

Despite the situation, Alice smiled at that. 'Valuables?' She looked over to the framed photograph of her wedding day and nodded. 'That's the only valuable thing I've got. And that's worth nothin', is it?'

He took note of the cheap metal frame and the photograph behind the glass. No, he reflected. Not worth much in terms of money.

'Apart from the letter you received, have you had any threats at all? Anyone shown any anger or resentment towards either you or your aunt recently?'

'No, Sergeant.'

Brennan looked at her for a while then said, 'We'll be moving your aunt soon.'

'Aye,' she said with a heavy sigh.

Then he asked, as a sort of inconsequential afterthought, 'Since she's been staying here, has she always slept in the front bedroom? I mean, it's bigger than the one at the back. I'd have thought as a guest that's where she'd be sleeping.'

Alice looked directly at him. He was struck by her eyes and the way the dim light was reflected and fragmented by the remnants of her tears.

'It were her idea, swapping bedrooms. Like I said, I've not been settlin' at night, an' she reckoned it was because of that room. It's where me an' Jack . . .'

Brennan looked first at Constable Corns, then at Jaggery, but neither of them registered any sort of awareness of what she had just said, other than the obvious.

Was it possible Doris Goodway had been murdered by mistake?

He motioned for Corns to vacate his chair, which he did with barely concealed relief. As Brennan took his place at the table, the young constable went over to the back door where Jaggery was examining the lock.

When she next spoke, there was a soft, dreamlike timbre to her words. 'We were warned, Sergeant. Not to meddle with such things. *An abomination*, it said in that letter. And this is the price.'

He suddenly felt a wave of sympathy for this young woman who, in a short space of time, had lost her husband to the tragedy of a pit explosion, and her aunt to the senseless violence of a murder. For reasons best known to herself, she had dealt with her grief by making preposterous claims of mediumship, aided and abetted by that fearsome aunt of hers. But if the disaster down the pit had been the hand of God, then what happened last night to her aunt was very definitely the hand of man – or woman.

Nothing supernatural about a suffocation.

'The last time I was here,' he said gently, 'I asked for a list of all the people who have visited you.'

She nodded and stood up, walking over to the rickety display cabinet with its small array of best plates, reached down to slide open the top drawer and slowly took out a single sheet of paper. She looked at it for a few seconds before moving back to the table and handing it to the policeman.

'My aunt's handwritin',' she said as if the paper were some holy relic. 'The last thing she ever wrote.'

Brennan looked down at the spidery writing. It took him only a second to discount any link with the menacing note that had dropped through the letterbox. There were seven names, he counted quickly. 'You only saw seven people?' he asked.

She gave a tired shrug. 'Even that was too many. All that sadness. But they're all . . .' she faltered and took a deep breath. 'I mean, all they've done is come to get some sort o' comfort.'

'And you gave it to them?'

''Course I did. I know what it's like to lose someone close. Folk need reassurin'.'

'But you turned some people away.'

She looked at him, and at first he thought she was going to take offence at his obvious cynicism. Then she seemed to control her emotions and gave a gentle smile.

'I didn't know any of them,' she said simply.

And so you'd be unable to tell them things they could cling onto. Personal touches you wouldn't be familiar with.

He left his thoughts unspoken.

He gave his two constables a glance. They too saw the disapproval in his eyes. Despite the tragedy that had taken place, he had little sympathy with what Alice Goodway had been doing – she called it reassurance; to him, it was simply lying. And lying for profit, at that.

Still, Brennan reflected, casting his eyes down the list of bereaved and misguided visitors, this wasn't the time to castigate the young woman after all she had been through. Instead, another thought struck him. 'There's no mention here of Mr Crankshaw.'

She gazed up at him. 'You asked for a list of visitors. He's never been here.'

'The last time I came, your aunt mentioned she'd had a few run-ins with Mr Crankshaw. What were they about?'

Despite the cold, sombre atmosphere in the room, a flicker of amusement appeared in her eyes.

'Aunty Doris was a law to herself right enough. But when Crankshaw found out she kept a pig in her backyard . . .'

Brennan knew the practice had been fairly common, especially among the Irish immigrants who routinely kept pigs back in the old country. It was part of the Inspector of Nuisance's role to make sure the practice was clamped down upon, and any disposal of swine dung made under the strictest of sanitary conditions.

'Anyroad, they had a right old set-to in the alleyway over on Canal Street, according to what Jack told me. He heard it all. She threatened to feed him to her pig if he didn't move.'

'What happened?'

'Oh he moved all right. Then next thing was she got a summons and was fined forty shillings for dumpin' its muck into t'canal. He'd followed her, see? That's the sort of man he is.'

He too gave a thin smile. Doris Goodway seemed to have been a lively character.

'An' then he kept his eye on us once she came to stay wi' me. Even though she got rid of the pig.' She let her eyes drift upwards as her tone grew softer, and he recognised the subtle change in her mood. That moment when raw grief is tempered by fonder memories of happier times.

'Kept his eye on both of you, you mean? You as well?'

She clasped her hands. 'He stopped her in the street only last week. Told her what I was doin' was wrong. Against God's teachings.'

Brennan gave Jaggery a quick glance. The big man nodded.

'Did he say anything else?'

She slowly shook her head. 'I don't really know. Aunty Doris was blazin' when she got back an' said she'd felt like givin' him a thick ear. I got the impression they'd 'ad a ding-dong in the street but she didn't let on about anythin' else. I reckon she was tryin' to protect me feelings, like.'

Something or nothing? thought Brennan. He'd look into it.

Then, quite unexpectedly, she said, 'You need to go easy, Sergeant Brennan.'

'What?'

'With the names on yon list. There's reasons – good reasons – why they've come to see me.'

'I'm sure you can tell me why they came.'

'I'm sure I can't.'

'Why not?'

"Cos they came to see me in private an' it's not my place to let on what they asked me.'

You sound like a priest, he thought. But this forlorn place was a far cry from the sanctity and the consolation of the confessional.

'Doesn't matter. I'll be seeing all of them anyway,' he said in a softer tone, remembering that she herself had just lost a loved one.

Constable Jaggery, who for the last few seconds had been leaning over the slop stone to examine the window, turned and said, 'Sergeant? You got a minute?'

Brennan folded the sheet of paper and put it in his inside pocket then left Alice Goodway at the table. When he got to Jaggery, he was pointing to the window.

'Wouldn't keep any bugger out,' he said. 'There's nothin' in the way of a lock, or a catch, or anythin'. My little lad could get in this road. All it needs is slidin' up.'

'If he were a burglar, Constable. Which of course he isn't.'

'Him bein' a matter of four-year-old,' Jaggery added, feeling it incumbent upon him to defend his son's fledgling honour.

'You and Constable Corns talk to the neighbours,' he said quietly. 'See if they heard or saw anything last night.'

'Yes, Sergeant.'

Brennan approached the back door and turned once more to Alice Goodway. 'Do you always lock this door?'

She looked up. 'Every night. From teatime onwards. Specially with it gettin' darker now.'

He swung the door open. 'So, the intruder climbs in through the window and calmly unlocks the back door to make good his escape.'

She stared at him and shivered.

'What is it?'

'It's just the thought of somebody creepin' about last night. Doin' what they did. An' all the time I were asleep.'

'Thank the Lord you were, Alice.'

Brennan let the implication sink in and frowned as he slowly closed the door. 'He had the forethought to unlock this door after climbing in. He's a planner all right, Mrs Goodway. A planner.' He paused before adding, 'Don't be alarmed if you see Constable Corns passing your door over the next few days.'

A look of alarm spread across her face. 'Why?'

'Oh, just a precaution, Mrs Goodway. It'll help keep the curious away.'

And someone who might want to return to finish the job, he thought, hiding the fear behind a smile.

*

Although Death was never far away from people's lives, especially in a town that had seen more than its fair share of pit disasters, there were occasions when it assumed a peculiar significance. Even though murder itself wasn't unheard of – casual brutality within the marital home occasionally degenerated into something fatal – this particular murder, of the shrewish Doris Goodway, aroused more than the usual doorstep gossip.

She had been related through marriage to Alice Goodway, who had shown over the last few months a rare gift of communication with the spirits of the departed. Doris's murder gave the poor young widow even more of an aura, and neighbourhood opinion was divided on whether this latest incident rendered her more mysterious and therefore someone to seek out, or more of a liability, a person who seemed to be increasingly surrounded by death and someone to be avoided.

It was common knowledge that Alice had no other relatives, which was quite unusual in a close-knit town like Wigan. But Alice had been an only child, and her parents were now both dead. They had moved to Wigan when Alice was three, having lived in Ormskirk, some twelve miles away, where Joshua Pritchard, Alice's father, had worked as drayman at the local Bath Spring Brewery until he was forced to leave when his spine became damaged because of the heavy lifting he carried out daily. His wife Mary had managed to get a job in one of the Wigan mills, and eventually Joshua was taken on there, too – working as overlooker for a while until even that task proved too much for his rapidly weakening frame.

It seemed to Alice that there had never been a time

when her father was fit and well. Her abiding memory had been of walking upstairs on tiptoe and in bare feet so that the noise wouldn't be too much for him. For a while, she had the impression that all fathers spent their time in bed with only a walking stick for communication. When he died, Alice was looked after by kind-hearted neighbours whose own children would see to it that Alice went to school and was met at the school gates every day, while her mother worked at the mill.

Last year, barely a month after her wedding to Jack, her mother contracted consumption and faded fast. It had seemed such a torment that the very church where Alice had been so happy four weeks earlier should now become a place of such desperate grief. As they lowered her mother into the ground, Alice let the tears flow as she realised that now she had no one, not a solitary person in the entire world, whom she could describe as blood kin.

Jack became everything to her then, and she clung to him in the weeks and months following, in the way she imagined a shipwrecked survivor holding onto a cork vest for dear life.

Jack Goodway, with his charming smile and ruggedly handsome looks.

When he too was taken from her (and when word began to spread of something *odd* about the things young Alice was saying), his aunt Doris's insistence that she stay for a while to *see to her* was welcome, Alice told everyone: she was, after all related to Jack and the aunt and nephew had been very close, a closeness that was reinforced several years earlier when Jack's mother had survived her husband by only a handful of months. Doris had done so much for her nephew despite the common perception of shrewishness that seemed to cling to her.

Alice's first visitor after Doris Goodway's body had been taken away and the police had left was her next-door neighbour, Mrs Brogan. She was well over seventy, with a stoop so pronounced she was almost hunchbacked. Her skeletal frame, grey and thinning hair, and eyes deeply set above hollowed cheekbones all added to the impression of frailty, but her physical diminution belied the sharpness of her mind and the generosity of her spirit.

She had knelt before the grate and built up the fire, before sitting with young Alice and watching the flames grow stronger, not a word spoken for over an hour.

Then, as coals shifted and sparks rose, the old woman said, 'At least she'll know now.'

Alice blinked, a trifle startled by both the sudden statement and its cryptic message. 'Who?'

'Your Aunty Doris.'

'Know what?'

The old woman didn't give her a direct answer, merely shaking her head before saying, 'When my Arthur passed away, I sat beside his bed for a long time, just lookin' at his face. An' I said to him, *well, lad, tha knows it all now.*'

Alice watched her face, its thin stretched skin almost clinging to the cheekbones beneath, and gave an involuntary shiver. This skeletal old woman, so close to death herself it was registered on her face, talking about dying . . .

'But knows what?'

'Arthur allus said to me how it never made him afraid. Dyin'. 'Cos he reckoned the minute you go, everything's made clear. Like scrapin' frost from a bedroom window. He were convinced o' that.'

Alice thought of her aunt. And Jack. Did they see clearly now?

'But what he didn't believe in were all this . . .' She let her voice trail off, but Alice knew what she was referring to. 'He told me once about goin' to the fair. Watched a foreign woman wi' a fortune-tellin' bird. Stuck in a wooden box wi' cards all spread out. Arthur said they were all queued up, waitin' to spend their money an' the woman gives the box a shake, the bird gives a squawk, then she opens a tiny door. The bird comes out an' pecks at a card. She turns it over an' it shows your fortune.'

'It's pinchin' money.'

'Oh aye. But Arthur said they all believed in it. Daft sods.'

It was the first time her neighbour had expressed any opinion about what Alice had been doing, albeit obliquely, and it struck her harder than she'd imagined. What difference was there between the fairground fortune-teller and herself? And Aunty Doris, come to that. Would folk say they'd simply been fooling those who were already suffering and made money out of grief?

Mrs Brogan must have read her thoughts. 'I reckon you'll rest easier now, love, if you leave all that in the past. There's only the dead can tell us what it's like – after. An' the dead can't talk, can they? Not to the livin', anyroad. You'd best grieve for Doris – an' your Jack – in private. I'm allus next door.'

They sat there for another twenty minutes in silence before her visitor rose, wrapped her shawl tightly around her shoulders, and bade her farewell.

*

Brennan and Jaggery sat in a small recess in The Crofter's Arms. It was early afternoon and the place was almost deserted. A man sat alone near the door, nursing a small whiskey and a sense of grievance, if the serious expression on his face were anything to go by. A suitcase lay on the floor beside him. A commercial traveller, thought Brennan, and a relatively unsuccessful one at that. The whiskey served as both commiseration and encouragement.

He hadn't needed a psychic medium to tell him that.

Jaggery wiped the froth from his mouth and gave a satisfied sigh. A pint at this time was a decided bonus, though he knew full well why they were here and not sitting in Brennan's cramped office. The chief constable had a disconcerting habit of entering without warning and asking silly questions about the progress of a case.

'Talkin' to them neighbours is thirsty work, Sergeant,' he said with a lugubrious shake of the head.

'I don't think they did much talking, did they? I mean, you said nobody saw or heard a thing. Doesn't take long to say that, does it?'

'No, Sergeant.' Jaggery took another gulp of ale, not sure if his professionalism were being made fun of.

Brennan took out the piece of paper Alice Goodway had given him with the list of people who had paid her a visit in the hope of contacting the dead. It wasn't the infantile scrawl on the page that made him shake his head, though Doris Goodway's handwriting was bad enough. No, it was the thought that each person on this list had gone to Alice expecting to achieve the impossible, and when she had fooled them sufficiently with bland nonsense they had gone away uplifted, as if they'd just heard the most inspirational sermon from the pulpit.

He shook his head to get rid of such thoughts. Time to get down to business. He looked quickly down the list of names:

Peggy Clayforth – Swann Street
Lucas Wesley – Taylor Street
Mabel Aspinall – Pennyhurst Street
Hazel Aspinall – Mason Street
Len Yates and Ettie Yates – Sharp Street
Betty Bennet – Herbert Street

He recognised one name immediately: Yates's Grocery Shop, on Sharp Street, where Len Yates and his wife traded goods and the customers traded gossip. He remembered what Ellen had told him about the man's visit to Alice and his reluctance to divulge anything about it. He also remembered what she'd said about Ettie Yates, how her eyes had shone after her visit, as if she'd received some divine revelation.

Was it possible that someone on this list had been so incensed by what young Alice had told them that he or she was driven to murder? What could make someone resort to such a drastic act after sitting in a kitchen and listening to nonsense from a young widow who should know better? Besides, the whole point of visiting a medium was to gain reassurance.

He gave a heavy sigh. He could spend time with each of them, ask the usual questions, especially concerning where they were last night, and come up with nothing for the simple reason that there was nothing to come up with. Doris Goodway could just as easily have been struck down by an intruder, a burglar intent on stealing what meagre possessions they had. Maybe Doris had woken up and seen him, even recognised him.

Still, there was the letter with its menacing tone. Had Crankshaw, the Inspector of Nuisances, really sent it, as Doris Goodway had suspected? Or was it a neighbour, someone who disliked living in the same street as a young widow who claimed to speak to the dead? That was stretching it a bit, he thought. If people started murdering their neighbours for sullying the name of the street, why, he'd be awash with corpses the length and breadth of Wigan.

The name on the front of the envelope was rather vague too: *The Goodway Woman*. It could be addressed to Alice Goodway, or equally to Doris Goodway. Although it had been delivered to Alice's house, it was common knowledge that Doris was also staying there on a temporary basis.

It was possible, of course, that the letter had nothing to do with what happened to Doris – the two could be completely unconnected. Yet he didn't like coincidences, even though he knew they existed.

But he had to start somewhere.

'At least it's not snowing, eh, Constable?'

Jaggery looked at his drained glass and his heart sank. He hadn't liked both the words nor the gesture that accompanied them, Brennan's slapping his thighs as a prelude to leaving the warmth of the place.

His heart sank to even lower depths when the sergeant stood up and said briskly, 'Let's pay the esteemed Mr Crankshaw a visit, shall we?'

'An' where does 'e live, Sergeant?' Jaggery's voice held a certain amount of apprehension. If it involved walking any great length . . .

'According to Captain Bell, who is sometimes a mine of information, not always useless, he lives in Hindley.'

Jaggery's heart sank. Almost three miles away. Surely he wasn't suggesting they walk?

'And then the rest of the afternoon back in Wigan,

strolling the streets of Victoria Ward to blow the cobwebs away, Constable. Exercise, that's the ticket! You'll enjoy your tea all the more.'

*

As they stepped from the tram at the Bridge Street terminus in Hindley, Brennan began to make his way along Ladies Lane. Behind him, he heard something that sounded very much like a suppressed groan from Constable Jaggery.

'What is it?' he asked, knowing full well what the matter was. Ladies Lane was a long thoroughfare, a steady incline to the tollgate at the top.

'Nothing, Sergeant,' came the surly reply.

'It's not far, Constable.'

'No, Sergeant.'

'But if you'd like me to give you a piggyback . . .'

Even Jaggery, not, as a rule, cognisant of irony in any of its forms, knew that the offer was made in jest.

It took a good ten minutes to reach the Pennygate tollhouse. The turnpikeman was busy opening the sturdy wooden gate to allow a carriage to proceed towards Hall Lane. He doffed his cap to the occupants of the vehicle – evidently from the more gentrified part of Hindley, where Hall Lane leads onto the village of Aspull – and pocketed the toll he had just collected from the driver. When he saw Jaggery's uniform, he gave a less than cheery wave in their direction and dragged the gate shut.

'Howdo,' he called out as the two policemen drew near,

Jaggery making a determined effort to control his breathing.

'We're looking for Makinson Avenue, which we are told is just beyond the tollhouse.'

'Aye,' came the reply. The man raised his arm and pointed to a street on the right some twenty yards away. 'Somebody not paid their rent?'

'None of your . . . business, pal,' was Jaggery's response, its acerbity somewhat diminished by his breathlessness.

Brennan merely gave the man a friendly nod and passed through the side gate. Once they reached number ten, Jaggery had regained his breath.

'This lot looks a cut above anythin' in Wallgate or Scholes, Sergeant,' he said with a sweep of the arm along the neat row of houses, all with a set of steps leading up to the front door. Each door, Brennan noted, was quite elaborately decorated with slender polished swirls, and small tinted windows rested above the door frames.

'Inspector of Nuisances must earn a bob or two,' Jaggery added.

A tall, thin man opened the door. His dark hair held flecks of grey; he was around forty years old, sharp of feature, his small moustache well groomed over thin and tightly set lips. He registered Jaggery's uniform and said simply, 'Well?'

'Mr Crankshaw?'

'Yes.'

Brennan introduced himself and his companion and waited to be invited in.

But the man stood resolutely by the door. 'What do you wish to see me about? My most recent report is awaiting a response. This, I presume, isn't it?'

'It concerns murder,' said Brennan.

For the first time the man's face betrayed an emotion other than ennui. His eyes flickered momentarily, and he glanced to his left, towards the end of the avenue, where the turnpikeman was even now idly leaning against a wall, whistling. He gave Crankshaw a cheery wave.

'Then you had better come in,' he said with little grace.

Brennan caught the briefest of glimpses of a small, slender woman who had emerged from a room further along the vestibule to see who their visitors were, but as soon as she caught Crankshaw's eye, she flitted back into the room and quietly closed the door.

They entered a small room that overlooked the avenue. It was quite cold, almost soulless, Brennan thought, and there was no grate from which a welcoming heat might blaze forth. Two upright chairs stood either side of the window, a small desk tucked into a corner opposite. Above the desk, a small collection of books, religious tracts mostly, with a copy of the Bible taking pride of place in the centre. There wasn't a work of fiction to be seen.

This must be where the man compiles his reports, he mused.

'My wife, whom you've just seen, Sergeant, is of a most nervous disposition. I hope she did not overhear your mention of murder.'

Brennan and Jaggery remained standing – they hadn't

been offered a seat – and the former moved straight to the point.

'A woman you have had several arguments with has been murdered.'

'Her name?'

From his question, Brennan wondered how many women this man had had run-ins with.

'Doris Goodway.'

Crankshaw placed his hands behind his back and moved to the window, gazing out at the deserted avenue beyond. 'Ah, if ever a surname was misapplied. Dreadful woman.'

'I gather you also harangued her in the street recently.'

Brennan saw his back straighten. 'A different matter entirely,' came the thin response.

'How so?'

Crankshaw wheeled round. There was a flash of anger in his eyes that was quickly extinguished. 'I merely pointed out to the harridan that her niece was playing with fire.'

'Why?'

'Well, if you must know, for two reasons. The unfortunate girl is committing a heinous sin by conspiring with the devil to bring forth spirits of the dead. Not that she is capable of doing so, you understand, but because she is attempting to do so, and in the process is spreading her corruption to others. That is a sin.'

'You said two reasons.'

'I heard that these attempts at communication had sometimes taken place on the Sabbath.'

'It isn't an offence.'

Suddenly, a fiery zeal appeared on his face, transforming his appearance in a way that caused Jaggery to step forward in case the man hurled himself at his sergeant.

'Do you know that the fourth commandment is the only one that contains the injunction, *Remember? Remember the Sabbath day, to keep it holy*? Many who profess to keep the Bible close to their hearts and their faith refuse to keep the day holy, styling it a *day of rest*. What could be less holy than languishing in some hostelry or even worse, making an attempt at conversing with the devil himself? The commandment urges us to *remember* and what the people do is *forget*.' He swallowed hard and took a deep breath. 'I am sorry, Sergeant. I can be a little overenthusiastic. But if you knew exactly what that foul woman was capable of . . .'

'Please remember, Mr Crankshaw, that the woman is dead. It might be better to show some respect.'

'Respect!' Crankshaw snorted. 'It isn't a word one normally associates with that woman.' He stopped, conscious, no doubt, that he had gone too far.

The expression on Jaggery's face suggested that he was finding the man more unpleasant by the second.

Brennan went straight to the point. 'Is that why you sent Alice Goodway a note of menace?'

'I beg your pardon?'

'It's a simple question.'

The man gave a cold smile. 'I sent Alice Goodway no

such letter. I don't even know the woman. Only by reputation as a fraudulent dealer in demonism. But she is part of the same brood, so it's entirely possible she incurred the wrath of the neighbourhood conscience. No one likes to have a viper in their midst.' He held Brennan's gaze for several seconds, and it was clear that the man had made his definitive statement on the matter.

'Do you mind telling me where you were last night in the early hours?'

'What a ridiculous question! Where in the Lord's name do you think I was? Swimming in the canal?'

Brennan remained silent. As the implications of the question sank in, Crankshaw gave a short, angry cough and moved to the door. He swung it open and called out, 'Charlotte!'

Within seconds, the door at the far end of the vestibule opened and Mrs Crankshaw emerged meekly. Brennan was reminded of a mouse coaxed from its hole.

'These are policemen,' he said unnecessarily. 'They wish to know where I was last night.'

She approached them, her eyes downcast and her hands held close together. 'You were here, Ralph. As always. You never leave the house at night.'

Her remarks were addressed to the carpet.

'Does that answer your question, Sergeant?'

Brennan tried to catch the woman's eye to see if there was any flicker, any trace of dissimilitude. But she was concentrating hard on the pattern below her feet.

'For the time being,' he answered, deliberately enigmatic.

'In that case . . .'

Once they were outside, Jaggery took a deep gulp of air.

'I didn't like that bugger, Sergeant. Bloody holier than thou. I'd like to see him stop me 'avin' me pint of a Sunday. So what do you reckon, Sergeant? Is meladdo tellin' the truth?'

But Brennan didn't respond. Instead he stood there, staring at the house and the now vacant window. He had the impression that Mrs Crankshaw wasn't simply supporting her husband, nor was she a naturally shy and taciturn woman.

No. It seemed to him that the woman was afraid of him. And fearful people will say anything to avoid goading their tormentor.

*

Once they caught the tram back to Wigan, Brennan gave Jaggery the briefest of respites in the form of a mug of hot tea in the station canteen before the two of them set off for Taylor Street, where Lucas Wesley lived. It was the closest to the town centre, so he had decided to start there. Luckily, all of the people on the list – Alice Goodway's visitors – lived within a short walking distance of each other, a sign that, so far, the widow's reputation had remained within the confines of a few streets along from Vere Street, where she herself lived.

A fog was slowly descending as they made their way down Wallgate. Through the haze, they could just make out the dim yellow light from the windows of Victoria Mills where the air would be filled with its own more fibrous mist. A thudding repetitive rattle from the huge weaving rooms made Brennan wonder once more how on earth the girls who worked the machinery could hear anything at all once they left that deafening place.

'At least them lasses'll be warm,' grumbled Jaggery with a nod to the building, as if he could read his superior's thoughts.

Once they reached Taylor Street, the fog had grown thicker, and the temperature had dropped so much that Jaggery had difficulty rubbing his hands together to ward off the chill. Brennan knocked on the door and waited. When no one answered, he moved to his right and cupped his hands, peering through the window. Inside the front room it was dark, but he could see furniture neatly arranged, a row of framed portraits along the mantelpiece, all apparently of the same young woman, and a small bookcase with a number of titles he couldn't quite make out.

After he knocked once more, a door swung open next door and a woman's face appeared. She looked at them coolly, her expression one of distaste when she registered Jaggery's uniform.

'If you want Lucas he's not in,' she snapped and was about to close the door having performed her neighbourly duty.

Brennan said quickly, 'Where is he?'

She leaned against the door and said, 'Where dost think he is at this time?'

'He's at work?'

She gave Jaggery a sarcastic glance. 'This mon a detective then?'

Jaggery, shivering now, said, 'Answer the bloody question, woman.'

'Aye.' She drew out the syllable to its ironic limit. 'At work.'

'An' where's work?' Jaggery asked.

'Bank.'

'Which bloody bank?'

She sniffed, a sure sign that she deemed the information she had given more than enough for one day and was once again in the process of closing her door when Brennan stepped forward and placed a firm hand against it.

'My constable asked you a question. Be so good as to answer him. Or he might well accept your kind invitation to come in and enjoy your blazing fire.'

'I've never . . .' she began but soon cottoned on. 'It's Parr's Bank. On Standishgate.'

'You've been most obliging,' Brennan said, relinquishing his hold on the door which promptly slammed shut.

'You're not thinkin' o' walkin' all the way back into town, Sergeant?' Jaggery's words were spoken through chattering teeth.

Brennan smiled and patted him on the back.

Did the bugger never feel the cold?

'That would be foolish, Constable, wouldn't it? We've other houses round here. They can't all be working in a bank, can they now?'

*

It's no easy matter to kill someone. Gives you a dry, stinking taste on the roof of your mouth.

No guilt, though. Despite what the commandment says. If Thou Shalt Not Kill was taken at face value, why, you wouldn't kill rats, or cockroaches – or those who did you harm. And it was the ones that did you harm that needed killing.

No, the best thing – the only thing – was to carry on. The job wasn't done yet, not by a long chalk.

But how could she just sit there and lie like that! You can't forgive that. One of them had paid the price right enough. It had felt - not good, that moment, but right. That grunt as the body finally realised there was no more breath to be had. And those eyes! Never to open again, and never to close again. And the hands, like a dead crow's claws, relaxing their grip. Never to scratch or maim again. Those last few seconds she must have realised that after death there's nothing but blackness. Eternal blackness. Not spirits floating about like ash from a house on fire.

But there'd been two of them, hadn't there?

And the other one had to pay, too.

Chapter Four

Fortunately for Constable Jaggery, Swann Street, where Peggy Clayforth lived, was just around the corner from Taylor Street, and they hadn't even got so far as knocking on the old woman's door when he realised with a smile that not only was she in residence, but the bright glow from her front window revealed a blazing fire and the prospect of a warming mug of tea. The older folk still knew how to be hospitable, he reflected, still showed a healthy respect for the uniform.

Five minutes later, he wasn't disappointed.

Not only had the kindly old woman ushered them both in from the thickening fog, she had also insisted on making them both sit on the threadbare settee with a steaming hot mug of tea and a small plate, each containing slices of the sweetest sponge cake Jaggery had tasted for many a month.

'It were a shock,' she said when Brennan moved the conversation along to the matter in hand. 'Nob'dy should go like that. Not afore their time.' She was seated in a rocking chair and leaned forward to the small table beside her, where an old briar pipe lay on a patterned handkerchief. She picked the pipe up and examined it. For a moment, Jaggery wondered if she were about to light it.

'What exactly makes you think Alice Goodway has, shall we say, a gift?' Brennan asked.

Before she could answer, she was struck by a violent coughing fit that forced her to lean forward with both hands gripping the arms of her chair. When it began to subside, she reached for the handkerchief with such a tremulous movement that the pipe tumbled to the floor. She brought the handkerchief to her mouth and held it there for a few seconds before wiping her lips and then briefly examining its contents.

It was at that point that Brennan realised the handkerchief wasn't patterned at all.

Peggy Clayforth cleared her throat and leaned forward to pick up the pipe. She held it tightly as she spoke.

'You never think anyone could speak to the dead. Not really. I've only been to one séance before, an' that was over in Standish. Posh house, big room, table filled wi' glass bowls of water so the medium could look into 'em an' see all sorts. It were a laugh more than anythin', I can tell you.'

Her voice lowered now.

'But at Alice's house, sat at her kitchen table, there was nothin'. Table was bare, save for a lit candle. There was none of that mumbo jumbo palaver. She just said as how my Matthew were with her Jack. I thought, well that's easy made up, that is. My Matthew worked wi' Jack Goodway down t'pit an' took him under his wing when he started. So it's hardly surprisin' they've got together, is it? But then she said how he wanted me to know summat.'

'And what was that?' The cynicism in Brennan's voice was very close to the surface.

Peggy held up the pipe. 'This were his favourite pipe. But when he started coughin' bad, I told him it had to go. So the daft beggar took to hidin' it so he could take it to the pub where he wouldn't get nagged. An' when he died wi' that poor chest an' all, I searched high an' low for this devil. I was goin' to bury it with him. But it were no use. It weren't to be found. Then young Alice said as how he wanted me to find it. An' she told me where the daft sod had put it.'

She nodded towards the grandfather clock in the corner. 'It were in that thing. Daft beggar had stuck it in the bottom.'

Brennan looked at Jaggery, who caught his glance and returned it with raised eyebrows.

'Thing is,' the old woman went on, 'I've never told anyone 'bout this pipe. So how did she know about it anyroad? An' t'other thing is this: how did she know exactly where I'd find it, eh? She's never even been inside this house. Doesn't even know I've got one o' them clocks.'

Jaggery shifted uncomfortably in his chair. He was feeling the heat from the blazing fire and could hear the *tock-tock* of the grandfather clock in the corner. He glanced furtively at it, as if it held some sort of ghostly trace and at any moment the door might swing open.

Brennan cleared his throat. 'Can you think of anyone who might want to harm Alice Goodway?'

Peggy frowned. 'It were that aunt of hers got done in, weren't it?'

'It was.'

'So shouldn't you be askin' me about Doris Goodway?'

'It's possible that whoever killed Doris Goodway was really after Alice Goodway.'

She raised the handkerchief to her mouth, this time to soothe her nerves.

'That'd mean they might try again.'

'It would.'

She looked at the flames dancing in the grate for a few seconds. 'Who'd want to do summat like that to young Alice? I mean, I didn't 'ave much time for Doris, truth be known. Money ruled that woman, mark my words. She'd sell her own mother for a shillin'. Not everybody's favourite, was Doris. An' there were things she did against –' She broke off, her eyes wide as if she'd suddenly realised something.

'Against who, Mrs Clayforth?'

'Nothin'. She did nowt against anyone. But I do know she took advantage of Alice. That were clear enough to a blind man. She were a frosty, hard-faced, connivin' old bat. God rest her soul.'

She spoke with such feeling that both Brennan and Jaggery gave each other a meaningful glance. Brennan wondered what the old woman had been on the verge of telling him.

Things she did against . . .

From the fixed expression on her face, he knew she would say nothing more about that.

Then she said, quite softly, 'You *sure* it weren't Doris they was after?'

'At the moment, Mrs Clayforth, we're not sure about anything. We're just making enquiries.'

'Well all I know is young Alice's done nowt but make folk happy in a sad sort o' way.'

And it may well be that she's made someone sad in an angry sort of way, mused Brennan.

He took out the slip of paper with the seven names, explained their relevance and read them out. 'Do you know any of these people?'

'Len Yates. He 'as a shop . . .'

'I know about him. Go on.'

'I know Mabel and their Hazel.'

Brennan glanced at the list. Both had the surname Aspinall.

Peggy added, 'Mabel's Hazel's mother-in-law. It's no

wonder they've both been to see Alice. Hazel's chap got killed in t'same blast as Jack Goodway. Bert Aspinall was Mabel's only lad.'

'Did Bert Aspinall and Jack Goodway know each other?'

The old woman gave him a cynical glance. 'I just said they were killed in t'same blast.'

Brennan accepted the rebuke, acknowledging the strong bonds of comradeship that existed among the miners. Of course they would know each other. They had shared the same darkness every day.

She paused, then added, 'An' I see Betty Bennet's on that list. Her lass ended up gormless.'

'How do you mean?'

'Betty had a daughter. Young Frances. Damn shame what 'appened to her.'

'Which was?'

She lowered her voice. 'Some devil interfered wi' her. Sent her funny.'

'When was this?' Brennan looked at Jaggery who gave a shrug of ignorance.

'Nigh on fifteen years ago. She were lookin' after a little 'un in the park, an' the little 'un ran off into the bushes. Poor Frances went lookin' for her an' that's where the swine grabbed the poor lass. She were nowt but a child herself. Twelve, thirteen.'

Both men gave a subtle sigh, relieved that the crime had been committed before they worked in the town.

'Did we catch whoever did it?'

She shook her head, a gesture that almost removed the flash of incrimination in her eyes. Then she said suddenly, 'Penny Gawp.'

'What?'

'It's what the childer round here used to call the poor lass. She'd wander round mutterin' all sorts to herself an' they'd shout after her. So she'd demand they give her a penny for gawpin' at her. They'd've got a thick ear off me.'

'Where is she now? Frances?'

'Oh, the lass is at peace now. Died last year in the asylum.'

People have their own ways of dealing with death, Brennan reflected. He supposed he shouldn't feel such annoyance when they sought comfort from the least likely sources, but it still rankled with him that there were those who were more than willing to take advantage of such grief. Alice Goodway might seem good-hearted in what she was doing – but it didn't alter the fact that she was fooling the very ones who had lost what she had lost, a loved one. Whatever Peggy Clayforth claimed, he refused to believe in the young widow's supernatural abilities, briar pipe or no briar pipe. To his way of thinking, those who are bereaved should seek what comfort they can from those trained to give it: men of the cloth. Or cope with the grief silently, head bowed in the sanctity of a church.

'You know any of the others?'

She nodded. 'I know Mr Wesley. Lives round t'corner. Bank clerk.'

'What can you tell me about him?'

'Lives on 'is own. Always seems to be on 'is own. I think most of 'em round here are put off by his wearin' a suit. You don't get many suits round here.'

'Why would he be paying Alice Goodway a visit?'

'Best ask him that. Keeps hisself to hisself does Lucas Wesley. You'll not find him proppin' a bar up. Reminds me sometimes of a dog that's lost its master.'

She couldn't add anything more to what he knew about Len and Ettie Yates.

'Well thank you, Mrs Clayforth. We'll leave you in peace.'

She looked at him for longer than was natural, and when she responded it was with a single utterance – 'Aye' – that came out more as a sigh than a syllable.

As Brennan stood up, Jaggery gave the fire a rueful look before following his superior to the door.

'You didn't ask her where she was last night, Sergeant,' Jaggery asked once they got outside.

'You think she's capable of such strength, Constable? A feeble old woman like that?'

'Don't suppose so.'

'Besides, the poor woman's dying. I don't think she'll be with us much longer.'

'Now how can you know that, Sergeant? She never said anythin'.'

'Handkerchief said it for her,' he replied and set off at a brisk pace.

*

Several customers at Parr's Bank on Standishgate remarked on the change in the young bank clerk. To them, today he was unlike his usual cheery self: he seemed preoccupied with something, and this lent a sombre shade to his personality, so much so that more than one of them had been heard to remark that the bank clerk had missed his true calling.

Bloody undertaker's gob, they whispered once he'd passed them their money. *Should be layin' folk out instead o' payin' folk out!*

Even his colleagues had noticed the change in his usual demeanour. Often, during slacker periods, and when Mr Voles was otherwise engaged, Lucas would spend a few minutes producing the most wonderful likenesses in pencil of some of the more memorable customers. He had even produced a remarkable caricature of Mr Grimes, one of the bank's senior partners, with his bulbous nose, rotund shape and small, bandy legs all exaggerated to humorous (if libellous) effect.

This afternoon, however, he was subdued and distracted. Every few minutes he would glance up at the large clock above the entrance to the bank, then at the thickening mist in the street beyond, and finally give a restrained sigh that suggested an uncharacteristic anxiety for the business of the day to come to a close.

'Tha's not wrote it down!'

Behind the counter, Lucas brought his full attention to the customer facing him through the wooden grille.

'I beg your pardon?' He glanced quickly at the name in the ledger that lay open beside him on the counter. 'Mr Farrimond.'

The man, who Lucas knew was a cabinet maker and ran a thriving business, waved the passbook that Lucas had just returned to him.

'Tha's wrote it down in thy book but there's nothin' wrote i' mine.'

He took the man's passbook back from him and examined the relevant page. Then he looked down at the ledger beside him. There he had written £5 DR, but the withdrawal hadn't been recorded in the passbook.

'Summat on thi mind, Mr Wesley?' said Farrimond with a sly nod and a wink to the customers queueing behind him. 'Missus put thi t'wrong butties up for thi snap?'

That brought a chortle from those in the queue at the idea of a bank clerk bringing a snap tin to work. It also brought Mr Voles, the assistant manager.

'Is there a problem here, Mr Wesley?' asked Voles.

Lucas felt his face turn white and said, 'Certainly not, sir.' Quickly he wrote down the necessary details in the passbook and handed it back to a grinning Mr Farrimond.

'Thanks,' said Farrimond, adding, as he turned away and addressed his remarks to the ones behind him,

'Could've got away wi' a fiver there. Good job I'm honest as the day's long!'

There was a conspiratorial murmur of admiration at the man's honesty, tinged just a little with the occasional glance of admonition towards the unfortunate Mr Wesley. What *was* up with him today?

Mr Voles gave his clerk the sternest of looks, straightened his tie and moved back to his office.

Lucas Wesley gave a curt nod to the next customer, glancing up at the clock and noting with displeasure that the time had progressed by a mere minute.

*

Brennan stood by the mortuary slab and looked down on Doris Goodway's body, with half its innards exposed. Dr Monroe was by the sink nearby, washing his hands and sighing intermittently, and Brennan wondered what lugubrious reflections were swirling around in the surgeon's mind. Finally, he wiped his hands and moved back to the corpse.

'You should think of taking my position as house surgeon here, Sergeant Brennan.'

'Why is that, Doctor?'

'Your guess was an accurate one. The woman was indeed suffocated. Yet the signs of suffocation are easily missed, especially if foul play is not suspected. So, man, tell me. How did you spot the signs?'

It was the doctor's idea of teasing, but when Brennan replied, there was no humour in his voice.

'I've seen suffocation before, Doctor. I'll never forget the bloodshot eyes and the blue skin of the face.'

'Quite. But those are superficial signs only. There could be a number of causes. Still, your guess proved correct. I, however, cannot rely on guesswork. My examination follows a more surgical and exploratory line. See here.' He gestured for Brennan to move over to a smaller table on which rested a pair of lungs.

'You'll no doubt notice the lungs are congested.'

'Obviously.'

'Yes, well. You'll also notice these.'

He indicated a rash of minute spots, as if the lungs had been splattered with ink from a fountain pen.

'Those are, you'll no doubt be aware, Tardieu's spots. Found more commonly in children who are suffocated accidentally or on purpose. *Very* common in the lungs of newborn babes.'

'Any idea of how the suffocation occurred?'

The doctor gave a thin smile. 'Great pressure on the face,' he said. 'And I managed with some difficulty to extract tiny fibres – cotton fibres – from the deceased's mouth and nostrils. Supporting your theory of a pillow, eh, Sergeant?'

'Would the murderer need great strength to carry this out?'

Monroe thought for a while, stroking his chin.

'It depends, of course. If the deceased were asleep and initially non-resistant, then it's possible that someone of average strength could carry it off. But sooner or later there would need to be greater force exerted as the victim struggled for breath. I would say it depends on how long the object was held there before the woman woke up.'

'Did you find any traces of anything that would render her incapacitated? Such as a dose of laudanum?'

He had an image of Alice Goodway depositing the opium compound into her aunt's food or drink and waiting for it to take effect. After all, she knew where Doris kept the stuff.

But the doctor's next words put paid to that theory.

'Nothing whatsoever, Sergeant. Sorry to ruin whatever idea had been forming in that brain of yours!'

Brennan frowned, thanked the doctor and left him to his corpse.

*

Alice Goodway stepped outside with her shawl wrapped tightly around her head and shoulders. The fog was thick and grey, and somehow it seemed to match her mood perfectly. The cold, too, was almost as welcome. She'd sat in that house, with its melancholy sounds of shifting coals and a clock whose ticking seemed to drag out each second, for far too long. It was as if the house itself, the home she had shared with Jack for twelve months, was conspiring against her, resentful now of her solitary presence and delighting in reminding her of the cruelty of life, of all that she had lost, and the slowness, the monotony, the predictability of her life from now on.

She saw a dim outline of the policeman standing on the corner of the street, with what appeared to be a warming mug of tea cradled in both hands like a shivering sparrow, and gave a resigned shrug. He was no protection, not really, and if someone wished to do her harm there were plenty of ways they could succeed.

Besides, she couldn't live the rest of her life like this. Best to get out, speak to others, make the world see that she had the strength of character in her to cope with what Fate had thrown at her. And so she had decided to do just that. All the spiritual stuff, well, that would end now. She would think of the future, once Doris's funeral was over and done with.

She knew well what Hazel Aspinall, whose husband Bert had perished in the same blast down the pit, would be going through right now. They would keep each other company for a while, talk about what they had both lost, even though Hazel and her mother-in-law had more reason to be positive than she had.

For a few seconds, she recalled the time Hazel and Mabel had visited her and their reaction at the message she brought them. They at least had a new life to look forward to, a reminder of . . . She shook the thought away.

As she turned the corner at the end of the street, she glanced back, sure she'd heard something. The opening of a door, perhaps? Was that a head, poking out?

There was no sign now of the police constable. Nothing

save the grey blankness of fog. With a heavy sigh, she moved on, thinking how easy it would be at this moment for someone to wrap an arm tightly around her neck and choke her to death.

Strange, how thoughts of death came unbidden now. Yet hadn't she spent the last few weeks bringing comfort to the living from the dead? There was a part of her that regretted that. Where was her comfort? She doled it out like boiled sweets in fancy wrappers, but there was no sweetness left for her, was there?

With a shudder, she increased her pace.

Daft, thinking like that.

Chapter Five

It's a curious thing, Brennan reflected as they made slow progress down Leeds Street in the direction of Herbert Street, where Betty Bennet lived. He knew these streets well – indeed, he himself lived only a ten-minute walk away – yet the fog had now become so impenetrable that the houses across the street were dim outlines fading in and out of vision as the mist seemed to hover and shift. All colour had vanished: even the curtains in the windows of the houses they passed on the pavement had become suffused with a uniform grey, and he had a wild fancy that the fog had somehow breathed its way through the glass and turned even the brightest fabric dull and monochrome.

'Bloody freezin'!' Jaggery exclaimed, emphasising the point by clapping his hands loudly before giving them a vigorous rub.

'A policeman's lot,' said Brennan cheerily.

Bastard, thought his constable.

Soon they came to the wider thoroughfare of Miry Lane. The muffled *clack-clack* of horses' hooves, along with the suggestion of carriage lamps and the rasping coughing and spitting from unseen pedestrians, helped to dispel the growing sensation that they had been cast adrift – the signs and sounds of life grew stronger as they ventured across the broader street towards the right where Herbert Street ended and Miry Lane began.

'Just our luck for the woman to be out when we get there!' grumbled Jaggery, whose last vestiges of optimism had been deadened by the fog.

'If she's out we'll just carry on to Len Yates's shop. That's only in the next street.'

'Aye, but in this bloody weather it's further than a duck's fart.'

Brennan, who had yet to work out the distances implied by the oft-used phrase, merely grunted.

Within a minute, they were standing outside the home of Betty Bennet.

The woman who opened the door was in her late forties, Brennan guessed, small of stature but with startlingly muscular arms. There was a powerful smell of soap that not only came from inside the house but also seemed to cling to her like scent. Once they were seated in her kitchen, the source of the aroma became obvious.

'You take in washing, Mrs Bennet?'

Brennan nodded in the direction of a mangle by the sink and, by the back door, a large galvanised dolly tub, half filled with soapy water and indeterminate items of clothing floating on top. Emerging from the mass of clothing was a wooden dolly, its arms extended as if in mute appeal. He could almost see this doughty woman rattling the dolly with both arms as its wooden feet crashed against the washing in a fearsome cleansing. For a second, he was reminded of his own mother, and how she used to strain every sinew in twisting the dolly *a hunnerd times, Michael, that's what gets 'em clean.*

'Ee, lad, you're a sharp un!' She sat opposite him, a humorous sparkle in her eyes.

Jaggery gave one of his supposedly subtle coughs.

'I just do it for a few of me neighbours,' she said. 'Them as can't manage. An' I do their steps an' all.'

Brennan was well aware of the immense pride the local women took over their front steps. Often, on his way to the station, he would see dozens of them on their hands and knees scrubbing with donkey stones and good-humoured determination to ensure their steps were scrubbed clean. There were occasions when he even had to step over his own wife Ellen on his way out – and woe betide him if he inadvertently placed a boot on her step. He'd never fathomed out the importance of such hard work. A doorstep was a doorstep.

He told her why he was here.

Betty Bennet shook her head. 'I heard about poor Doris.

I know she 'ad a sharp tongue on her. Not everyone's cup o' tea was Doris. Still.'

'She was unpleasant?'

Again, a smile broke out on Betty's face. She turned to Jaggery, who was now resting a hand on the iron dolly tub to catch some of the fading heat of the water. 'Told you he was a smart un!' Then, when she saw the detective sergeant bristle a little at her gentle mockery she added, 'Aye, she didn't do many favours for folk, did Doris, unless you count –' She pursed her lips.

'Unless you count what?'

She shook her head. Just like Peggy Clayforth, he reflected. *There's something people aren't telling me about Doris Goodway.* He was growing more than a little annoyed.

He leaned forward and stared directly into her eyes. 'I said, unless you count what?'

It must have been the note of steel in his voice, or the flash of anger in his eyes, for she gave a heavy sigh and said, 'Don't suppose it matters now though, eh?'

'What matters?'

'Doris Goodway didn't do many favours for folk. An' I reckon what she did for some of 'em don't rate as favours anyroad.' She saw him bite his lip and added quickly, 'She helped 'em get rid.'

'Get rid? Of what?'

The woman looked down at her strong hands and suddenly he knew what she meant.

Doris Goodway was an abortionist.

That was what Peggy Clayforth had been about to say. *An' there were things she did against the law.*

Was Doris the intended victim after all? Everything he'd heard about the shrew suggested someone who might well have made enemies.

But Betty Bennet was continuing to speak, as though by carrying on she could avoid the accusation of spreading unsavoury gossip, or, worse still, snitching to the police. Abortion was illegal under the 1861 Offences Against the Person Act. He'd brought several old crones in on that particular charge, although the evil practice wasn't as prevalent these days.

Or were the perpetrators getting more cunning in its concealment?

'Always looked after herself, did Doris. It were no secret she 'ad her hand in young Alice's purse these last few weeks. Ever since she started all that with the spirits.'

'How long have you been a widow?'

She closed her eyes for a second. 'I'm not.'

'I'm sorry, I just took it for granted.' He waved an arm at the washing paraphernalia, evidence that no man's wage was coming into the house.

'I was married an' then one day he up an' left. That were fifteen years ago. Haven't heard from him since.'

Around the time her daughter Frances was attacked, mused Brennan, recalling what he'd been told by Peggy Clayforth.

'What took you to see Alice, Mrs Bennet?'

She stood up and reached out for the dolly, twisting it

this way and that until the water began to splash over the rim of the dolly tub.

'Alice not tell you?'

'No. She gave us no details of anyone's visit. She told us it was up to you. If you didn't want us to know . . .'

She stooped over the tub and bent low with her arms extended. There was a gurgling sound as she heaved on something and hauled it from the water. It was a man's shirt. She grabbed it firmly between her hands and gave it a hard squeeze, forcing the excess water from it with great force. Then she moved to the slop stone and placed it inside, ready for its rinse along with the rest of the items.

With her head bent low over the slop stone, she said quietly, 'You got any childer?'

Brennan replied, 'A boy.'

'How old?'

'Six.'

She raised her head and turned to Jaggery. 'You?'

'Same as him. Only my lad's a bit younger.'

'You'd die for 'em, wouldn't you?'

Jaggery looked at Brennan before saying solemnly, 'Aye. An' kill.'

Slowly she wiped her wet hands on the front of her pinny. 'I 'ad three childer. Two of 'em died just after they were born, but the third one – our Frances – she were a bonny lass an' no mistake. Grew strong an' all.' She paused, as if she were trying to keep her emotions in check. 'Anyroad, when I say strong . . . she got sick another way.'

She raised a finger and touched her head. 'She were thirteen at the time.'

Somehow he felt it would be wrong to let her know that Peggy Clayforth had already given them the gist of what had taken place. 'What happened?'

She bit her lip before replying. 'Some devil attacked her. She were lookin' after . . . after a child who ran off, so our Frances went lookin'. Only she found a monster instead of a child. An' she were never the same after that. Later on, that swine left me, said he couldn't cope with it all, an' hadn't she cost him enough? He weren't forkin' out any more for a *backward wench*. I kept her with me for as long as I could but she took to wanderin' off, lookin' for summat she could never find. I reckoned she were lookin' for that young lass who'd run off when our Frances were lookin' after her. I'd find her down by t'canal or near t'railway tracks. Sometimes she'd point to the black water an' say, *She's in there, mam!* Or she'd stand in the middle of a railway track an' tell me she were waitin' for someone an' they wouldn't be long.' She sighed, the memories pressing heavily on her consciousness. 'She were a danger to herself.' She gave a bitter smile. 'I even thought o' takin' the poor lass to that church in Ashton. The one with the hand.'

Brennan knew the reference, the hand of Edmund Arrowsmith, a Catholic priest who'd been hanged, drawn and quartered for his faith and whose hand had been cut off and preserved as a holy relic in St Oswald's in nearby

Ashton. It was reputed to have miraculous powers to cure the sick.

Mrs Bennet shook her head. 'Shows how desperate I was, eh, Sergeant? A chopped-off bit of a corpse three hundred years old. Anyroad, they say relics like that cure the sick in body, an' to hell with the sick in mind. In the end, I had no choice.'

She seemed on the verge of breaking down, so he asked in a sombre tone, 'How old was she when she died?'

'Twenty-seven. Died last year. In the asylum. Been in there eleven years. Poor, poor soul.'

The silence in the room was total. Jaggery, normally fidgeting in his seat or coughing at something that was said, sat frozen, his face pale and rigid. Both men held a hellish vision of their own child locked away with sickness of the brain. It was the stuff of nightmares. When Brennan at last broke the silence, his voice was low and gentle.

'You went to see Alice Goodway to . . . get in touch with Frances?'

There was an infinitesimal pause before she nodded.

'And did you? Get in touch?'

'I always got told it was usual for everyone to hold hands, close their eyes while the gifted one stares into a crystal ball an' starts makin' daft noises. But there were no crystal ball, nowt like that. Table were empty but for a flickerin' candle. I watched that flame sway this way an' that for a while, an' then Alice lifted her head an' says straight off, *He's here, my Jack*. Then she strains to hear what he's sayin' for a bit, until her face sort of brightens an' she says he's gone and found my Frances and she's now with him. An' she spoke through him. Jack told Alice an' Alice told me.'

'What did she tell you?'

'Stuff me and Frances used to talk about. Before she lost her mind. But the main thing was, it made me feel better in another way.'

'How?'

'Frances were right again. In her head, I mean. None o' the gibberish an' the screamin'. Alice said she were calm, spoke normal. She were better, see? Once she'd gone to a better place. All that sickness in her head had vanished. An' Frances told me how happy she was now an' how she had so many friends who loved her wi' not one of 'em callin' her names. I wasn't to worry no more.'

Brennan caught the note of pleading as her voice trailed off. She was anxious, desperate almost, to believe what she'd been told, although there was some fear in her eyes that it might all be nothing but fantasy.

Again, he felt a confusing set of emotions. And he asked himself for the first time if Alice Goodway's claims of communicating with the dead, ridiculous and unbeliev-able as they sounded, might carry with them motives more altruistic than financial. Certainly, this woman appeared to be largely content with what she had been told. Wasn't that a good thing?

'Do you know anyone who'd want to harm Alice or her aunt?'

Again, she leaned over the dolly tub to take out some article of clothing. 'Alice can't be held responsible for doin' folk a favour. Nowt bad about that. As for Doris – bein' the way she was is no reason for killin' the woman. Whatever you might think o' what she used to do, it all came down to givin' some poor soul a helpin' hand, even if she did charge for the privilege.'

She lifted up another shirt, held it dripping over the water. 'Not bein' rude or owt, but I've another load to wash afore I've done.'

Brennan thanked her for her time and motioned to his constable that it was time to leave.

Something Betty Bennet had said back there was gnawing at him, but for the life of him he couldn't now think what it was.

*

Every time he walked past the parish church in the centre of town, tucked away behind a row of shops, on his way home from the bank, Lucas Wesley felt a lowering of his spirits. Tonight, even though the fog had come down thicker than ever and the church's exterior was veiled and indistinct, he could see it clearly in his mind's eye. For some reason he couldn't fathom, it brought back memories of the place he was born and where he spent the first fourteen years of his life.

Style Street, Manchester, lay in the notorious district of Angel's Meadow, and for as long as he could remember, he thought that the phrase *fresh air* was inextricably linked with the pungent stench that filled every corner of the place. Indeed, living so close to both St Michael's and All Angels Church and the vast parochial burial ground close by, his five-year-old self became convinced that the ever-present smell came from the rotting corpses below the ground.

It was only when he began to attend Sharp Street Ragged School that he realised where the smell was really coming from.

Susan Corbett told him.

Lucas, it's River Irk. Stinks, it does. Dead bodies can't do a thing. All that soil stops 'em. It's River Irk.

It was strange, he reflected as the ghostly outline of a tram heading down Wallgate shunted slowly past him, how the slightest thing could bring back the memory of Susan Corbett. Had it been a week since he'd sat in Mrs Goodway's front room and listened to the message Susan had sent him? The way his heart had throbbed when the words came soaring through the ether!

I will always love you, Lucas. You can depend on that.
Susan.

How her words, her ghostly words, had upset him. Because something hadn't been right.

After taking a look at his fob watch and noting the time, he increased his pace, almost colliding with a murky figure with a blackened face who muttered, 'Watch wheer tha gooin', pal.'

Lucas mumbled an apology and carried on down the incline towards Poolstock, and his home.

Where he held great hopes of something waiting for him.

*

There was a murderous expression on Detective Sergeant Brennan's face. Jaggery was often slow on the uptake, but even he, at that moment, knew exactly what the cause of the man's anger was. Constable Corns had been given a simple order, and he had failed to carry it out.

"Appen summat 'appened,' said Jaggery, feeling it incumbent upon him to offer some words of support in defence of his young colleague.

'I left the strictest of instructions that Alice Goodway should be kept under watch at all times.' Brennan's voice was low and menacing, a tribute not to his powers of self-control but to the fact that the two of them were at that very moment gazing through the window of the next one on their list, Hazel Aspinall. Alice Goodway herself, large as life, was on the point of pulling the front room curtains together when the two policemen suddenly came into view. The way she slapped her hand to her mouth showed that she was as shocked to see them as they were to see her.

Once they were invited in, Brennan came straight to the point.

'Mrs Goodway, do you think it wise to leave the safety of your own home and walk through thick fog? God knows who could be waiting for you.'

Alice blushed. She was seated in one of the two armchairs in the tiny front room. In the other, Hazel Aspinall sat with her hand on her chin, looking at Brennan with some interest.

He himself was struck by the way the woman's eyes held him. She wasn't quite beautiful, he could see that, but there was something alluring about the way her gaze never wavered, a challenging look almost. He noted too, how her cheekbones were firm and smooth, her blonde hair hanging loosely at her shoulders.

Alice smiled gently as she caught him appraising her friend.

'I just had to get out. It's my home, but it shouldn't be a prison. Nor a funeral parlour. Everythin' just reminds me of what 'appened to Aunty Doris. And to Jack.' She gave her friend a weak smile that indicated a sharing of loss.

Brennan nodded. 'I can see that. But I wanted you safe, not walking the streets in this fog. My constable was given orders to keep a sharp eye out – not a blind eye – to make sure you stayed safe.'

'I told her she were daft, comin' here.' Hazel Aspinall spoke in a low, slightly hoarse voice.

'We share a lot, Sergeant Brennan, Hazel an' me.' Alice reached out and held her friend's hand. 'Hazel's chap – her

Bert – was in the same blast as killed my Jack. The two of 'em were best pals.'

Suddenly the mood in the room changed. Hazel's eyes sought the floor, and the amused expression on her face had vanished. Brennan recognised their common grief. Widowed over three months ago, both of these young women's efforts to accept the injustice of what had happened were spasmodic, fleeting, like a leaf harried by the wind. Sometimes settled, at others disturbed. Alice had resorted to the nonsense of spiritualism. Hazel had sought comfort in it.

Alice went on. 'But I didn't leave home just for me. I just had a feelin' Hazel was a bit, y'know, down in the dumps.'

'An' I *were feelin' that way!*' Hazel's tone seemed to suggest something supernatural about her friend's *feeling*, proof positive of her psychic abilities.

'Well, I just need to ask Mrs Aspinall a few questions.' Brennan said, turning to Alice, 'and I'd appreciate it if you allowed Constable Jaggery here to make sure you get back home safely.'

For a moment, it looked as though she were about to object.

Then Hazel said, 'Aye, I reckon that's best, Alice. I'd only fret if you went back on your own. Specially in this fog. Anythin' could happen.'

Accepting the inevitable, Alice Goodway stood up and gave her friend's arm a gentle pat.

'Constable?' Brennan said as Jaggery was already opening the front door. 'I'll see you back at the station. Stay alert, do you hear?'

'Like a barn owl,' came the reply. Jaggery's annoyance at being told to do the obvious was tempered by the prospect of getting his feet up in the station canteen before a coal fire. The image blazed merrily away in his imagination.

Once they had left, Brennan sat opposite Hazel and began.

'I couldn't ask you this while Mrs Goodway was here, Hazel, but can you tell me if anyone wished her or her aunt any harm?'

She again held his gaze for a few seconds before replying. 'Who would want to hurt Alice? She's done nothin' wrong. Talkin' to the spirits is a good thing, isn't it?'

He parried the question. 'And Doris Goodway?'

Hazel sniffed. 'Doris were all right in her own way. It's just that folk tended to get the wrong idea.'

'What do you mean?'

Hazel gave a small shrug. 'I don't reckon she was as bad as folk make out. She'd do you a favour if you asked her right.'

Brennan thought about that for a while. Others he had spoken to were unanimous in their dislike of the aunt, who he himself felt had come across as being a mercenary one, to say the least. But now here was someone almost pledging a defence of the woman. It was curious.

'There's people who might disagree, Mrs Aspinall.'

'My mam always told me to take folk as I find 'em. Wi' me, Doris were all right.'

'In what way?'

She shifted in her chair. 'Lots o' ways.'

'Such as?'

'Just the way she was, that's all. Besides, she was good to Alice after she lost Jack.'

He gave a sigh. Then he chose another tack. 'Can you tell me why you went to see Alice?'

'You know why.'

'To get in touch with your husband?'

'Aye.'

'Your mother-in-law went at the same time?'

'She did. It were her what talked me into it. I didn't feel up to doin' summat like that. But she always gets her own road does Mabel.'

He thought he detected some rancour in her voice.

'And you really believe Alice is able to reach those who have passed away?'

She thought for a while before replying. 'All I know is she told me things my Bert said. From 'is grave. Things she couldn't know anythin' about.'

'Give me an example.'

Now he could see her eyes glistening as the tears began to gather. He felt a pang of guilt for putting this recently bereaved widow through what must be agony for her.

Finally, she swallowed hard and took a deep breath.

'There was only one person in the world who knew. Me. I'd only just found out, an' when Bert went down the pit that day I was goin' to greet him with the news that night. Only he never came back, did he? I said nowt to nobody. I . . . I just didn't know what to do for the best. Alice couldn't have known.'

'Known what?'

She placed a hand on her stomach, stroked it gently but said nothing.

Brennan gave a nod of understanding. She didn't have to put it into words.

'When I heard what Bert had said . . . it fair sent a shiver through me.'

'What did he say?'

'He hoped the little bugger looked like him.' Her lower lip began to quiver. 'How could he know about that, eh? *I* never told him. Never got the chance. An' as God is my witness, I didn't tell a soul. But it might be that the dead see everythin'. Know everythin'.'

Despite the folly of her words, he felt a sudden wave of sympathy for the poor woman. Her life would soon become much harder once the child was born. He shook his head, dismissing such thoughts.

'But Alice is your closest friend, isn't she? Perhaps you mentioned your condition to her, let it slip somehow?'

Hazel shook her head. 'I can assure you, Sergeant, I told nobody. Specially not Alice.'

'Why not?'

111

She smiled sadly. 'Alice and Jack wanted a baby. It was all she talked about. Can you imagine how she would have felt if I'd told her my news after what happened to her Jack? No, Sergeant, I swear to you I told nobody. So how could Alice have known? Come to that, how could my Bert have known? When she passed on that message from him, she was as shocked as the rest of us.'

'Can you tell me where you were when Doris Goodway was murdered?'

There was shock in her features as she realised the implication of the question. 'Where would I be in the middle of the night, Sergeant? On a cold night like that an' all?'

*

Jaggery had taken especial care with his escort duties. He insisted on the two of them walking slowly – it wouldn't do if Alice Goodway bumped into a street lamp or tripped and cracked her head open on the slippery cobbles. He could just imagine Sergeant Brennan's fury if that happened.

But there was another reason for his care. A feeling that had gradually stolen over him every time he looked at the young widow. Occasionally, as they walked along in the fog he would shake his head and silently scold himself for such thoughts, but it worried him the more it preyed on his mind.

When they got to Alice's street, with the fog as thick as

ever, he saw a large figure – vague and indistinct – standing outside her front door. As they got closer, he saw Constable Corns, rubbing his hands and trying with little success to keep warm. When he saw Jaggery he half-raised a hand in greeting, only to let it drop unceremoniously when he saw Jaggery's companion.

'Aye, lad,' said Jaggery with mock venom, 'you might well pull your face. What are you doin', might I ask?'

'Standin' guard here, like I was told to.'

'Guardin' who?'

'Her yonder,' came the quick reply, as if the question were quite nonsensical.

'But she's here, wi' me, lad.'

'Aye, I can see that.'

'So how did she get here wi' me instead of bein' inside this house wi' you keepin' guard, like?'

Constable Corns thought for a moment and said with a slow-dawning sheepishness, 'She must've got out.'

'And where were you then when she got out?'

The unfortunate constable pointed up to the grey murkiness at the end of the street. 'I must've been up yonder. I only walked up an' down. Keepin' warm. An' somebody took pity on me an' made me a cup of tea. There's some nice folk round here.'

All the while, Alice Goodway had gently detached herself from this professional difference of opinion and unlocked her front door, stooping low as she spotted something behind the door.

Jaggery watched her stand erect. She was holding an envelope in her hand.

'What's up?' he asked.

He saw her hands tremble as she held out the envelope.

'I . . . I 'ave a bad feelin', Constable. You'd best open it.'

Jaggery took it from her. He threw Constable Corns an accusatory glance before tearing open the envelope. He took out a single sheet of paper, read its contents and said, 'Bloody 'ell fire!' before ushering Alice inside.

Even in the fog, he could see she had suddenly grown excessively pale.

Chapter Six

On his way to Sharp Street, and Len Yates's grocery shop, Brennan couldn't stop thinking about the woman he had just left. What frenzied thoughts and feelings must be swirling around Hazel Aspinall's mind. She had lost her husband over three months ago, after discovering she was with child. The grief and the deepening sense of loss she must have endured – would they be rendered almost unbearable by the prospect of giving birth and bringing up a fatherless child? Or would the new arrival bring her comfort, a daily reminder of something her husband had left her?

But then Alice Goodway supposedly brings her a message from the spirit world.

I hope the little bugger looks like me.

A simple communication.

But how could Alice have known? If what Hazel told him was true, then there were only two possibilities he could think of: one, Alice Goodway was a genuine medium with powers beyond human understanding, or two – and by far the more likely explanation – she already knew of Hazel's condition.

Hadn't both she and Hazel told him that Bert Aspinall and Jack Goodway were the best of friends who worked together and no doubt shared a few pints together? She said she hadn't told him of her condition, that she was going to tell him on the day of the explosion. But what if that was simply a lie? What if she told him on the morning of the blast? And wouldn't it be reasonable to suppose that he was so thrilled with the news that naturally he'd share it with Jack as soon as he could?

Keep it to yourself, Jack, owd lad. Wife's told me to say nowt to nobody. But anyroad . . .

And didn't Alice Goodway tell him she sat with her husband as he lay dying in the hospital and they spoke a few last sad words? Isn't it possible he told her then? Sharing with her a meagre morsel of good news amidst all the carnage of the accident?

Don't let on, though, Alice. I promised I'd say nowt.

A logical explanation.

As he found himself standing outside Len Yates's shop on Sharp Street, Brennan nodded to himself, satisfied that rational thought had for once overcome superstitious nonsense.

*

Lucas Wesley sat in his favourite armchair and tried to focus on the book he was reading, *The Night Side of Nature* by Catherine Crowe. Under normal circumstances he would find himself thoroughly involved and transported by its pot pourri of legends and family tales of ghosts, poltergeists, apparitions, allegorical dreams and presentiments, in fact the whole plethora of strange and inexplicable occurrences.

This evening, though, he found his attention drifting. He would watch the flames in the grate, listen to the occasional spit as the coals shifted their position and the smoke flickered wildly at some invisible downdraught from the chimney, and find his thoughts similarly agitated. The thing he had been expecting hadn't arrived, despite the note of urgency he had imbued the letter with. The Manchester Private Investigation Agency, based in the middle of the city's theatre district just off Peter Street, had informed him several days ago that they had every expectation of finding Miss Susan Corbett.

We have received most credible information that she is alive and well and living in the Liverpool area. Our finest investigator has taken up the challenge of finding a needle in a haystack.

And yet there was no word of the man's progress.

One thing was almost certain though: *credible information that she is alive* gave him a renewed hope of finding her.

He knew, of course, that she wasn't dead. Hadn't needed a letter from a private investigation agency to tell him that. There were many examples cited by Catherine Crowe herself of the souls of the recently departed travelling many hundreds of miles to manifest themselves before their loved ones to let them know that Death had taken them. He particularly liked the case of the comatose woman who, as she lay dying in the Mediterranean, was said to have visited her family in England. When she revived briefly before taking her final breath, she told those around her death bed that she had seen her children, a fact later confirmed by her family back home who spoke of a mysterious visitation they'd all had.

Proof positive!

So, if Susan had indeed passed away in the intervening years, surely her soul, her spirit, would have found its way to him and given him the dreadful news?

Yet he had had no such visit.

It was Susan. It was always Susan who drew him.

She drew him now as he looked above the flames at the row of portraits, all done in pencil and all depicting Susan as he hoped she would look now. There were times when he couldn't bring himself to look at those features, for they represented an ideal, an image that he couldn't be sure existed – only in his imagination, and that was kindled more by the desire for a girl grown into woman-hood, who had shed the soiled past she had emerged from, than by anything rooted in reality.

Sometimes he would try to bring her childhood face to memory, see the mischief and the sparkle in her eyes, a sparkle that shone despite the filth that clung to her cheeks and the matted brown hair that drooped down to her shoulders. He remembered, too, the way her eyes would light up as they sat huddled in the paupers' grave-yard, ignoring the foul air around them that oozed not only from the nearby river but the slaughter houses and the boneyards and the catgut factory, and Susan would give free rein to that imagination of hers.

And she would tell him such tales!

The best times were at night, when the light had gone and they couldn't see the small mounds where the dead lay, though they knew they were there, right enough. She had a world, she would tell him, a world that you could only reach if you dived into the River Irk and got beneath its surface of green slime and the stink of the bubbling gases, deep, deep down to the bottom where there was a secret opening that took you to a special place. There, everybody had a different mam and dad.

They look t'same, Lukey, but they're always laughin', never shoutin'. An' they 'ave lots o' money, an' it never rains. At night, there's a red sun – imagine that, eh? A red sun in a dark sky! An' at daytime there's a bright yellow one. An' both of 'em keep you warm.

She swore she'd been there many times, and although he didn't really believe that bit – who in their right minds would jump into the Irk? – he loved the idea of the two of them leaving Angel Meadow for good and being together forever. One day, she always promised, she'd take him there, to her secret world where he'd never feel the cold again, never be hungry again.

Someone walked past his front window – he watched

the shadow glide past his closed curtains – and he listened to the footsteps growing fainter. Someone – a miner, or a foundry worker, or an overlooker at the mill – on his way to the pub, he thought, and though it would be nice sometimes to stand at a public bar and have some form of communion with others, he knew well that he would hate it after five minutes. He didn't really belong in their company – not because he wore a collar and tie and dressed smartly to work every day. No, it was more than that. A friendly nod in the street from some of the men, perhaps, but he could see beyond their affable nods and half-hearted smiles. He wasn't one of them.

Because his hands were clean when he got home. That was actually something they judged him by – clean hands!

Look at 'em – never done a hard day's graft in 'is life!

And also because he thought about things other than rugby and pigeon shoots and cockfighting and pitch and toss. Try discussing spectral lights or doppelgangers or poltergeists with those men! There was nothing below the surface with that sort – what you saw was what you got. Such an impassable gulf between them. Their conversations were so shallow, so ordinary, completely bereft of any kind of imagination or sense of wonder about what lay beyond the five senses, while he longed to share a depth of feeling, of ideas, the concept of things on a spiritual and, yes, supernatural level.

He shook his head before returning his gaze to the fire and his mind to memories of Susan.

They kept him warm on nights like this.

She was his red sun.

*

Jaggery held the single sheet of paper close to the oil lamp and read its contents. Just two words:

'*Lying bitch*'

In the kitchen, Alice Goodway sat at the table with her head in her hands. He could see that she was shaking, and not from the cold.

'Sergeant Brennan'll know what to do, Miss. Don't you worry 'bout that.'

She removed her hands and he noticed the tears now flowing freely down her face. He cleared his throat and rested a large hand on her shoulder. He flinched as he felt the thinning flesh and the thin bonework beneath. *One squeeze*, he told himself, *and she'd snap in two*. She reached up and placed her hand on his. It felt cold, and he could sense the trembling in her light touch. It reminded him of something from a long time ago, something he had buried in more ways than one.

'I wish it'd been me who died, not my Jack.' Her voice was like a whisper at the graveside. 'I'm scared. More than scared. An' all I've tried to do is help folk.'

She tightened her grip on his hand. 'There's nowt wrong with helpin' folk cope, is there?'

121

'No, Miss,' Jaggery said with a heavy sigh. 'Nothin'
wrong wi' that.'

*

Five large wicker baskets stood outside Len Yates's
Grocery Shop, each one filled with potatoes. Brennan
wondered if it would be better to get the baskets inside,
for the swirling fog couldn't be doing their contents any
good. Then, as if he had read the grocer's thoughts, he
saw Len Yates himself suddenly emerge from the front
door of the shop and reach down to grab the nearest
basket with a huge pair of arms.

Perhaps I could go in for all this psychic malarkey, Brennan
thought.

'Mr Yates?'

With a grunt, the grocer said, 'Aye, that's me,' before
heaving the basket back into his shop.

'Do you need a hand?' Brennan asked.

'I need two strong arms, pal,' came the reply.

Five minutes later, Brennan, having shown the grocer
just how strong his arms were, was sitting in the back
room of the shop wiping the sweat from his brow. Mrs
Yates was in the shop, serving customers with a cheery
voice that belied the gloom of the weather outside.

'An' them sprigs o' mint was only picked this mornin','
she was telling one woman, 'so if your old man fancies a
nice bit o' mint sauce wi' his roast lamb . . .'

'Roast lamb?' exclaimed her customer. 'Be lucky if 'e

gets a plate o' scrag end, state his lordship rolled in last night . . .'

Brennan smiled.

In the dim light from the oil lamp on the table, he could make out Len Yates more distinctly. He was a large man, ruddy complexioned, with a broken nose and ears that were grossly misshapen. He wondered if he had been in the ring at one time, and was on the verge of making some wry comment about a greengrocer with cauliflower ears when he stopped himself in time. The scowl on the man's face put paid to any humour.

'I'm sorry Doris Goodway died the way she did. But I won't miss the malicious old sow, that's for sure.'

'In what way was she malicious?'

Yates leaned back in his chair and pushed the connecting door shut.

'She had a tongue on her. She'd stand in my shop, listenin' to what other folk were talkin' about an' takin' it all in. Then she'd spread it round like shit on a field, only when she'd finished it stank worse than any field, 'cos she'd add shit of her own.'

'Did she gossip about anyone in particular?'

The grocer gave a shrug. 'Anyone were fair game. If a woman complained about her 'usband rollin' in drunk, then by the time Doris had finished, the poor chap 'ad given his wife a real good leatherin'. If someone said her son were feelin' a bit offside, then before you knew it the poor little sod had smallpox.'

It seemed to be a common impression, Brennan thought. A thoroughly unlikeable character was Doris. Only Hazel Aspinall had been more equivocal about her.

'If you don't mind my asking, Mr Yates, can you tell me why you went to see Mrs Goodway?'

The man flicked a glance at the door that led to the shop. It was still closed, and muted chatter drifted from beyond the door.

'It weren't me. I've no time for all that stuff. It were her.' He gave a curt nod in the direction of the shop, where his wife was still engaged in lively discussion with a small group of customers who preferred the relative warmth of the grocery than the freezing fog outside.

'And why did your wife wish to see a so-called medium?'

Yates gave him a quick glance in acknowledgment of a cynicism he shared.

'We 'ad a daughter – our Eve – an' she died last year. She were twenty-two.'

'I'm sorry. How did she die?'

Len Yates cleared his throat. 'Givin' birth. Only she couldn't. The little one was dead 'cos our Eve couldn't bring him out.' His voice was low now. Almost a whisper.

Brennan waited for the man to continue.

'It were on account of the rickets she'd had as a child. She got through that all right, but doctor warned us that if she ever got wed, then she'd be in real danger. She had to . . . avoid it.'

Brennan knew what he meant. Any woman who'd had

that most debilitating of diseases, where the bones soften – in particular those surrounding the pelvis – was in mortal danger if she ever became pregnant.

'We warned her and warned her but it were like talkin' to a turnip.'

'Didn't you – or she – discuss the condition with her husband?'

For a moment, he thought the big man was about to launch himself across the table, so dark and menacing were his eyes. Then he clenched his fists in some sort of self-control and merely said, 'There were no husband, Sergeant.'

An all-too-common story, thought Brennan. Every so often an infant is found on the steps of a church, abandoned but with the dubious good fortune of being alive. Many were found in the canal, a sad and pathetic end to a moment of illicit pleasure.

He let the man's anger subside before asking his next question.

'What happened when you went to see Alice Goodway?'

Yates took a deep breath. 'Ettie – that's my wife – heard how good she was. *Contacting the dead.*' He coated the phrase with as much bitterness as he could muster.

'And I presume she did just that?'

A sneer distorted the grocer's face.

'Oh, she contacted the dead all right.'

'And what was the message?'

'Oh, it were just a few words. But they made my Ettie collapse.'

'It would help me if you could tell me exactly what was said. I'm sorry if it's painful but . . .'

Len Yates held up his large hand. Brennan saw the dirt ingrained in his creased palm. 'Ettie wanted to hear from our Eve, wanted to make sure she were all right. Over yonder.'

'And?'

'Alice Goodway said her Jack had someone with him.'

'Eve?'

He closed his eyes briefly before opening them again. 'Oh aye. But she had someone with her an' all. It were a little lad. An' he had a message for us both. *I'm glad you've come, Grandma. I'm glad you've come, Grandad.*'

Despite his cynicism, Brennan shivered.

'My Ettie just dropped. Sat at that table wi' nowt but a flickerin' candle an' she dropped to the floor like a bloody stone.'

Brennan chose his words carefully. 'Did Alice Goodway know about your daughter? About how she died?'

There was a slight hesitation before he gave his reply. 'That bloody aunt of hers.'

'Do you believe it? Or do you think she just made it all up? About the message?'

Another sneer. ''Course she made it up. I told Ettie before we went but she insisted so we went anyroad. An' she's not been the same since. Every bloody sound in the shop she thinks it's Eve, bringin' our grandson to see us. Our *grandson*!'

'Just one final question, Mr Yates. Where were the two of you last night?'

'Last night? When?'

'Late on. Early hours.'

'An' where the bloody hellfire d'you think we were?'

Brennan didn't answer. He knew very well that anybody who was asked such a question would consider it foolish. Where would any sane person be at that time? And the guilty one would hardly admit it, would he? But he gave a shrug that implied he had to ask anyway.

'We were here, all day an' all night. Servin' all day an' sleepin' through the night. Isn't that what most folk do, Sergeant?'

Brennan agreed and stood up. As he reached the door to the main part of the shop, he heard the grocer give a bitter, humourless laugh.

'What sort of nonsense is that, eh? All this medium-talkin'-to-the-dead stuff? It's all my bloody arse, Sergeant. All my rancid fat arse.'

*

As he left the grocer's shop, Brennan stood on the pavement and looked across the street. He couldn't even see the houses opposite, yet he knew full well they were there. This case felt like that. Obscured by fog, the answer was out there and was built on the firm foundations of truth. He wouldn't allow himself to be distracted by all this nonsense about spirits and contact with the dead.

That was nothing more than a sideshow. The truth was simple: a woman, an unpleasant and shrewish harridan, by all accounts, had been murdered. Had she been killed because of something she'd done? An abortionist runs not only the risk of arrest, but of things going wrong. Had she botched an abortion? Was the murder an act of revenge?

But the letter might have been targeted at Alice, not Doris, and it accused her of lying. It might well be then that the aunt was murdered in a case of mistaken identity. Doris Goodway was, after all, sleeping in the front bedroom which had been where Alice and her husband Jack had slept. A natural assumption by anyone that that would be the place to find the young widow.

But if the real target was Alice herself, because of her meddlings with spiritualism, why hadn't the murderer simply finished her off too that same night?

Unless he thought he'd got the right one. It was Alice's bedroom, after all. And in the darkness of that hour, he would see nothing more than a woman asleep.

If Alice were being threatened by someone, what was the reason?

He was sure it had something to do with the young widow's growing reputation as a medium. People in the town – some of them, at any rate – were prone to superstition and an irrational belief in the dead somehow lingering and passing on messages of the utmost banality. He smiled in spite of his scornful dismissal of such things as a sudden memory of his own grandmother came to him.

She was swirling the dregs of a cup of tea, staring down at the dark pattern the tea leaves made as they clung to the sides of the cup.

Ah sure ye'll work in the circus, young Mickey. See now, if you look inside this cup with the eyes of a believer ye'll see that there is a lion sittin' on its hind legs an' its paws in the air, an' them leaves yonder are your sweet little self all brave an' tellin' the king o' the jungle what to do. Sure ye'll be tamin' lions right enough, young Mickey. The leaves don't lie.

In a daft way, he reflected, the leaves hadn't lied.

Wigan had more than its share of wild beasts.

He took out his fob watch and looked at the time: almost five o'clock. He had two people still to call on – Mr Lucas Wesley, who worked at Parr's Bank according to his neighbour, and Mabel Aspinall, Hazel's mother. But somehow he hadn't the stomach to speak to yet more misguided folk whose sad tales of bereavement would undoubtedly echo what he'd already heard – they could wait till the following morning – so instead he turned to head back to the station, where Constable Jaggery would doubtless be waiting, hopefully with Constable Corns's scalp dangling from his belt.

He was therefore understandably speechless, in a murderous kind of way, when the first person he saw on entering the Wigan Borough Police Station was Constable Corns himself, scalp intact and standing by the sergeant's desk with a relieved smile on his face.

'Is something amusing you, Constable?' Brennan asked in his frostiest tone.

Immediately the smile vanished.

'No, Sergeant. Just glad to see you.'

'You won't be in a minute, lad. Now let's go to my office, shall we?' Brennan was watching the desk sergeant's curious expression and gave him a belated nod. But what he had to say to a constable who deserted his post and could have brought about another brutal murder needed to be said in private. He was willing to scalp the bugger, but not humiliate him.

'I don't think we'd best do that, Sergeant,' came the unexpected reply.

'What did you say?'

'I mean, Freddie – sorry, Constable Jaggery – sent me to get you.'

'Get me?'

'Yes, Sergeant. He's wi' that Goodway woman an' said as how I was to come an' get you. He says it's important an' didn't want to leave her wi' me.'

He said it in a tone that showed how completely oblivious he was to the implied criticism. Then he smiled again.

Brennan gave the desk sergeant a subtle shake of the head before heading back outside into the fog.

*

Len Yates slid the bolt across his front door, gave the shop a last glance to check that everything was where it should be, then he stepped through into the living quarters – a small parlour with the kitchen accessed through a doorway – and slumped into his chair by the fire with an angry grunt. On the range, his tea was simmering in a large earthenware pot.

'What's got into you?' his wife Ettie asked as she gave the stew a slow stir. 'That policeman?'

He clasped his hands and placed them on his sizeable chest but said nothing.

'He'll be round to everyone who called on Alice Goodway,' she said. 'I hope he doesn't scare the poor lass.'

'Why?'

'You know why.'

He sat upright, ramming his fists onto the arms of the chair. 'Get that out of your bloody daft head! There'll be no more visits to that one. It upset you enough last time.'

'I'm not upset, Len. I'm not. I'm the opposite.' She spoke softly, almost dreamily. It was a tone she often used now. Either that, or loud laughter.

'There's no such thing, woman.'

'I don't know what you mean.'

'There's no grandson. How the bloody hell can there be?'

'Not here, perhaps, but out yonder . . .' She tossed her head in the direction of the greyness beyond the window. Then, as she stirred the pot, her eyes drifted to his hands. She could see the knuckles begin to whiten as his grip on the chair arms intensified.

Finally, he cleared his throat. He would bring her back to earth all right. 'I told him about our Evie.'

She blinked, and for a moment stopped her stirring. She half-lifted the wooden spoon from the stew, and lumps of meat, glistening with the thick gravy, slithered to the edge before falling back into the pot.

'I imagined you would. It's why we went there, after all.'

He sighed. 'Aye, but I might've told him more than I should.'

She held his gaze for a few seconds until he glanced away, finding something of interest in the dancing flames of the coal fire.

'An' what does that mean?'

Slowly, he unclasped his hands and rubbed his forehead vigorously, as if he were striving to remove a fierce pain.

'Don't matter none,' he said. 'He'll not have noticed. No reason why he should.'

With a weariness that had little to do with the day's work in the shop, Ettie Yates lifted the pot from the range and moved through to the kitchen. And yet, despite the lethargy of her actions, the hymn she was humming, *Angels We Have Heard On High*, was lively and a reminder of happier times.

Len shook his head slowly.

*

Brennan held the letter in his hand and read the short message it contained. Handwritten once more, but even though there were only the two words written down, he could tell at a glance that the writing wasn't the same. The first letter had small, neat writing, but this was hurried, angry, the indentations on the paper forceful and the penmanship untidy. The envelope, too, was different, cheaper, and contained not her name at all but the single word, '*Bitch*'.

And that was puzzling. Two letters. Two different authors?

Or one author trying to fool them into thinking there were two?

He then turned his gaze onto Alice Goodway, who was sitting at the table, her hands holding each other tightly. Constable Jaggery was standing behind her, to Brennan's mind looking more like some grotesque parody of a guardian angel than a representative of law and order.

'And this came after you left the house?'

A nod.

'You sure you didn't just miss it? Might have been there earlier and you just didn't see it.'

'It weren't on my doormat when I left for Hazel's. I'm sure o' that.'

He turned his gaze onto Jaggery. 'Did Constable Corns see anyone pushing this through the letterbox? Between gulps of tea?'

Jaggery shook his head. 'First thing I asked, Sergeant. But in all this fog . . .'

Brennan waved away the excuse and said, 'It isn't the same handwriting.'

Alice flicked a glance sideways, as if silently pleading with her new protector, but Jaggery remained stolidly mute.

'What does that mean?' There was a tremor in her voice. 'There's more than one after me?'

'I don't know what it means at the moment.' Brennan put the note back in its envelope and placed it in his inside pocket. 'What you must understand, Alice, is folk don't like anything that's out of the ordinary. The first note you got made references to the Bible. This one seems to be a bit more personal, more aggressive. But they're similar in one respect. Both accuse you of lying.'

'Meanin'?' There was a slight note of resentment in her voice.

Brennan smiled to take away the barb in what he'd implied. 'You must admit, having a neighbour in the street who claims she's talking with the spirits of the dead isn't common, now, is it?'

'You're sayin' it's one of that lot?' She threw her head streetwards, a gesture prompted by both anger and fear.

'I'm not saying anything like that. Just that this note doesn't contain an actual threat. More of an accusation. Might just be from someone who feels what you've told them is just nonsense. And they're upset because you've used a loved one – a departed loved one – and somehow got it wrong.'

'Wrong?' There was defiance now in her voice. 'Everythin' I told all of 'em was true.'

'You mean you think it was true. Seeing as how you can't actually prove you were talking to the dead.'

She was about to offer some retort but remained silent.

'If someone were serious about harming you, do you think he or she would advertise the fact like this?' He patted his inside pocket, his voice now assuming a more reassuring note. 'Put the police on alert?'

Now she turned round and looked up at Jaggery, who gave a supportive nod in return. Slowly, she unclasped her hands and placed them flat on the table. 'Does that mean you think what happened to Aunt Doris was *meant* to happen? To her an' not me?'

Brennan shrugged. 'I'm keeping an open mind, Alice. I've not completed my investigations yet.'

She cast anxious glances around the room. 'I'll be safe here, won't I?'

Brennan smiled reassuringly. 'Of course. But just to be on the safe side, I wonder if there's someone you can stay with. Away from this house for a while.'

Alice frowned. 'So you do reckon I'm in danger?'

'No. I'm just being very cautious. Far better to be careful, don't you think?'

She gave the matter some thought then appeared to accept what he said. 'I could go to Hazel's. She's me closest friend.'

'That would be an excellent idea.'

'If she'll 'ave me.'

'I'm sure she'll be glad of the company.'

135

Alice smiled. 'She has her mother-in-law call round sometimes. Though I don't reckon you could call Mabel Aspinall *company*.'

Brennan smiled and nodded. 'And I've still got to have a little chat with Mrs Aspinall, don't forget. She's on your list of visitors. I've spoken to Hazel but I'd still like to see what her mother-in-law has to say.'

'You seen 'em all then, apart from her?'

He shook his head. 'I've still got to see Mr Lucas Wesley. He was at work when we called round.'

With a sigh she said, 'He were a funny 'un, though.'

'How do you mean?'

'When he came, he asked if I could put him in touch with somebody called Susan.'

'And did you?'

She thought for a few seconds, and Brennan got the feeling she was making things up now when she said, 'There *was* a girl called Susan who came through, but my Jack said she weren't fussed about stayin' for long. She said a few things an' left.'

'Why would a spirit do that?' There was more than a touch of cynicism in his voice.

Alice, however, accepted the question at face value and replied simply, 'Sometimes they get afraid.'

'Well that's a strange turn of affairs, is it not? The dead afraid of the living?'

A blush spread across her cheeks as she realised the mockery in his tone.

'It upset Mr Wesley though. Kept sayin' I'd got it wrong an' that I'd got the wrong Susan.'

'What did he mean by that?'

Alice shrugged. 'He had a go at Aunty Doris, told her he wanted his money back, but she told him in that cruel way she had that he'd more chance of drainin' t'canal wi' a straw.' She smiled guiltily at the memory. Then she stood up and smoothed out her skirts. 'I'll go upstairs and get a few things to take with me to Hazel's. I won't be long.'

Once she'd left the room, Jaggery stepped from behind the woman's chair and produced a ferocious clearing of the throat.

'Constable?' said Brennan, alarmed in case the man was about to suffer some sort of fit.

'I reckon you upset the lass,' he said, his tones an unusual blend of servility and recrimination.

His superior gave him a stern look. 'Because I don't swallow all that spiritualist nonsense?'

'I reckon *she* believes it.'

'*Sergeant.*'

'Sergeant.'

Jaggery licked his lips, and Brennan wondered if the man was about to add to his insubordination. Instead he spoke in what for Jaggery were almost meek tones. 'Might as well be me then, Sergeant.'

'What might?'

'As escorts the lass to her friend's house.'

'Why, that's very noble of you, Constable.'

'Yes, Sergeant.'

They could hear drawers being slid open above them, Alice Goodway's footsteps on the floor of the bedroom as she gathered a few items of clothing.

'You feeling all right, Constable?'

''Course I am.'

'Only, it's not the usual run of things for you to volunteer an extra duty, especially walking these streets in this weather.'

Jaggery once more cleared his throat. ''Tis nowt. Won't take more than a few minutes.'

'As long as you don't get lost in this damned fog, eh?' said Brennan, giving the volunteer an amicable pat on the shoulder.

'Besides, as you said, Sergeant, there's nowt really for the lass to worry about, is there? Yon letter were just neighbours blowin' off steam.'

Brennan shook his head. 'I don't think so. This letter is a serious threat.'

'But I thought you said . . .'

'Should I have told her the truth, or try to allay her fears?'

Jaggery frowned, uncertain as to the exact meaning of *allay*.

'Just make sure you keep those eyes well and truly peeled, eh? And I'll make a point of asking for an extra patrol around Mason Street.'

Brennan gave him another, firmer pat on the shoulder

as Alice Goodway appeared with a small canvas bag. 'You got everything you need, Alice?'

She flashed him a nervous smile. 'Everythin' I need. Except me crystal ball.'

*

From across the street, a figure saw only dim shadows through the window and wondered what was happening inside. Whatever it was, it meant a rapid reappraisal of plans.

Perhaps tonight had been a bad idea.

Chapter Seven

The morning sun shone so brightly that it seemed to turn the smoothed cobblestones into an impossible legion of burnished gold. As Brennan made his way down King Street to the police station, he smiled at the fanciful image that had just flashed unbidden into his head.

Streets of Wigan cobbled with gold! He'd keep that particular vision to himself.

He hadn't been in his office more than five minutes, when his door swung open and the chief constable breezed in. From the expression on his face, everything, for once, seemed right with his world. His first words, however, were rather confusing.

'Have you ever listened to your own voice, Detective Sergeant?'

'How do you mean, sir?'

Captain Bell grinned. It was an extraordinary sight on a face more suited to solemnity and disapproval, and Brennan gave an involuntary shiver.

'I mean what I say. I attended the fifth annual ball of the Royal Antediluvian Order of Buffaloes last night. In the Public Hall.'

If it had been intended to clarify his opening statement, it failed miserably, although Brennan made a manful attempt to nod understanding.

'And over seven hundred people were in attendance.'

Brennan thought he understood now. 'You gave a speech, sir?'

Again alarmingly, the chief constable laughed. 'In a manner of speaking!' he chortled, leaning his thin frame forward, arms behind his back. 'I was invited to help in a demonstration.'

'Really, sir?'

'Have you heard of Edison's tin foil phonograph?'

'Can't say that I have.'

Captain Bell resumed the upright position, still beaming. 'It's a marvellous invention, and it was brought into the hall to entertain. I was asked to lean into its trumpet extension and speak into it.'

'And you heard it echo back?'

'No, Sergeant. That is the whole point. With a small adjustment of the tubular cylinder that held the tin foil, I was able to hear my words once more.'

Brennan made suitably impressed noises.

'And then people were queuing up to listen for themselves. It was quite the highlight of a most enjoyable evening.'

Before Brennan could make some sort of suggestive move – picking up his pen, flinging open a sheath of papers – that would indicate the mountain of work he really needed to get started on, there was a knock on the door and Constable Corns burst in without waiting for permission.

'What is it, Constable?' Brennan snapped, albeit with relief at the intrusion.

Corns hesitated when he saw Brennan's visitor. 'Freddie . . . I mean Constable Jaggery's at the front desk with some bloke wi' a busted nose.'

'Has the poor fellow been attacked?' the chief constable asked.

'You could say that, sir.'

'So who is he?'

'Dunno, sir.'

'Well who's attacked him?' asked Brennan.

'Constable Jaggery, Sergeant. Caught him lookin' through Alice Goodway's window earlier this mornin'. So he give him some fist.'

*

Lucas Wesley dabbed very gingerly at his nose with the cloth Brennan had given him. He seemed relieved that at last the bleeding had stopped. Only the throbbing and discolouration remained to indicate he had been the victim of an unprovoked assault. From time to time during this process he threw a glance at the impassive presence of his assailant, Constable Jaggery, who stood by the door.

Constable Corns knocked and entered, bearing a steaming hot mug of tea, which he placed very gently before Sergeant Brennan's guest. He then left, closing the door quietly behind him.

'There,' said Brennan with a generous wave of his right hand, 'the cup that cheers, not inebriates.'

Wesley ignored the attempt at levity, although he lifted the mug to his lips, taking care not to bring its rim into contact with the devastation to his nose.

'Constable Jaggery was merely doing his duty,' Brennan said as he watched his visitor swallow his first sip. There was something dainty and meticulous about the man, as if every action required careful thought.

'I should like to see the police manual that advises unwarranted brutality as a facet of one's duty.'

Jaggery shifted his position and gave a small cough.

Brennan looked at the man more closely. He was smartly dressed, as befits a bank clerk, and his face – the part thereof not damaged by Jaggery's sense of duty – was smooth and cleanly shaven. He caught an occasional whiff of coconut, presumably emanating from the macassar oil Wesley wore. His receding hair was tousled now, despite the man's efforts to return it to some kind of equilibrium on either side of his centre parting. But it was his eyes that struck Brennan the most: they were bright blue, intense, almost burning with a deep sense of injustice.

'What exactly were you doing at Alice Goodway's house this morning?' Brennan needed to move the interview away from Jaggery's overzealousness and onto more pertinent ground.

'I was hoping to speak with her before I went into work.'

'Why?'

'That is between Mrs Goodway and myself.'

'Unfortunately, it isn't.'

'I beg your pardon?'

'I need to know what you were doing there. You've visited her before, have you not?'

A slight hesitation, then, 'Yes.'

'So in a way, it's a stroke of good luck that my constable brought you in this morning, as I was planning to call on you today at any rate.'

'Surely not at the bank? Mr Voles would take a very dim view of that.'

Brennan let the question hover in the air to allow the horror of such a scenario sink into Wesley's consciousness.

After a few seconds, the bank clerk seemed to come to a decision. 'I wanted to have a very short conversation with Mrs Goodway this morning on my way to the bank.'

'About what?'

A sigh, followed by another careful sip of tea.

'I wasn't entirely convinced by my first visit. She offered only vague answers to my questions.'

Brennan decided not to reveal what he already knew of the man's reasons for visiting Alice Goodway. 'And what, or whom, did your questions concern? A late relative?'

Wesley placed the mug gently on the table then turned it round slowly so that the handle faced him. 'When I first went to the house, it was because I'd overheard one of my neighbours talking about Mrs Goodway's remarkable gifts, so I decided to see for myself. I lost someone very close to me a long time ago and I wondered if she could be of help. Tell me if she was happy where she is. Missing me. That sort of thing. When I got to the house I was met by her aunt who told me the cost of a visit was a pound.'

Brennan lifted an eyebrow.

'I know. An extortionate amount. But if Mrs Goodway were able to . . . at any rate, I agreed and went the next day.'

'What happened?'

'The situation felt absurd from the beginning. I have an interest in such things. I've been to séances where one hears strange noises, rappings on the table and so on; one sees sudden apparitions and balls rolling from one end of the table to the other. But on Mrs Goodway's table – a small kitchen table, not big enough to hold much – there was just the candle in its holder with a flame flickering from side to side. Not even a mug of tea to fortify the senses, Sergeant!'

When he saw that his attempt at humour had fallen flat, he resumed his narrative.

'Oh, she went through the routine of having some private conversation with her late husband. Asked him to seek out an old friend of mine called Susan Corbett, the one I was anxious to communicate with.'

'And was she successful?' Brennan tried to keep the cynicism in check, but a flicker of a glance from the young man told him he'd failed.

'She passed on some messages from beyond. Her late husband had miraculously bumped into Susan in the ether.'

'And she wanted you to know she was quite content? That you weren't to worry?'

For the first time, Lucas Wesley smiled. He gave a nod in acknowledgement. 'That was the gist of the message, yes. And of course the spirit world held no fears for her and she would be waiting for me when my time came.'

'But isn't that the same sort of message she passes on to everyone?'

The young man shrugged. 'I suppose it is. But there's one vital difference between Susan's message and the usual ones from the world beyond the grave.'

'Oh?' Brennan's curiosity was aroused, especially when he saw a flash of anger in Wesley's eyes.

'I went to Mrs Goodway because I'd heard she was a genuine medium. And they are few and far between. I know. I've looked. I wanted her to give me news about Susan Corbett, but not from the grave.'

'I don't understand.'

'Neither did Mrs Goodway. You see, as far as I'm aware,

Susan isn't dead. When I say I lost her, I mean just that. She moved away from Angel Meadow in Manchester, where we were brought up. It was a horrible place, Sergeant, and we both hated it. The one good thing about living there was the prospect of seeing Susan every day, sharing our dreams.' He smiled bitterly. 'We were nothing but children. But then, one day, her family did a moonlight and left, chased, no doubt, by the tallyman. And I had no idea where she went. There have been occasions since then when I've been sure I've seen her, passing on a tram or strolling through a park. But these were illusions. Not even doppelgangers, thank God.'

'Doppel-what?'

Wesley gave a superior smile. 'A German word, Sergeant. A doppelganger is a double. Someone who looks exactly the same as another.'

At that point Jaggery stepped forward as if about to join in the conversation, but he evidently thought better of it and resumed his stationary position by the door. Brennan gave him a curious look.

Wesley went on. 'But it was a relief that these women weren't doppelgangers.'

'Why?'

'Because when you see a double of someone, it invariably means that person will soon meet an untimely end.' He paused, a smirk now appearing on his face. 'I didn't go to this so-called medium to contact the dead. I went to contact the living. It shocked me when the message came from Susan that she was in the spirit world. It greatly upset me, I must admit. Everything I'd felt inside told me she was still alive, but here was this so-called medium telling me she was dead. I asked for a reimbursement but the harridan refused.'

Brennan recalled the framed portraits he had seen through Wesley's front window. He asked him about the curious fact that they all seemed to be of the same person.

'Yes. They're all of Susan. Or what I suspect she might look like now. One can never tell how people grow up.'

'You drew them?' Brennan asked, surprised and more than a little impressed.

Wesley nodded. 'I sometimes while away my spare time drawing people. Caricatures, mostly. Though the ones I've drawn of Susan are as far from caricature as you can get. With a caricature you take the most ridiculous aspect of someone's appearance and exaggerate it to poke fun. But with Susan . . .' His voice lowered, as if he were speaking of a revered saint. 'With Susan, I exaggerated nothing. I just used my imagination to show how she would look now. The beauty inside as well as out.' He paused then and took a deep breath. 'After my visit to Mrs Goodway, I did what I should have done from the start. I hired a private detective agency to find out exactly what happened. And I was most surprised when they informed me she is probably still alive and living in Liverpool. Somewhere.'

Brennan shifted in his chair. 'So you aren't sure really whether she's alive or dead?'

Wesley shook his head angrily. 'She isn't dead! I'd *know* if she was.'

He saw that the young clerk's eyes had narrowed, and the anger that had shone from them earlier had now been replaced by something akin to fear.

'I'm afraid I don't quite understand, Mr Wesley. You're saying you went to a supposed psychic medium to put you in touch with the living? That's not how it works, is it?'

'I thought if she had these strange powers, then she might be able to seek out the spirit of the living as well as the dead. It's a fanciful theory, I accept, and one which some spiritualists disdain. They deal only in spirits of the dead. But my firm belief is that the spirits of the living are active, too. Perhaps stronger than those of the dead. Are you familiar with the works produced by the Society for Psychical Research?'

Brennan was forced to admit ignorance of such a body.

'Some of them have undertaken research on thought transference.'

'Thought transference?'

'Yes. There are those who are referred to as *agents* and others called *percipients*. A percipient has the ability to transfer thoughts to an agent, and I wondered if Mrs Goodway had such ability, in which case . . .'

Brennan held up his hand. He looked at the young man closely. He seemed sane enough, but to believe that there's some sort of other world filled with the spirits of the living all anxious to connect with each other like a monstrous telephone exchange . . . ?

Wesley must have seen the scorn flicker in the detective's eyes, for he averted his gaze and picked up the mug, sipping the tea slowly. Then he said, 'You don't believe in the spirit world, do you, Sergeant?'

'No,' he replied flatly.

'But you do believe in the Bible?'

'Yes.'

'The Bible is filled with instances of spirit appearances. From Moses to Ezra, from Job to Isaiah, from Peter to John, there you'll find them. So you believe those spirits appeared back then, but not today, almost two thousand years after Christ died and reappeared?'

Brennan cleared his throat, annoyed with himself for getting dragged into theological debate with a bank clerk.

'I believe there are fakes and fools everywhere, Mr Wesley.'

Instead of taking umbrage at his words, Wesley ignored them.

'There are very few people in this world who are truly psychic, Sergeant. But from what I'd heard of Mrs Goodway, I had hoped that perhaps she did have that rarest of gifts. I listened to what she said with a growing anger, and a growing sense of loss. I have no idea where Susan is now, but I have a firm belief that she is still alive. The private detectives have received information she's living in Liverpool somewhere. But to be told in such stark terms that she was on the other side of nature . . .' He paused, took a deep breath then continued. 'But later, after I'd left, I sat at home with nothing but the mocking flames before me, and I tried to bring to mind what Susan would be doing at that precise moment. It's something I do often. Is she laughing? Or crying? Or carrying out the most mundane of chores? Or is she sitting there with that vacant expression on her face and thinking somehow of me, and what we meant to each other so many years ago? Is her spirit really trying to reach out to me? There have been times when I've almost heard a whisper in the darkness . . .'

His voice had grown steadily lower. Brennan was reminded of his own voice, in the confessional.

'But then, after my visit to Mrs Goodway, *I couldn't bring Susan to mind*. It was as if there had suddenly appeared a void in my head where *she* had always been. In the gloom of the night I stared at those portraits and could almost swear they were fading. I imagined some unseen force slowly erasing the contours of her face, the locks of her hair. Why should that be? And the awful prospect came to me: what if Mrs Goodway had been right after all? What if the private detectives were wrong and Susan Corbett *had* passed from this world and was really trying to contact me?'

'So you decided to pay her another visit, pay another pound?'

Wesley shook his head. 'I just wanted to talk to her. It had been impossible to have any sort of conversation with her the last time. Not with that aunt of hers hovering around.'

'The aunt who's been murdered, you mean?'

A flush spread across the young man's face. 'That was thoughtless of me. I am sorry.'

Brennan slapped his hands on his thighs, indicating that he'd heard enough. His instinct was to grab this fellow by his lapels and rattle him wildly around the room until he could shake some sense *into* him and all talk of thought transference *out* of him.

'Where were you two nights ago, Mr Wesley? The night Doris Goodway was murdered?'

Wesley smiled. 'I was home all night. I'm there most nights, unless I go to the theatre, if there's something worth watching. I go alone. I've never understood someone taking a female friend to the theatre when all you want to do is wallow in the drama, not listen to inconsequential babble.' He paused, then added, 'But that's the problem, isn't it? I live alone, so if I say I was at home on that particular night you just have to take my word for it, don't you?'

Brennan smiled back. 'Well then, Mr Wesley, I think that will be all for the moment.'

Wesley suddenly seemed to remember he was in pain. 'And my nose?'

'As with all things, Time is a great healer, wouldn't you agree?'

Before he had the chance to disagree, Wesley was

ushered from the office and out onto the street, shielding his ruddy nose from the bright morning sunshine.

*

'But why were you in Vere Street this morning? You hadn't even come on duty then.'

Constable Jaggery, walking alongside his sergeant, looked abashed.

'I just thought I'd take a look, Sergeant. I know Mrs Goodway's at her friend's house but I thought I'd see if the 'ouse were secure. An' I saw meladdo with his hands to the window like a peepin' Tom.'

'Was it necessary to hit him?'

'Only the once, Sergeant. Only the once.'

Brennan smiled at the man's ability to answer a question by avoiding it.

With the sun shining, and a freshening breeze in their faces as they walked down Wallgate towards their destination, it seemed a wonder to Brennan that these same streets, with their same sounds of trams shunting and rattling and the *clack-clack* of horses' hooves from passing wagons laden with all manner of fruit, fish or vegetables, had only yesterday been transformed into sinister and murky places where all manner of devilry was possible. This morning, though, they could smell the salt tang of the sea from the fish in their several boxes and the earthy freshness of the recently dug vegetables. Strange, he thought, how fog deadens more than the sense of sight.

Before they reached Pennyhurst Street, where Mabel Aspinall lived, Brennan placed an arm on Jaggery's shoulder.

'It might be an idea for you to cut down Miry Lane to Mason Street, Constable. Make sure Alice Goodway's safe and well at Hazel Aspinall's.'

Jaggery suppressed a smile and gave an elaborate salute before turning right into Miry Lane with a jaunty spring in his step.

Either the fellow's carrying a torch for the young widow, or she's bringing the father out in him, Brennan mused. He hoped it was the latter.

Five minutes later he was seated in Mabel Aspinall's front room, explaining why he was there. She sat opposite him, a suspicious expression on her face. She was in her late forties, he guessed, and already he could see incipient lines etching their way down from her lips, and slivers of grey in her black hair. There was a greyish pallor to her skin, which seemed to sag around the cheeks, as if they had once been fuller but now looked only drained. She still wore black for her late son, he noticed. There were two framed photographs on her mantelpiece, one of them showing a small boy dressed in a sailor suit with a mock-up pirate ship in the background; the other showed a man and woman posing for a studio photograph, the woman a younger version of Mabel. Even then she had a stern expression.

'He was a bonny lad, my Bert, eh?' she said with a nod at the young boy.

'He was indeed, Mrs Aspinall.'

She paused then said, 'So you reckon whoever did Doris was after Alice?'

'It's a possibility.' He didn't mention the second letter she had received that lent more credence to the possibility.

'Well, I'll be honest, Sergeant. I couldn't stand the woman. We'd had more than our share of rows, I can tell you. But it were bad, what 'appened to her. I'll grant you that. Still, I don't know how I can help.'

'I'm simply asking everyone who went to see Mrs Goodway about their visit.'

'Why?'

'To give me a better picture of what took place.'

She sniffed. 'Well, it were nowt like I'd imagined.'

'And why was that?'

'I've been to few sittings in my time. Not long back I went to a big house where a medium from Preston sat us all round a table an' had us all holdin' hands an' all that. An' she told us the spirits were with us an' lo an' be-bloody-hold the table starts rockin' from side to side. A bunch of flowers appears from nowhere.'

'Flowers?'

'Aye. From the ceilin'. Only I'm not bloody stupid. We could hear summat slidin' from the ceilin'. Them flowers were no more ghostly than I am. Amazin' what you can do with a bunch of flowers an' a piece of string. And a hole in the bloody ceilin'! When we got to Alice's house an' saw them rose petals on her table I thought, here we go again. But I were wrong. She spent more time talkin' about them rose petals than anythin' else. I were watchin' them petals, waitin' for 'em to disappear, but they didn't.'

'So if you think it's all a waste of time . . .'

'Didn't say that. I reckon there's summat in it right enough. It's just there's some what takes advantage an' they're no more psychic than next door's cat. What I'm sayin' is there's allus a chance. An' if there's a chance I can speak to my son, I take it.'

'According to your daughter-in-law, Alice told you some startling things.'

'What? Like Hazel were expectin'?'

'Yes.'

'It were a shock, I admit. But since then I've give it some thought. I mean, it were three months ago after all when my lad got killed. So it stands to reason she'd say summat to her closest friend, don't it? An' if Alice knew beforehand, well . . . Thick as thieves, them two. Nothin' supernatural about Alice knowin', is there?'

'Your daughter-in-law insists she told no one. Not even your son. She had planned to on the day of the accident.'

She sniffed. 'Aye well. Our Hazel might not want to tell the truth.'

'What do you mean?'

'She must've told Alice. That stands to reason. But she'd be shamed to high heaven if I found out she'd told Alice an' not me. I'll be its grandma when all's said an' done. And I reckon Alice only brought it up at the so-called séance 'cos I'd have found out in a few weeks anyroad. She's over three months gone an' she won't keep her shape much longer. They cooked the bloody thing up between 'em.'

Brennan was confused. This woman, according to her daughter-in-law, was a great believer in the spirit world and had more or less forced Hazel to attend the séance. Yet here she was offering a rational explanation for what was revealed that day. She must have seen the confusion on his face for she began to explain.

'I'm not sayin' Alice Goodway's a fraud, Sergeant. I believe she can make contact with the spirits. Only I don't think it worked that day.'

'Why not?'

She took a deep breath, and Brennan could see that she had been working herself up into a lather. She took a few moments to compose herself then continued.

'Well it's a fine thing, me findin' out like that. Bert wouldn't have blurted it out like that. Anyroad, I don't reckon it were a séance. Not a proper one. I said nowt at the time. But I don't reckon my lad's spirit was there that night.'

'Why not?'

'Because I'd've felt him there. An' I felt bugger all.'

He could see it played hard with Mabel Aspinall: a mother finding out something as important as that in such circumstances. Death and the promise of new life all in one cramped room . . .

She was about to say something else. He saw her lips compress together, but then she folded her arms to indicate her silence.

'You want to tell me something?' he asked.

'Only what I said. There were no spirits there that night. I think if my son had been in that room I'd 'ave been the first to know about it. I weren't. So he weren't. Besides, the smell of them dried rose petals made me feel sick. Too sweet by half.'

'Do you live alone, Mrs Aspinall?'

She bridled at that, nodding sharply at the photograph above the fireplace. 'I lost my husband years ago. An' I've been to a few séances where he's come through to me, told me to make sure I looked after little Bert.'

'So, the night Doris Goodway was murdered you were here alone?'

'I've just said so, haven't I?'

As he stepped outside into the bright sunshine, Brennan cast a glance down Pennyhurst Street. How many more conflicts, simmering and unresolved, lay behind each door?

Don't be a bloody fool, Mickey, he chided himself. *You're a policeman, not a priest.*

*

A problem, the police always around. But a problem's only a problem till it's dealt with. She has no means of knowing what's coming. And she'll get such a shock! Serve her right, though — no thought for who gets hurt through her lies.

Still, a lie's only a lie till it's dealt with.

Chapter Eight

Father Fergal Clooney had been parish priest at St Joseph's Roman Catholic Church, in Caroline Street for sixteen years now. He was, in fact, the first incumbent at the new church when the old one had been torn down to make way for a newer, larger building. He often looked back with fondness, and not a little pride, at the day the church was officially opened by the Right Reverend Dr O'Reilly, Bishop of Liverpool. It was a glorious day in more ways than one: the sun was beaming down, the streets of Wallgate were teeming with onlookers and those eager to catch a glimpse of the bishop, the visiting priests and deacons, and of course Father Clooney himself.

Often, in the intervening years, he had made reference to His Lordship's sermon that day, how Man's life was empty, restless, with nothing but a craving hunger and thirst, and that once those cravings were satisfied then

Man yearned for more, and more, until he must realise that there is nothing on this earth that can truly be said to satisfy what Man desires.

He thought of these things now, as he sat with Ettie Yates in the living room of the grocer's shop. It frustrated him more than he could say, how foolish, how *dangerous*, was this growing belief in the mystic power of Alice Goodway and her outlandish claims of communication with the dead.

'Have you heard of the Witch of Endor, Ettie?'

The grocer's wife shook her head. Ever since her visit to Alice Goodway, she had tried in vain to suppress the excitement she felt, either when dealing with customers or in the relative solitude of her home. When the tears came, as they did often, they were tears of joy. Even now, although grateful for the Father's visits, her eyes betrayed her.

'Saul had heard that a medium existed, one who could conjure up the spirits of the dead. So he visited this witch of Endor and asked her to bring to him the spirit of Samuel. And she did bring a spirit to him. One who brought terrible news to Saul, that the Lord will bring about the defeat of Saul and the Israelites to the Philistines.'

She looked at him, saw the pink flush on his cheeks as he leaned forward, hands clasped. She said, 'So this medium Saul saw were a success? She did what he asked.'

'It's believed that the spirit she conjured up was a false one, a demon, not Samuel at all.'

'I don't understand, Father. How can that have anythin' to do wi' Alice Goodway an' our Eve?'

He reached out and folded her hands in his. 'Because when you deal with the devil, there's nothing good can come. You thrust your hand into a beehive and it comes out covered with stings, not honey. Forgive me, child – Mrs Goodway brought forth no spirit, did she?'

'She did! She said . . .'

He held up one hand to calm her. 'No, Ettie. You *saw* nothing. It was just words, spoken by Alice. It was Alice who told you she could see her poor husband, was it not? Saul, at least, saw the demon posing as Samuel for himself. You – none of you – saw anything at all.'

'You sayin' she lied?'

The priest held up his hands, a gesture both of despair and denial.

At that moment, the door leading from the shop swung open and Len Yates came in. He gave their visitor a cursory nod and was moving through into the kitchen at the back of the house when Father Clooney spoke.

'And how are you keepin', Len?'

The grocer stopped and gave the priest a long, hard stare. Then he said, 'I'm keepin' meself to meself. Isn't that t'best way?'

Ettie raised her face to her husband's in mute appeal. *Be civil, at least.*

But Father Clooney merely smiled. He knew why Len Yates resented him. Why he resented the church itself.

There had been hard words spoken when their poor daughter Evie was taken from them, but he did not regret for an instant the way he had spoken to Len, and Ettie for that matter. The girl died, but the manner of her death was unforgiveable. They had deliberately flouted God's law and the teaching of the Holy Roman Church and the poor girl suffered as a result. He went along with the falsehood they had created surrounding her death – he was a merciful man, after all, and had no wish to add to their burdens by speaking the truth – but for them now to involve themselves with the ramblings of that poor deluded widow and her nonsense about the spirit world, well, he would do all he could to keep them away from such sinfulness.

They had sinned enough.

As Len Yates walked through into the kitchen, Father Clooney reached out to hold Ettie's hands once more. They felt frail, cold, a slight tremor running through them.

'Will you ask Len to come to church this Sunday? It's been a while.'

She shook her head. 'He won't.'

'He needs to. To find comfort.'

'You condemned him once. When all he were doin' was lookin' out for our Eve. He's a proud chap.'

'He looks troubled, Ettie.'

'Aye. An' not just about our Eve. It were what 'appened at Alice Goodway's.'

'Tell me.'

She remained silent for a while. From the expression on her face, it was clear she was making her mind up whether to reveal something important. Finally, she took a deep breath and spoke. 'Alice told us her Jack's spirit had brought a child. An' it were our grandchild. A grandson.'

Father Clooney gave a heavy sigh of frustration. 'You had no grandson, Ettie. We both know that. Nothing was born.'

She leaned forward, a fierce sparkle in her eyes. 'Aye, but what if the poor thing were just as alive as the rest of us? When 'e were inside our Eve, eh? An' a baby that dies inside the womb is just as much a livin' creature . . .'

Again, the priest held up his hand, this time in warning. 'Ettie. You're deceiving yourself and deceiving God Himself. We both know that what was taken from poor Eve's womb had no soul. How could it have? And it was still cursed with Original Sin that only Baptism can cleanse. Perhaps if the foetus had been allowed to grow . . . but you and Len took the decision to intervene. To bring that dreadful woman into your house and perform the work of the devil himself.'

'We did it to save our Eve's life! She couldn't give birth, not in her condition!'

'But she *wasn't* saved, was she?' said Father Clooney, more harshly than he intended. 'The abortion killed two, not one.'

He regretted the outburst as soon as it had left his lips

and leaned forward to apologise. But then he felt a sudden draught of air on the back of his neck as the kitchen door swung open and a huge figure hurtled towards him. He had no idea how long Len Yates had been listening there, but he could tell from the murderous expression on the grocer's face what was coming next.

*

The last thing Brennan expected to see, as he reached the place where Pennyhurst Street and Sharp Street intersected, was a bloodstained priest. And not any bloodstained priest either – old Father Clooney was his own parish priest, had dutifully listened and tutted his way through countless confessions Brennan had given at St Joseph's. So it was with some shock and anger that he watched the old man shambling along Sharp Street with a bloody handkerchief arresting the flow of blood from his nose. Two women whom he vaguely recognised were either side of the priest, supporting him with one arm and carrying their shopping baskets with the other.

'Father?' Brennan said as he approached. 'What's happened?'

The priest shook his head. 'It's nothing, Michael. Just a nosebleed.'

Brennan frowned. 'I can see that. But what's caused it?' He turned to face the women.

'You need to do your duty,' one of them said. She placed her basket on the pavement, ignoring a single potato that rolled into the gutter. 'Never seen anythin' like it in all my days.'

'Me neither!' declared her shopping companion, who also dropped her basket and fussed around the priest, irrelevantly stroking his grey hair back from his forehead.

'Like what?' Brennan felt his anger rising. Why couldn't people just say what they meant?

So the two women told him exactly what they had seen.

*

Lucas Wesley sat in Mesnes Park eating a sandwich and congratulated himself. He would never make a habit of lying to Mr Voles, but he had been left with no option once the assistant manager spotted the bruising around the bridge of his nose.

'A skipping rope?' Mr Voles's voice, while maintaining its professional pitch, had betrayed his shock at the unexpected response from his young clerk.

'Yes, Mr Voles. Tied from lamppost to railing, inches from the ground. It's a wonder I wasn't concussed.'

'Quite.' Voles's expression acknowledged his gratitude to small mercies. 'These children are the spawn of the devil himself.' And with a lugubrious shake of the head, he left his injured clerk to serve his customers.

Nearby, a group of mill girls sat on a small grass mound, enjoying the sudden burst of warm weather. Occasionally one of them would glance towards him and turn to her friends with a whispered comment.

More than likely an obscenity, he told himself, looking right through them and watching the slow movement of a family of ducks in the small pond behind them. Girls like that seemed such strange creatures, coarse and unlovable, a far cry from Susan and her wondrous imagination. It would never enter their minds to think of a world beyond their own midden, to create a fantasy world where everything had the sweetness and the joy of everything that Life had to offer. He'd seen them, as he made his occasional visit to the theatre, walking along with some rough-looking fellow linked as if by chains, or sitting in the snug of a public house and coyly making eyes at the men standing by the bar. It would be impossible to find beauty in them.

At that moment, they giggled and one of them said, loudly for his benefit, 'No! *You* ask him.'

He watched as one of them – a dark-haired girl, pert-faced and with hair tied tightly in a bun, like all of them from the mill – stood up and made her way towards him.

'Nah then,' she said by way of introduction.

He swallowed the last of his sandwich and brushed the few crumbs of bread from his waistcoat.

'I'm sorry,' he said. 'But I was just leaving.' He stood up.

The girl seemed undaunted. 'Only we was wonderin' where you work, like.'

'Why?'

'I reckon I've seen you in Ranicar's.'

He shook his head. Ranicar's specialised in funeral attire. Did he really seem so grave?

'Only we've seen you somewhere but we can't work out where, like.'

'The Royal Court Theatre, perhaps? I saw *The Case of Rebellious Susan* there last week.'

He gave the girl, and her friends, a cold smile and turned to go. It gave him a small thrill to name the production in front of them all, just as it gave him a thrill when he saw the posters around town advertising the play. With *her* name!

*

Never let it be said that Freddie Jaggery was one to disobey an order, especially from Detective Sergeant Brennan.

Cut down to Mason Street, and make sure Alice Goodway's safe and well at Hazel Aspinall's.

And so here he was, sitting in a most comfortable armchair with not one but two women fussing around him with mugs of tea and the nicest almond cake he had ever tasted.

'I can taste summat in this, like sweet an' tarty at the same time.'

Hazel Aspinall, kneeling before the fire and carefully placing coals in the grate, smiled. 'It were Bert's favourite, almond cake. His mam used to bring it round every week till . . . Anyroad, she still brings it. Religiously. I reckon it's her way of keepin' him here. Some I throw away. I've lost me appetite for it since Bert passed away. It's the lemon rind she grates in the mixture you can taste.'

'Well, it's very nice.'

'I bet you could eat another slice?' said Hazel, looking down at her hands stained with coal dust. 'Soon as I've give these a swill.'

Jaggery would never dream of upsetting a woman by refusing.

'I'll get it,' said Alice, who had been helping Hazel with her dusting.

No sooner had she left the front room than Hazel nodded in her direction and spoke in almost a whisper. 'She had some bad dreams last night.'

'No wonder,' Jaggery said. 'She's frightened to death.'

'She told me about the letters.'

Jaggery shifted in his seat. He was now on uncertain ground, not knowing if Sergeant Brennan wanted it to become public knowledge. There were times when he said it was better keeping things back from the public.

'Aye, well,' he said with a sniff, hoping she would accept that as his response.

She didn't. 'What I don't understand is why Doris was done in then. If this devil's threatenin' Alice.'

'Aye.'

'So what's Detective Sergeant Brennan doin' about it?'

'Investigatin'.'

'But he must 'ave some idea? I mean, it's not normal, is it, gettin' stuff like that shoved through your letterbox?'

Before he could answer, Alice came back with a fresh slice of almond cake. From the look in her eyes, Jaggery could tell she'd heard every word.

'Sergeant Brennan is doin' all he can,' she said, kneeling on the rug before the fire, alongside Hazel.

'That's true,' he agreed and took a larger-than-usual bite from the cake to forestall any further questioning.

At that point, a dark shadow passed across the front window, and there was a sharp knock on the door.

Jaggery, recognising the owner of the shadow, leaned forward and hurled the half-eaten slice of almond cake onto the fire, bringing a gasp of rebuke from Hazel Aspinall.

'It's his lordship,' Jaggery offered by way of explanation. 'An' he's not sent me here to eat cake.'

'I'll go,' Alice said and went to open the door.

Jaggery stood up as Sergeant Brennan entered.

'I hope my constable has been taking good care of you?' He was addressing the women but observing Jaggery.

'Been a good help,' Hazel Aspinall said and patted the object of her praise on his shoulder.

'And he's been helping himself to your delicious cake,' Brennan replied. 'I trust you'll clean those crumbs before we leave, Constable? They add nothing to your uniform.' He pointed to Jaggery's large chest. 'You settled in for a while, Mrs Goodway?'

Alice pursed her lips. 'I'm settled with Hazel here, if that's what you mean. But we're not stayin' in like prisoners in one of your cells.'

Brennan gave a curt nod in acknowledgement. 'Very well. As long as the two of you are together there's no problem. Constable, we have a small bit of police business to attend to.'

He bade both women farewell and the two policemen stepped out into the midday sun.

'What's this bit o' business, Sergeant?'

'We're making an arrest, and I might need some assistance. It's Len Yates.'

Jaggery smiled and flicked an errant crumb from his tunic. 'Piece o' cake, Sergeant. Piece o' cake.'

*

Brennan had asked the two women to escort Father Clooney back to his house which stood next door to St Joseph's Church. The old priest had been most adamant in his refusal to make any sort of complaint against Len Yates, but Brennan had told him with equal firmness that an assault on a man of the cloth was an assault on the church itself, and that no one should be allowed to get away with such a foul deed. Perhaps because of his injuries and the blood stubbornly refusing to stop flowing, Father Clooney had reluctantly allowed himself to be led back to Caroline Street and the tender care of his housekeeper, muttering vague phrases on the theme of forgiveness and how the whole sorry business was his fault.

But Brennan wasn't in a forgiving frame of mind, as

he had explained to Jaggery on their way to Len Yates's shop. Now, as they marched into the shop, they were greeted by Ettie Yates, her hands held up as in surrender.

'My Len's sorry for what he did.'

'I'll bet he is!' Brennan snapped.

'Only he didn't mean to burst Father Clooney's nose.'

'Where is he?'

Before she could answer, the door from the living room swung open and Len Yates emerged, his dark expression not lightened a jot by the passage of time.

'Out!' he yelled. 'It's my bloody shop an' I'll serve who I soddin' well please.'

Brennan took a step towards him. 'I'm not here to be served, Len. I'm here to arrest you for assaulting Father Clooney.'

He felt Constable Jaggery tense beside him.

'No man comes into my shop an' accuses me o' . . .'

'Len!' Ettie Yates's voice was ice-cold.

But her husband waved her away. From the flushed condition of his face, he was beyond the point where caution could control him.

'Him an' his holy shite! He got what he deserved an' if tha takes one more step in this shop I'll give you both the same as that bastard got!'

It always amazed Brennan how lightning-fast Freddie Jaggery could be. He flew across the shop and grabbed the grocer by the neck, forcing his head down onto the counter. With equal speed, though, Yates hurled himself

171

forward using his head as battering ram and launching his huge frame over the counter, swinging his right fist in such a violent flurry of blows that, had Jaggery been a tenth of a second slower in pulling his head back, it would more than likely have been wrenched from his shoulders by the force of the attack.

But despite his near brush with decapitation, Jaggery had a smile on his face that Brennan recognised only too well. It was almost a serene acknowledgement of pure joy in facing someone who could land a punch or two but who, sooner or later, would walk straight into his fearsome left.

Ettie Yates was screaming. Several passers-by now stood in the entrance to the shop and shouted their support for the grocer, Jaggery's uniform being a distinct disadvantage in garnering any sort of support.

With such an audience, though, and with both combatants squaring up to each other with fists clenched and circling each other as if they were in a boxing booth, Brennan made a decision. As Yates shuffled menacingly towards Jaggery, his fists poised ready to strike any second, Brennan reached down to a wooden box on a stand below the counter and removed one of the items lying there on display. Yates took one step too close to Jaggery, who swung a ferocious left that caught his opponent flush on the jaw. It wasn't enough to stop him, but then Brennan crept up behind him and raised his improvised weapon high in the air, causing both Jaggery and Ettie Yates to shout their objections, albeit for different reasons, before bringing it down hard on the back of the grocer's skull.

Len Yates staggered under the blow and stumbled forward, finally crumbling to the floor of his shop. His wife let out an almighty scream.

'You've burst his bloody head wide open! Them's his brains all over the shop!'

Before Brennan could point out to her that the squashed mess that even now was slithering from the counter and down the shop window was nothing to do with her husband's brains but rather more to do with the huge marrow he'd wielded, Ettie Yates fainted.

Jaggery again moved quickly and caught her, before carrying her through to the rear of the shop. When he came back, Brennan was once more improvising. He'd found some twine by the counter and was even now tying Yates's hands tightly behind his back.

'I didn't need no bloody vegetable!' said Jaggery as they both raised the half-conscious grocer to his feet. 'What'll folk think, eh?'

'Sergeant,' Brennan reminded him.

But for once, Jaggery ignored him. His pride and his prowess had taken a beating.

*

It was a different Len Yates who sat slumped in his chair facing Detective Sergeant Brennan. It wasn't the menacing presence of Constable Jaggery standing by the interview room door that subdued him, although privately Yates had to admit that, having felt the sheer brute force of the constable's left fist, he had been quite happy to be knocked senseless by one of his own marrows. The lack of aggression now had more to do with something deeper having been extinguished: the anger and the resentment that had been building up inside him these last few weeks – fuelled by the visit to Alice Goodway that Ettie had insisted they make – seemed to have erupted into violence, and now, once the explosion had subsided, he was left with nothing but emptiness.

'What possessed you to hit a priest, Len?' Brennan asked.

'Had it comin'. Thinks 'cos he wears that thing round his neck it gives him the right to stand as judge an' bloody jury.'

'How did he do that?'

Yates looked down at his hands. They were trembling slightly. 'It's between him an' me. Private.'

'Well it won't be private for long, will it?'

Yates looked up. 'What?'

'When it gets to court, well, it'll be all over the Wigan Observer. Do you read the Wigan Observer, Len?'

'Do I bloody 'ell as like.'

'Well there's a section in there that gives reports of what's been happening in court.'

'So?'

'So, when your trial is reported for all to read, how do

you think it's going to look? I mean, it's hardly likely to boost your trade, is it?'

Len Yates gave an ironic laugh. 'My customers don't need the Wigan bloody Observer to know what happened this mornin'. It'll be all round Wallgate by now. Faster than any newspaper report, that's for bloody certain.'

Brennan tried another tack. 'Gossip's one thing, Len. But think of the shame it'll bring on your wife, seeing your name in the paper.'

Len shook his head. 'Well there's sod all I can do about it now, is there? I gave him a crack an' that's the end of it.'

Brennan leaned forward. Although he knew Father Clooney had no intention of making a complaint and wouldn't dream of standing up in court and giving evidence against one of his own parishioners, Len Yates was unaware of that.

'I might be able to talk to Father Clooney. Get him to forget about it. Though his nose is quite a mess, I'm afraid.'

The prisoner looked at him. There was defeat in his eyes, Brennan could see, but also something else. What was it?

'So what dost want?' Yates's tone contained an element of suspicion.

'Just tell me the truth, Len. That's all I want. Why did you hit Father Clooney?'

Yates hesitated, then said, 'If I tell you, I need a guarantee.'

'Of what?'

'What I tell thee doesn't bring about another charge.'

'What sort of charge?'

'Summat that 'appened a while ago.'

Brennan looked across at Jaggery, who simply shrugged. 'If it was illegal . . .'

'It *were* illegal!' Yates slammed a fist down on the table. 'But it were *right*. She'd have died anyroad.'

Brennan began to realise what the man was referring to. They'd told him his daughter Eve had died giving birth because of the rickets she'd contracted as a child. But what if she didn't die in childbirth? What if . . .

'Are we talking about Doris Goodway, Len?'

The grocer flashed a glance at him, a mixture of respect and fear. But he said nothing.

'I think we are, aren't we?' Brennan now spoke slowly, deliberately. 'Let's say this is a theory of mine, shall we? No need to admit to anything.'

Yates gave a wary nod.

'Perhaps you arranged for Doris Goodway to perform an abortion on your daughter, to prevent the pregnancy going its full term.'

He paused, waiting for a reaction. But Yates merely stared at him, no flicker of emotion now, although Brennan could sense there was another build-up of feeling inside the man. This was the sorest of subjects.

'But perhaps the abortion went wrong and your daughter died. And both you and your wife have blamed yourselves ever since. Does that sound a good theory to you?'

Carefully, Yates gave a nod.

'Did you blame Doris Goodway as well, Len?'

He spoke the words so softly, with no trace of accusation in them, that they took the prisoner off guard. He swallowed hard and gripped both hands tightly together.

'She did what we'd asked. Weren't her fault my little Eve was weak. Doris said her stomach just couldn't take what she'd give her.'

'And what did she give her, Len?'

Again, a slow, sad shake of the head.

'It were nothin' like I thought it would be. She said me an' Ettie could stay, there'd be nothin' gruesome about it, no blood or anythin' like that. All she gave her were a cup o' tea.'

'Tea?'

'Aye. Funny smell to it, though. Like mint tea it were. An' our Eve drank it an' Doris left, sayin' we was to give it time to work its road through. So we did.'

His voice was now barely more than a whisper, and there was something in his simple words and the way he uttered them that seemed to darken the atmosphere in the room. Shadows that hadn't been there before now showed themselves, and from the street outside, the harsh rattle of carriages and the shouts of passers-by were muted.

'But later that night she started wi' a nosebleed, an' it

fair gushed out. Then as she were lied there in bed she said her fingers were tinglin' an' she felt sick. She stayed in bed for two days. We daren't send for the doctor 'cos he'd have reported us. But we did send word to Doris an' she came an' said it was just the stuff workin' its way through her system. Nothin' to worry about. An' then on the third night she screamed an' said she were wet. I've never seen as much blood in me life. She started gibberin' then an' said me an' her mam were nowt but butchers. Them were the last words she said. We were butchers.'

By the door, Jaggery shifted his stance.

Brennan stood up, heard the chair scrape back, for now every sound in the room was clear, sharp, piercing.

He cleared his throat and said quietly, 'I think it's time you got yourself home, Len. Don't you?'

*

Lucas Wesley was justifiably proud of his attendance record. In his four years at Parr's Bank, he had never once taken a day off, for any reason. Yet tonight, with his whole world disintegrating, he couldn't really see where he would ever get the strength again to stand behind the counter and engage with customers on any sort of personal level. At the slightest provocation, he could well find himself leaping across the counter and gripping the offending customer by the throat and throttling the life out of him.

On his return from work that evening, his heart had lifted when he picked up the letter postmarked in

Manchester. The detective agency would only be writing to him if they had some news as to Susan's whereabouts, and it was therefore with some excited trembling and fumbling that he finally managed to tear open the envelope and devour its contents.

Within a few seconds, the past had grown very much darker:

> '*Dear Sir. It is with some regret that we must inform you of our most recent findings. According to our extensive and exhaustive enquiries to date, we ascertained that Susan Corbett was residing in the Liverpool area. We have since discovered that the information was only partially correct. Sadly, Miss Corbett passed away two months ago after a prolonged period of illness at Prestwich Asylum, where she was held under the Lunacy Act. She is buried in an unmarked grave in the graveyard at nearby St Mary's Church.*
>
> '*Please accept our heartfelt condolences and find attached to this letter our final notice of payment.*'

*

The Inspector of Nuisances, Ralph Crankshaw, had had a good day.

For most of the afternoon and evening he had spent a profitable time in the market hall and fish market, and his small notebook contained several names of those stallholders soon to be appearing in court. Two fishmongers had been reported for allowing garbage and shells arising from the cleansing of fish to be left exposed around the stall, instead of placed in the statutory tub for the disposal thereof. A butcher had failed to wash down his stall and all blocks and boards thereunto belonging, and one stallholder had been heard hawking, shouting out his wares to all passers-by in direct contravention of By-Law Number 24, which the Inspector of Nuisances had been delighted to quote for him verbatim:

'No person shall hawk or cry any article for sale in any market or ring any bell, blow any horn, or use any other noisy instrument to attract any attention to his or her stall, or standing therein.'

All of the contraventions he had recorded in his note-book, and they would each bring in fines of ten shillings. 'A by-law is a by-law,' was his standard response to the inevitable, and occasionally blasphemous, abuse he suffered.

Tonight, as he walked up Market Street with an air of satisfaction at a job well done, he allowed his mind to drift towards other matters.

Doris Goodway, for instance.

The woman had been an abomination.

And while every Sunday he espoused the magnanimity and the virtues of the New Testament and the grace of God, during the week he couldn't help reflecting how the Old Testament, with its focus more on the punishment of sin and the iron will of God, was far closer to his views of how one should live.

That the Goodway woman had broken more than one commandment, he knew full well. The neighbourhood she lived in – and which contained its fair share of shops that occasionally transgressed his laws – was awash with rumours of her wickedness. Whereas the New Testament would urge him to pray for her, the Old Testament would advocate a just punishment.

Now, her niece by marriage was involving herself in matters that weren't far off devil worship.

As he stepped onto the tram at the top of Market Street, he recalled the words of Leviticus:

A woman that hath a familiar spirit shall surely be put to death.

The thought gave him comfort on his journey.

*

It was growing dark when Betty Bennet made the short journey from Herbert Street to Mason Street, where Florrie Wignall lived. The old woman lived alone, was almost blind and spent most of her time rocking in her chair and listening to the crackle of coal from the grate.

The gas lamps were lit, and she noticed small globes of mist around the glass that were a forewarning of a more powerful mist to come. *I'll be back home long before that*, she told herself. She held a large bag in front of her – Florrie's monthly washing load – and gave the few people she passed a friendly enough nod of greeting. Yet there was something slightly distant in the smile she gave them, as if it was formed too quickly to contain any real fondness.

There was always something in their eyes, an unspoken acknowledgement of what they regarded as the invisible blemish she still bore. Until her Frances died last year, she'd heard them whisper in the street, or as she left a shop, or even as she sat on a tram.

Bloody shame, the way her daughter went. Bonny lass before her brain melted.

'Appen it were for t'best, though, eh? Bein' put i' that place. My littluns were that scared when she shouted at 'em. All they did was say 'ello an' that.

Aye. Penny Gawp, eh?

An' they reckon poor Betty goes every week to see her in that asylum.

Wouldn't get me goin' yonder. They reckon it's catchin'.

Aye. If a dog goes mad we have the poor bugger put down, don't we?

Now that Frances was gone, the whispers had stopped, but the looks she still got carried their own whispers.

When she reached the alleyway that ran parallel to Mason Street, she walked down to Florrie's back gate and pushed it open. Once she'd dropped the bag of washing off on the back doorstep, she knocked on the door and waited. Normally, she would spend as little time as possible passing the time of day with any of her customers: a back-door drop was her customary and unobtrusive way of delivering. They always paid her beforehand, so the delivery of clean washing was merely a fulfilment of that contract. But she did like to spend a few minutes with old Florrie, making sure she was coping. And she felt a little ashamed that, in her semi-blindness, Florrie's eyes held no reprimand for her for having a daughter whose mind had been scrambled.

As she was waiting for Florrie to come to the door, Betty looked at the houses further along. At the third house down, she saw in the upstairs window a young woman standing there, both arms stretched out as if preparing to pull the bedroom curtains together. It was with something akin to shock that Betty recognised the woman.

Alice Goodway.

There was something a little strange about the young widow's actions. Both arms remained raised for action, but they stayed there, suspended in mid-air, with the feeble yellow light from an oil lamp casting grotesque shadows against the bedroom wall. It was as if she were staring out into the gathering gloom and searching for something, and the expression on her face seemed to suggest she would never find what she was looking for again.

For some reason, she was reminded of Frances, and the way she too had stared out, searching for something she could never find. Thirteen-year-old Frances, happily skipping into the park and urging the child she was with not to run off.

But the child had run off.

What had she been thinking, that moment she stooped low and pushed her way through the bushes to where she thought the foolish child was hiding?

Betty posed the questions she'd posed a thousand times since that day: what if, oh God help her, what if dear Frances hadn't gone looking for her?

And what if the child hadn't run away in the first place?

Such a simple act. With such devastating consequences.

At that moment, the back door opened and old Florrie stood there peering out into the gloom.

'Who's that?' she snapped.

Betty saw Alice Goodway pull the curtains together.

'Only me, Florrie,' came the reply.

'Ah, Betty, love. Come on in. It's gettin' colder than a petty latch out yonder.'

Betty picked up the washing and stepped inside.

Chapter Nine

The chief constable was in a tetchy mood that morning. Brennan knew there had been a meeting of the Watch Committee the previous evening, and more often than not, Captain Bell's ire was roused by his attendance there. By the very nature of the committee, it meant that occasionally its members, including the chairman the mayor, had some bone to pick, and it was clear, from his opening words, that the bone in question had been sharp and uncomfortable.

'Too much drunkenness in the town!' he quoted, his skeletal face taut and furious. 'Drunkenness! I ask you, Sergeant!'

Brennan, standing before the chief constable's desk, felt it prudent to refrain from stating the obvious. Which was what the Watch Committee had done.

'And they ask me what am I going to do about it! What

do they expect? Fill the constabulary with banner-waving Methodists? Or drum-banging zealots from the Salvation Army?'

Again, Brennan considered the question rhetorical.

'The mayor himself sits on the magistrates' bench and spends half of his time discharging the filth before him with a nod and a sympathetic wink. It's hypocrisy of the vilest kind. Punishment, that's what the devils need. Not a hail-fellow-well-met form of justice!'

He stood up and moved to the window overlooking King Street.

'There are times when I miss the simple life of the army.' His voice was now low, tinged with nostalgia. 'At least you knew if you transgressed you'd get the punishment you deserved. No winking there.'

Brennan sighed. He hadn't asked to be called into the man's office. He had much to do, and listening to the usual lamentations kept him from his task.

Captain Bell turned round, the expression on his face only fractionally less aggressive. 'Well?'

Brennan blinked. 'Well what, sir?'

'Do you think I asked you in here to while away the morning?'

'No, sir.'

'Well then.'

At a loss as to what he was expected to say, he said, 'Perhaps we could send our men into the local public houses and have a quiet word with . . .'

'Public houses? Quiet word? What on earth are you talking about, man?'

'The drunkenness, sir. I thought . . .'

'And I was asking about the progress you've made in the murder case.'

No you bloody well weren't! was what Brennan felt like saying. Instead, he said, 'It's a complicated case, sir.'

'Complicated? Seems clear cut to me. The aunt is murdered after receiving a threatening letter. Look for the sender, Sergeant. Look for the sender.'

'Actually, sir, the letter was addressed to *The Goodway Woman*. Could've been Alice *or* Doris Goodway. And while I have my suspicions about the sender . . .'

'Whom do you suspect?'

'It's only a suspicion. But it may have been sent by Mr Ralph Crankshaw.'

Captain Bell gave a rare smile. 'Indeed? The Inspector of Nuisances making a nuisance of himself, eh?'

Brennan took it as one of those rarest of utterances from the chief constable – a joke – so he returned the smile.

'This is no laughing matter, Sergeant,' came the immediate response. 'What have you charged him with?'

'Nothing, sir.'

'Nothing? He threatens a woman and she is later found murdered – or at least her aunt is – and you charge him with nothing? Did you wink at him, by any chance?'

'No, sir. I've no proof. And his wife has stated he was at home with her on the night of the murder.'

'His wife? You surely cannot put faith in the word of a *wife*?' Captain Bell raised his arms in the air. 'Oh well that clears that up. His *wife* says.'

'I have little choice, sir.'

'And you define that as progress?'

'And since then,' Brennan added quickly, 'the young widow, Alice Goodway, has received another note. This time of a viler nature, accusing her of being a *lying bitch*. It would suggest that Alice Goodway is the target after all. Whether Doris Goodway was murdered by mistake, or whether she was deliberately targeted too, I'm not yet sure.'

'And have you again questioned our esteemed Inspector of Nuisances or sent him a basket of fruit?'

Brennan shook his head. 'The handwriting wasn't the same. He could have got someone else to write it – his wife perhaps – or disguised it himself, but I'm not convinced.'

'I see. Any more *progress* I should hear about?'

'There are several people who called upon Alice Goodway to . . . contact departed ones. I've spoken to all of them now. I'm convinced the answer lies with one of them. Something I haven't worked out yet.'

'Well, see that you do work it out, Sergeant.' He waved at the door. 'We don't want another murder on your hands.'

'No, sir.'

As he opened the door, the chief constable said, 'Oh, and it might be worthwhile to send some of our constables to the more notorious public houses. Have a quiet word, you know?'

'Yes, sir,' said Brennan. 'An excellent idea.'

*

Hazel Aspinall felt decidedly uncomfortable that morning. Her mother-in-law had developed an awkward blend of coldness and warmth towards her ever since she discovered she was pregnant. The coldness was caused by her feeling of exclusion; that her own daughter-in-law hadn't seen fit to share with her the news she was soon to be a grandmother had rankled with her: she had known for three months, after all. Now that her son had gone, it was Hazel herself who bore the brunt of her resentment. And yet there were other times when she showed her daughter-in-law a deal of warmth and an evident desire to make sure the pregnancy ran its full course and her grandson – for she was convinced the child would be male – be welcomed into the family and brought up in the very image of his father.

Hazel wondered if she'd ever be able to exercise enough control over the woman to prevent her from regarding the child as her own son.

This morning, Mabel had called round with a sponge cake, some beef tea and oatmeal, and a large bottle of castor oil, the latter a response to Hazel's throwaway comment the other day that she was feeling *a little bunged up*.

'It's by far the best,' her mother-in-law pointed out as she emptied her basket of treats. 'Better than Epsom. Just make sure you don't overdo it, 'cos then you'll be swappin' constipation for bein' sick.'

Alice, who had volunteered to make their visitor some tea, tried to suppress a smile, but the ever-sharp Mabel caught it.

'Oh, well may you smirk, Alice Goodway, but when I had our Bert, I never went for a week. An' the joy when I swallowed a few spoons of castor oil. The bloody lot came out.'

Hazel steadfastly refused to take even a drop of the castor oil, made a vague promise to take some later, and looked positively relieved when her mother-in-law suggested that perhaps she should go upstairs and have a lie down *'cos there's two of you needs restin' now, don't forget.*

As soon as Hazel had left the kitchen, it was clear that Mabel's concern for her condition was coloured by other considerations.

'I'm glad we can 'ave a little chat, Alice, love,' she said in a low voice. 'Just us two, like.'

'Oh aye?' replied Alice. She placed the teapot on the table between them.

'It's just that I've been thinkin'.'

'About what?' Alice had a good idea what the answer would be.

'Oh, I know ever since Doris was . . . since Doris passed away you've not done anythin' in the spirit way o' things.'

'No, I've not.'

'An' I know I might have said a few things that cast doubt on what you can do. But what with our Hazel lettin' you stay here while the police do their job, well, I was wonderin' if you could see your way to havin' a sittin' here? Just for me.'

Alice gave a little cough. 'I've said I've done wi' all that.'

'But you've got a gift, Alice, love. Believe me, I've seen frauds all right. But you . . .'

Alice reached for the teapot and poured out their drinks.

'I mean, I know what I said last time . . . but that were because I'd found out about our Hazel's condition. Send anyone round the bend, summat like that. But I've been lied awake in the early hours an' got to thinkin'.'

'You said you didn't think Bert was there. Or my Jack, for that matter.'

'Aye, well, I were upset. An' I did reckon Hazel had told you. About her condition.'

'She'd said nothin' to me,' said Alice.

'I accept that. But I were lied there last night, thinkin'. If I can just get in touch wi' my lad once more. I said some harsh things . . . I just want to make things right with him.'

But Alice picked up her cup, took a small sip and slowly shook her head.

'I'm sorry, Mabel. But like I said. I've done with all that. All it's brought is misery.'

191

Mabel leaned forward. 'I'll pay,' she said. 'I wouldn't expect it done for nothin'.'

'I won't do it again. I've made me mind up.'

Mabel's lips pressed together until they lost their redness. 'You don't think that's a bit bloody selfish?'

'I'm sorry.'

'You're leavin' my lad stuck out yonder like a lost soul?'

'He's not lost, Mabel, he's . . .'

But Mabel had had enough. She stood up, slammed her fists down on the table with such force that the cups rattled and tea stained the surface.

'You bloody selfish stuck-up little bitch!'

There was no attempt to keep her voice down now.

'After all my Hazel's done for you, keepin' you safe an' sound while she's not only weighed down with grief but expectin' her dead husband's child. My son's child!'

Alice sat there but the expression in her eyes was one of matching anger. The meekness of a second ago had been replaced by a fiery passion.

'And what do you think I'm feelin', eh? My Jack's dead, Aunty Doris is murdered in my bed an' some madman's after killin' me. What 'ave I got to look forward to? At least you've got summat on its way and so has Hazel. Me? It's all black. Nothin' but black.'

Her outburst caused Mabel to blink several times. When the door opened and Hazel walked in, she stood there, silent.

'What's all this shoutin' about?' Hazel asked.

Neither Mabel nor Alice gave any reply.

'You don't need to tell me 'cos I know. I heard it all.' She moved over to stand before her mother-in-law and gave her a steely glare. The older woman returned it, defiance almost spitting from her eyes.

'Hazel,' Alice began.

But her friend raised a hand to forestall any further comment.

'Mabel here said last time was all a lie, that my husband never came. But your Jack brought him, didn't he, Alice? I never told you about bein' with child, no matter what Mabel says. An' I never told Bert neither.' She turned to her mother-in-law. 'Believe what you want about that. I told no one.'

Mabel sat down and wrapped her hands around the teacup.

Hazel placed a hand on her friend's arm. 'I know you can speak to Jack. I know he's there. With my Bert. But I reckon you're right, not doin' any of that stuff anymore. We should let the spirits rest, eh, Alice? Leave 'em be. I think they've been disturbed enough.'

Her mother-in-law looked up from her cup and gave the two of them a look of such venom that Alice was forced to look away.

*

There were still traces of ground frost around the graves at Wigan Cemetery in Lower Ince. Ettie Yates was on her knees arranging the small spray of flowers she had brought. She was humming an old lullaby, and then she stopped and spoke very gently, the way she used to do when tucking little Eve into bed.

'Now, you'll like these flowers, my love. And he'll *love* the colours.'

Her husband Len was standing a few feet away. He frowned, thought about interrupting, but remained silent. Instead he gazed at the headstone that bore Eve's name.

A little more than a year ago, he thought, this headstone did not exist. It was lying in the stonemason's backyard, or in a quarry somewhere just waiting to be cut free to serve its melancholy purpose. Back then, his daughter had changed from the silly carefree lass who often spoke to him as if he were the child and she the parent, into a pale and sullen shadow of what she had once been.

He never got the chance to lay hands on the bastard who ruined her. Eve had steadfastly refused to name him, despite his dire threats, which she well knew he would never have carried out. She was his angel. Then and now. But she was a stubborn lass, too, and in her mind she was saving whoever he was from a thundering and possibly fatal attack. She knew that her father was a lamb towards her but a rabid dog to anyone causing her harm.

If the swine had been any sort of man and owned up to what he'd done, then perhaps Len could have forgiven him after giving him the beating of his life. But as long as he did the right thing by his little Eve, then she may have been happy. But she never gave him a name.

Even as such thoughts entered his head, he dismissed them. Whether he'd known the swine or not, they still had to face the dreadful reality of her condition: the rickets she'd suffered as a child meant that she must never get pregnant.

And there she was. Pregnant.

An abortion was the only way. Ettie had said that Doris Goodway had heard from the usual sources and approached her with the solution. And to the very small band of those who knew what was happening – namely Len and Ettie – Doris had done all she could and it wasn't her fault that the procedure went wrong.

'Whose bloody fault was it then?' Len asked, addressing his remarks to the cold stone on his daughter's grave.

'What did you say?' said Ettie, who heaved herself up and wiped the dirt from her hands, a half-smile on her lips.

'Nothin'!' he snapped.

'Well just you watch your language, Len Yates.' She turned and nodded in the direction of their daughter's grave. 'We don't want her disturbin'. An' the little one shouldn't be hearin' stuff like that anyroad.'

At the far end of the cemetery, he saw a group of gravediggers carrying out their melancholy duty, their spades slicing into the hard, unyielding soil.

'*Little one?*'

He shook his head sadly and was about to rebuke her for such nonsense. Instead, he pointed to the flowers laid out on the grave. 'I don't know why tha's bothered. Them things'll be dead this time tomorrow. Frost shows no pity.'

*

Although he had a professed interest in the world of mediums and séances and contact with the departed in general, Lucas Wesley had come across some nonsense in his researches. People visit mediums out of grief, or fascination, or doubt, or for more mercenary reasons, such as those who would dearly love to know where that missing money had got to. He'd read widely, too, and he recalled the experiences of a Swedish believer named Helleberg whose son Emil had passed away. During a séance, a beautiful passion flower miraculously appeared before them with a slate-written message from the child.

Lucas had almost burst his sides laughing at that one. Especially when, at a later séance, the child's spirit told his father that if he were to examine the flower more closely (he'd had it preserved in a glass jar with deodorised alcohol) he'd find hidden among its petals a small dove. And would you believe it – he found it!

The sad gullibility of it all.

And yet, he had read of other séances, other experiences, where the revelations were not only feasible but indisputable.

It was those he clung to as he left Parr's Bank that

lunchtime, his face still flushed from the confrontation in Mr Voles's office. The manager, dissatisfied with his clerk's excuse that he *felt rather unwell* the previous day and had decided to stay at home, had shown scant sympathy.

'*Unwell covers a multitude of sins, does it not, Wesley?*'

'*I don't know what you mean, sir.*'

'*It ranges from a malingering lassitude, to over-indulgence, through to diphtheria. Where on that scale would you place your unwellness?*'

'*I had a stomach upset, sir.*'

'*Is that all? Where would we all be if we succumbed to what the working classes hereabouts term* bellywarch?'

'*And I was vomiting, sir.*'

A pause, while a nightmare scenario involving bank clerks, five pound notes and a counter swimming in vile matter, flickered across the manager's mind.

'*Well. Indeed. I have always sworn by effervescent draughts myself,*' came the slightly less abrasive reply. '*And today? The sensation has thankfully passed?*'

'*Indeed it has, sir.*'

'*Right. Well, you may return to your position. But if there is the slightest twinge . . .*'

'*I shall remove myself, sir. Of course.*'

Lucas couldn't muster a smile at the memory – the devastating news he'd received yesterday that his dearest Susan was dead and buried in an unmarked grave put paid to any smiling – but he felt some satisfaction at the man's discomfiture.

He had a full hour to do what he had to do. If it were

really true that Susan Corbett was dead – and he had no reason to doubt it – then his quest became far more difficult and far less rewarding, yet he was absolutely convinced that her spirit would be waiting to be reached. His first meeting with Alice Goodway could hardly have been called a séance: there had been none of the paraphernalia he'd come to associate with such things, and yet it was that very simplicity, almost a naivety, that had intrigued him. Of course, he had doubted her when she gave him mere platitudes, and he had been sure that both she and that aunt of hers had been fraudulent. And when they refused to return his money he had been quite justified in losing his temper. But now? Had she really made contact with his beloved Susan? He'd gone there convinced she was alive and left angry to be told she was dead.

Had his anger been misplaced after all?

Perhaps the aunt's death – her murder – served to intensify Alice Goodway's psychic gifts? He'd heard that deep personal grief serves well as a psychic conduit, renders the medium more receptive to the bidding of the spirit world.

Things may work for the best after all.

There was only one way to find out. But going to see her had now become a complicated business. He knew, from his unfortunate run-in with the bear-like constable, that her house was now empty and that Mrs Goodway was staying elsewhere. He needed to find her, but that wasn't really a problem.

He knew just where to get that information.

No, the problem would be two-fold, as he saw it. If the police were to find him anywhere near the woman, he'd doubtless be hauled into the station again, so he needed to be extra vigilant when seeking her out. The second problem might prove to be the more difficult, though: persuading an anxious young widow to contact her spirit guide – her late husband – in order to bring forth dear Susan's spirit from the ether if, as he'd been forcibly informed by Sergeant Brennan and his odious gorilla, she had decided to leave the psychic world behind her.

He would do everything he could to change her mind on that.

*

Brennan sat at his desk, listening to the subdued mutterings from the front desk along the corridor from his office. A constable was making a short statement to the desk sergeant enumerating the short catalogue of crimes the one he'd just dragged in was to be charged with. From what he could hear through the closed door, it was a depressingly mundane set of offences: drunkenness; begging; threatening behaviour; assault with a clog.

He shook his head and gazed down at the sheet of paper on which he had been idly drawing. The case was beginning to annoy him, and he tried to put his thoughts into some kind of order.

Doris Goodway, a woman of dubious character, an

abortionist, was suffocated in her niece's home. She had been sleeping in the front room, a bedroom usually occupied by Alice Goodway. So, was Doris the intended victim or the young widow who should have been in the bed?

The two of them had been carrying on some kind of fraud, convincing locals that Alice could speak to the dead: namely her late husband, killed down the pit three months ago. He would be the one to escort the dead from their resting place. Even as he thought about it, the sheer stupidity of people swallowing such nonsense was hard to believe.

Still, the ones who paid them a visit had all suffered the loss of a loved one.

Peggy Clayforth, an old woman longing to speak with her late husband once more before Death consumed her too. From the evidence of her soiled handkerchief, he guessed she hadn't long left.

Lucas Wesley, a bank clerk whose search for his one-time sweetheart was a quest to find a living person, not a dead one. A nonsensical belief that there are those in this world who can read the thoughts and feelings of distant people.

Len and Ettie Yates, whose daughter Eve so tragically died during an abortion carried out by Doris Goodway. According to Len, the man who got the poor girl pregnant was never found.

Betty Bennet, whose daughter Frances was brutally attacked at such a tender age and whose innocent mind couldn't cope with the horror of such a vile act. Again, as with Eve Yates, the one responsible was never caught.

Hazel Aspinall, a young widow expecting a child, who only visited her friend Alice because her mother-in-law urged her to. She had a firm belief in Alice's powers, especially as she swore she told neither Alice nor her husband about being with child.

And Mabel Aspinall, who was hoping to speak once more with her son Bert who died in the same pit blast that fatally injured Jack Goodway, the so-called *spirit guide*.

He shook his head. The one common thread linking them all was an intense sadness, a sense of bitter loss. Anyone taking advantage of people like that was beneath contempt. And yet Alice Goodway didn't come across as contemptible at all. Unlike her aunt by marriage. Perhaps Alice really did believe she was communicating with the spirit world? It would be a sign of mental disturbance, of course. But grief can have that effect. She had only been married a year and the loss of her husband must have dealt her a devastating blow.

He sighed heavily.

There was also Mr Ralph Crankshaw, Inspector of Nuisances, who in all likelihood had sent Alice Goodway a biblical quotation out of his sense of outrage at her meddling with what he regarded as unholy matters. He had also had strong words with Doris Goodway and brought her to court. But did his sense of righteousness turn him into a murderer, breaking one commandment to reinforce another?

But the second note, this one more direct and abusive, accusing Alice Goodway of being a *lying bitch*. Who had sent that particular message? The handwriting was completely different from the first letter. And the sentiment was expressed with a coarseness that seemed alien to the austere Ralph Crankshaw. Yet was it within the realm of possibility that *two* people should send menacing letters quite independently of each other?

Was anyone on that list responsible for the murder of Doris Goodway?

He gazed down at the drawing he had made on the sheet of paper before him. It was a flower, a misshapen unrecognisable flower with petals and a stem no gardener would recognise. With a smile, he placed his pencil in the small compartment reserved for his writing material and screwed up the paper, aiming for the basket in the corner by the door. He missed, sighed, then frowned as something struck him as odd. He stood up, walked over to the basket and retrieved the ball of writing paper.

He then took it back to his desk and smoothed it out, so that the flower appeared once more.

*

Fascinated though he was by the story Peggy Clayforth told him of her husband's briar pipe, Lucas Wesley couldn't help growing slightly frustrated.

He'd knocked on her door and asked her how she was doing. The question had thrown the old woman at first:

she had told no one of the blood she was now regularly coughing up, and she would accept no pity even if she had. But then he told her he'd paid Alice Goodway a visit, and he was simply wondering if what she had been told had left her wanting more from the young widow. He told her of his relationship with Susan Corbett, and how desperate he was to hear from her once more.

Now, as they sat in her kitchen nursing cups of tea, Peggy could see that there was something in the young clerk's eyes, a deep sadness, and a yearning that could never be satisfied in this world.

'I got what I wanted,' she said quietly. 'I know my Matthew's there, waitin' for me. Gave me comfort, did that. Now it's just a matter o' bidin' me time.'

'It left me wondering,' he said. 'I would dearly love to pay her another visit.'

'Ah,' said the old woman with a shake of the head. 'I've heard she's stopped all that. Since Doris got killed.'

'I know. It's just . . . I have some very important questions I need to ask Susan.' He took a deep breath and justified the coming lie with the prospect of what it might lead to. 'You see, there's some other girl I'm seeing and, well, I just wanted to know if she approved. We were so close and . . .'

His eyes showed such longing that Peggy had no sense of the falsehood he'd just told her. The fact that she now felt so close to death herself gave her a sense of power: here was a young man tormented by his contact with the spirits and she had the wherewithal to help him resolve his difficulty. It would be a neighbourly kindness.

'I'm not sayin' you'll get anywhere with her,' she said with a shake of the head, 'but there's nowt wrong with tryin', is there?'

Lucas's heart fluttered.

'Anyroad, a friend of mine, Betty Bennet, told me she's stayin' with her friend Hazel Aspinall. Betty saw Alice in an upstairs window. I don't think she feels right stayin' in her own house, not with what happened to Doris an' all.'

Lucas made suitably sympathetic noises and waited for the old woman to give him the address.

As he stepped outside after thanking her profusely, he checked his fob watch. He had a ten-minute walk back into town and the bank. He felt some frustration, now that he knew exactly where to find Alice Goodway, that he couldn't simply march round to Mason Street right away and seek out some resolution. But he had a respectable situation at Parr's Bank, and it would do no good to place that in jeopardy for the sake of a few hours. But rest assured, he promised himself as he made his way quickly back towards town, he would be face to face with Mrs Goodway soon, come hell or high water.

*

If Lucas Wesley had bothered to call at Yates's Grocery Shop, he could have saved himself some trouble, for the information he sought from old Peggy Clayforth was being distributed freely at that very moment to those customers who stood in the shop patiently waiting for Ettie Yates to arrange the counterweights for her scales. As she took particular care with reaching the exact weight with every purchase, her usual customers regularly took the opportunity to swap tales and hear the latest scandals, more often than not concerning marital strife or moral laxity.

Betty Bennet stood at the front of the queue, having placed her order for onions and potatoes. She watched the grocer's wife take one potato at a time and place it in the curved brass bowl on one end of the scales, and the woman's attempt at precision was irking her.

'Are them spuds heavier than normal?' she asked with a note of irritation in her voice.

'No potato weighs the same, Mrs Bennet. They're all different.'

'Aye, so why not pour the lot in an' take 'em out one at a time, eh?'

Ettie Yates gave the woman behind Betty a patronising smile then pointed a potato at Betty's folded arms. 'We don't all have your strength, Mrs Bennet. Some of us have the arms of ladies, not coalbaggers.'

There was a snigger from the group of women standing behind Betty.

Betty felt herself blush and was aware that the general hubbub in the shop had now become more subdued, wary, with the promise of a confrontation. Ettie Yates had seemed in a queer sort of mood this lunchtime, her eyes sparkling and her smile just that little bit forced.

Betty pursed her lips and said nothing. If she'd launched into the attack, the others would inevitably put it down to the family trait of mental instability. But Frances's memory deserved better than what Betty had felt like saying. So she kept silent.

But the mood Ettie Yates was in, coupled with the impression that silence meant weakness, caused the grocer's wife to add a further comment.

'Is it right, Mrs Bennet, that when you went to see Alice Goodway your daughter was talkin' sense?'

Betty felt the muscles in her arms grow taut.

'Where did you hear that?' she said.

'Oh, it were no secret. It were Doris what told me. God rest her soul, like.'

'Well she'd no right. It were private.'

Some of them muttered behind her. She couldn't tell everything they were saying, but it would inevitably involve poor Frances, and when she heard one of them say *Penny Gawp* followed by a snigger she gritted her teeth and flushed a deep scarlet. One of the women – she couldn't tell which one because she knew if she turned round all hell would break loose – had tried to quieten the gossips down, had even told them they should be ashamed of themselves which only occasioned a chorus of sniffs.

Ettie smiled broadly. 'Well it must've been a comfort to you, Mrs Bennet. Knowin' she weren't that way anymore.'

Before Betty could respond, one of the women behind her said, 'I've heard that young lass has stopped all that anyroad.'

Ettie placed a final potato on the scales and gave a smile of achievement. 'Oh, I'm sure she'll find her way of doin' some of us a good turn, eh, Mrs Bennet?'

Betty remained silent, not trusting her own voice.

The woman who'd spoken up went on. 'Well, it were Mabel Aspinall told me an' she should know.'

'An' why should she know?' Ettie's smile had now frozen.

'Because that young lass is stayin' with their Hazel, that's why. Thick as thieves, Hazel an' Alice.'

'Stands to reason,' said another of the customers. 'Both lost their husbands in the blast. Only natural they should look after each other.'

'That doesn't mean Alice'll stop reachin' out to the spirits,' said Ettie. Her words contained a note of both defiance and uncertainty.

'My fella's been doin' that for years!' quipped one of them.

'She's done wi' all that,' said another. 'Mark my words.'

'There's plenty more young Alice'll be tellin' us. Don't you think so, Betty?'

Betty Bennet now turned round and faced the woman who spoke. 'They don't call my lass names anymore. Not where she is now. Where no devil can hurt her. An' we can talk in peace.'

She turned her back on the woman and faced the counter. Both Betty Bennet and Ettie Yates looked at each other in some sort of communion of minds. They were both thinking the same thing.

*

People trusted Betty Bennet with their washing, but they kept their distance any other time. She'd felt that even more keenly only that afternoon when the whole of Yates's shop seemed to conspire against her with their sniggering comments about her darling Frances. Sometimes, she felt she had to protect her poor confused daughter more in death than she ever did in life: and on those occasions, the bitterness and unfairness of what happened back then came rushing back to her with all the force of a tidal wave.

Tonight, she sat in her armchair, watching the coals glow and the sparks fly and sipped at the gin slowly.

In a way, she reflected, her Frances had had the better of the deal. After the monster had attacked her so vilely when she was barely thirteen, Frances at least had had the comfort of madness, a warm and deluding blanket to wrap around herself to keep all other monsters at bay and dwell in a world where such creatures lived far, far away. Even her constant searching for something or someone gave her some mad purpose in life. For Betty, though, seeing her poor daughter drift towards madness like an unmanned ship, the pain had grown almost unbearable.

Almost, that is, as long as her husband had stayed with them. Once he flew the coop, then the pain grew so much that it reached the point of numbness.

The one who'd done what he'd done . . . he had no face she could loathe, no back she could stab. Frances had given the police no description, nothing at all to help. He had vanished into oblivion. Or perhaps he was still among them, walking the streets with a cheery wave and a hearty smile?

But there was one other person to blame for what had happened to her daughter that day.

The young girl whom Frances had been looking after, who ran off and forced her to seek her out in the bushes where *he* was waiting.

If she hadn't run away like that, if Frances hadn't been compelled to follow her, then today, tonight, this moment before the flickering flames, she and her Frances might even now be sharing a tale or two, might be watching a child play with dolls before the hearth . . .

A child.

She thought then of Doris Goodway, and what she had done.

No point in telling Sergeant Brennan about that. Nothing whatsoever to do with him. At least that pig of a husband had coughed up enough to . . . But what fools men are. He'd imagined that once Doris Goodway had done her work on Frances, that the madness would leave her, along with the foetus.

She shook the thoughts out of her head. It was daft, thinking like that.

She drained the last of the gin and rested her head back. She closed one eye and watched a flame dance in the grate. Then she opened her eye and closed the other, noticing that the position of the flame had changed – one eye seemed to see one thing while the other saw it differently. But with both eyes open, the flame seemed to merge into the middle.

How many gins had she had?

She shook her head, lifted her powerful hands to her face and covered it.

Then she removed them.

An idea!

The last time she visited Alice Goodway, her daughter had spoken so clearly, as if the madness had been lifted from her like a veil. She could speak and therefore reason and, God help us, remember!

What if, after all these years, Frances's spirit could remember what her poor benighted mind had blocked out all those years ago? The face, the name, of the one who'd attacked her!

Wouldn't that be a thing, eh?

*

It was late afternoon, and the premature gloom, rendered heavier by the unlit gas lamps awaiting the arrival of the lamplighter, had seemed to reflect Brennan's mood as he

and Constable Jaggery made their way along Mason Street
to Hazel Aspinall's house. Usually, at this time, the front
doors would be open, the women would be leaning in
their doorways arms folded and sharing the minutiae of
the day until their husbands turned the corner of the
street ready for their tea, but the temperature had dropped
over the last few hours, and that meant that neighbours
stayed indoors making sure the warmth did the same.

Jaggery knocked on Hazel's door and waited. Brennan
moved to the front window, where the curtains were still
pulled back. There was no light from the front room,
which overlooked the pavement, unlike the other houses
in the street, although there seemed to be a thin sliver of
light from the rear of the house where the kitchen was.
He saw shadows move in the narrow gap beneath the
kitchen door, and he got the impression these movements
were urgent, almost frantic. He was about to order Jaggery
to make his way to the alleyway at the back when he saw
the kitchen door open and a dark figure move quickly to
the front door.

When the door swung open, he could see that it was
Hazel Aspinall, and when she peered out into the gloom
there seemed to be a wildness in her eyes, as if she had
only seconds earlier received a great shock. She seemed
taken aback when she registered Constable Jaggery's
uniform.

'Constable?' she said in a feeble voice. When Brennan
moved into view she gave a small gasp.

'What's the matter, Mrs Aspinall?' Brennan asked.

She swallowed hard. 'Nothin'. It's just . . . you appearin' like that. Out of the dark an' all.'

'Like a ghost, you mean?'

He'd meant it as a joke, not a very good one, he realised immediately as she raised a hand to her mouth and began to cry.

Suddenly, another figure showed up behind her. It was her mother-in-law, Mabel Aspinall.

'What do you lot want?'

Although there was resentment in her tone, Brennan could see traces of the same emotion Hazel had shown. Both women had been disturbed by something very recently. Suddenly, Brennan felt his throat turn dry.

'Where's Alice?' he asked. Without waiting for a reply, he brushed his way past the two of them and entered the house. He made his way immediately to the door to the kitchen and swung it open.

Alice Goodway was lying on the floor, not moving.

Chapter Ten

It was quite a spectacle, seeing Constable Jaggery fussing around the now-conscious Alice Goodway like a giant moth.

He'd heard Sergeant Brennan call out from the kitchen doorway and moved past the women with surprising speed. Once he saw the young widow sprawled out on the floor he gave an audible gasp and stood over his superior as he knelt beside her.

'Tell me she's not dead!' said Jaggery.

'She's not dead,' came the reply. 'Looks like she fainted. You might help by picking her up and taking her through to the front room. There's a couch she can lie on.'

Jaggery did as he was told. As he placed both hands beneath her waist, he saw her eyes flicker open, and she gave him a look of sheer helplessness. She tried to speak but nothing came out. Within seconds, he'd laid her down on the couch and rested her head on a small cushion. Her skin felt cold.

By now, the two women had closed the front door and were standing before the hearth, where the last ashes were slowly subsiding, tiny sparks floating upwards being the only signs that the coals had once been lit. Jaggery gazed anxiously at the prostrate form, noticed her face was a deathly pale, and her lips were cracked and dry.

'I'll get some water for the lass,' he said to Brennan. Without waiting for his superior's assent, he walked into the kitchen.

Brennan glared at the two women. 'Do you mind telling me what's been going on?'

It was Mabel Aspinall who spoke. 'It's no secret. Alice yonder was doin' a sittin' for us. When you knocked on the door she collapsed. I think you frightened her.'

'A sitting? You mean, talking to the spirits and that?'

'Yes.'

'I thought she'd done with all that nonsense?'

'It's not nonsense!' Hazel's voice was high pitched, almost a screech. To Brennan, her nerves seemed taut, ready to snap. 'I didn't want her to do it. It were Mabel here, started on an' on about it. So Alice agreed to do it just once more.'

'Why?'

'Because I wanted to make contact,' Mabel spoke in a

harsh tone. 'Say things to my lad an' ask things we didn't get the chance to last time. Then you knocked on the door an' madam yonder decided to keel over.' She gave a curt nod in the direction of the couch.

Brennan gave a heavy sigh of irritation. He'd just about had enough of this spiritualist rubbish, and he felt like grabbing hold of the two women and shaking the superstitious nonsense out of them once and for all. But before he could say anything, two things happened. Alice Goodway opened her eyes and blinked several times before she registered Brennan's presence. Then Jaggery came from the kitchen with a cup of water in his hand. However, instead of reaching down to the still prostrate Alice, he pushed the cup into Hazel's hand and leaned into Brennan, pulling him towards him with his giant fist.

'Sergeant,' he whispered in his ear. 'I'm goin' outside. Round the front.'

Brennan pulled back and looked at his constable as if he'd completely lost his senses. 'Why?'

'Because there's some bugger lurkin' out at the back, just near the alley gate. If he sees me come out the back door he'll scarper. I'll get the sod, whoever he is.'

Before Brennan could say another word, Jaggery was opening the front door and disappearing into the gloom beyond.

*

'What's goin' on?' Alice Goodway's voice was thin, brittle. She heaved herself up and looked at Brennan, then Hazel and Mabel Aspinall. She raised a hand and pressed it against her head. 'What am I doin' here?'

'You fainted, Alice,' said Mabel, looking not at the patient on the couch but directly at Brennan whom she evidently blamed for Alice's condition.

'You were talkin' to Jack when the sergeant here knocked.' Hazel knelt beside her friend and stroked some stray wisps of hair from her forehead.

Brennan remained tight-lipped, moving towards the kitchen once it became clear that Alice was conscious and aware of her surroundings. Through the curtainless window he saw only the darkening shadows of backyard paraphernalia: mangle draped in tarpaulin, a dolly tub with its peg lying against it at an angle, and what looked like the remnants of what had once been an armchair. He saw no one lurking there now.

As his eyes adjusted themselves to the gloom, he could see the gate resting half open, but the alley beyond was now swathed in darkness.

There was a silence that lasted a minute, and he could sense tension in the air.

Then he saw the gate swing inwards, and a huge shape – Jaggery's – come bursting through. Brennan marched quickly to the back door and opened it.

'Well?' he said to his constable who was by now breathing quite heavily.

Jaggery placed one hand against the door jamb and leaned on his outstretched arm. He shook his head and said, 'No bugger there, Sergeant. I could've sworn . . .'

Brennan slapped him hard on the shoulder. 'Never mind. You did your best.'

'Aye,' came the reply. 'How's the lass?'

'Come and see for yourself.'

As his constable brushed past him, Brennan stepped out into the small yard. He moved to the gate and pushed it further open, stepping out into the alleyway. A small row of lavatories – four in all – stood there in the dark. The doors were all closed, and he wondered if Jaggery had had the idea of looking in them. He moved as silently as he could to the first one, pressed a hand against the crumbling wooden door and forced it open.

Empty.

He moved along the other three, with equally disappointing results. Then, as he stepped back inside Hazel Aspinall's backyard he closed the yard gate behind him. Had there really been someone out here, or had his constable merely imagined it?

He shivered and went back inside.

There he found Alice Goodway sitting upright, handing the cup back to Jaggery with her thanks.

'Are you feeling all right?' he asked.

Alice nodded.

'I gather you were doing it again, Mrs Goodway.'

'Doin' what?' She looked at Hazel and Mabel who

were now sitting in the two armchairs either side of the hearth.

'Contacting the spirits of the departed.' The way he intoned the words left his listeners in no doubt as to what he thought of the practice.

'I was doin' a favour. That's all.'

Mabel gave a harsh cough. 'An' there's no crime in that, is there, Sergeant?'

'No.'

'An' there's no crime in contactin' the departed either, is there?'

Brennan stared at her. 'In my opinion, Mrs Aspinall, the only way you can contact the departed is writing them a letter, sending a telegram or using a telephone.'

'I meant the dead. It's no crime.'

'No, it isn't. Unless there's some kind of fraud going on.'

'Fraud? What do you mean?'

Brennan shook his head. 'Well, if Mrs Goodway here was charging you money for what she did . . . that could be taken as fraud.'

Alice spoke next. 'It was never my idea to charge folk.'

'No,' said Mabel with asperity. 'It were your Aunty Doris, God rest her blessed soul.'

'Besides,' added Hazel, 'Alice here weren't chargin' us a single penny – not a farthin' – for doin' the sittin' this afternoon. It was a favour, like she said.'

Suddenly, Alice stood up and swayed a little. Constable

Jaggery was immediately at her side, placing an arm around her shoulder.

'I'm all right,' she told him with a thin smile. 'I was just wonderin', what brought you here this afternoon, Sergeant? I must admit it gave me a bit of a shock to hear you knockin' at the very moment I could feel my Jack approachin' but that's 'cos we weren't expectin' nobody, were we, Hazel?'

'No, we weren't.'

'So what *are* you doin' here?' asked Mabel.

'Well,' said Brennan, 'I was hoping to ask Mrs Goodway here a few more questions. In private, if I could.'

Hazel stood up and beckoned for her mother-in-law to follow her into the kitchen, but it was clear the older woman had had enough of being ordered about by the police for one day.

She made straight for the front door, unhooking her coat from the back of the door.

'I'll feel more comfortable in me own house, thank you very much.'

With that parting comment, accompanied by a valedictory sniff, she opened the front door and slammed it on her way out.

'Constable? See that Hazel's all right,' said Brennan with a nod in Hazel's direction.

Jaggery gave him a surly look, which transformed itself into an expression of concern when he addressed the young widow. 'Don't you go taxin' yourself,' he said with an admonitory glance at the one he felt would be doing the taxing.

Once they had the front room to themselves, Brennan invited Alice to sit once more. He sat in one of the armchairs and moved it round slightly so he could face her.

'Now then, Mrs Goodway, what's all this about rose petals?'

*

Len Yates was beginning to worry about his wife. Ettie had always been deep, he knew that – there were times when she would let the smallest squabble gnaw away at her and she would sulk for a week or more – but since Eve's death last year, she had gradually grown even deeper, her long silences suddenly ending with bouts of spiteful recriminations that intimated that he was to blame for their daughter's death. Yet it had been Ettie herself who had sought out Doris Goodway to carry out the abortion. He affirmed that there was only one person responsible for Eve's death and it wasn't him, nor her. It might be that Doris held a share of the blame, but the one who bore most of it was the bastard who'd got her pregnant in the first place.

Since their first visit to Alice Goodway, however, Ettie's behaviour had changed. Where she had once allowed her grief to manifest itself in drawn-out silences, now she was alert, breezy almost, as if she had been given something special to cling onto.

He knew what it was, of course. The mention of a ghostly grandson.

A *grandson*, for God's sake!

And all it gave her was the falsest of hopes. How the blazes could she expect to gain comfort from that? There was no grandson, dead or roaming about in the spirit world. Of that he was sure. But Ettie had been given something and she would burn in hell before she would let go of it now.

While she had been serving the last of the customers, he had moved quickly to the front of the shop and brought in the baskets of produce on pavement display. He'd noticed that as the day wore on her mood grew more and more cheerful, almost as if she were anticipating something and couldn't wait for it to happen.

As he brought in the last of the baskets and was wiping his brow, he was surprised to see her emerge from the living quarters with her coat on and a small basket on her arm.

'An' where do you think you're goin'?' he asked.

'I said I'd call round see how old Peggy Clayforth is. She's not been in today an' she always calls in. Might be poorly. I've just put a few things in.' She held up the basket. 'I won't be long. Tea's in the oven.'

She gave his face a playful slap and, before he could raise any sort of objection, she was through the front door to the accompaniment of the entry bell.

*

Brennan was surprised when, instead of answering his question, Alice Goodway stood up and said, 'I need some fresh air, Sergeant.'

Before he could respond, she had gone over to the front door, where several coats were hanging on a peg, and taken one down.

He stood up, gave a frown and then realised the reason for her sudden desire for some air.

She was about to tell him something she didn't want her closest friend to overhear. The kitchen door would be an unlikely deterrent if Hazel were intent on eaves-dropping, and he knew it would be too much to expect Constable Jaggery to be alert to such a thing.

He shrugged. 'As you wish, but it's not exactly summer out there you know.'

She gave a smile. 'I need the cold. It's bracin'.'

So they opened the front door and stepped onto the pavement. Brennan noticed at the far end of the street, the lamplighter was making his slow progress, reaching up and bringing the gas to life inside its glass casing. He guided her towards the freshly lit lamp.

'Now then, Sergeant. You were askin' me summat.'

'You held these séances . . .'

'Sittings,' she corrected him. '*Séances* sounds too grand for what I do.'

'These sittings, then. From what I can gather, all of them involved nothing more than you and the . . .

customer sitting at an empty table with just a solitary flickering candle waiting for the spirits to turn up.'

'Aye. That's right. And Aunty Doris, of course. She always insisted on sittin' in.'

'Yet there was something a bit different about the sitting you did for Hazel Aspinall and her mother.'

'Was there?'

'They told me you'd put a scattering of dried rose petals in the middle of the table. None of the others who visited you mentioned the rose petals.'

She stared ahead, watching the lamplighter cross the cobbled street and stretch his long pole upwards once more. Then she turned to look at him.

'Them rose petals weren't my idea, Sergeant.'

'Whose were they then?'

'Aunty Doris brought 'em.'

'Did she say why?'

She looked away, as if she were staring not at the present but at the past. 'I don't know. Me an' Jack used to go for walks in the woods an' we'd smell the wild roses. But I never wanted 'em in the house. They remind me too much . . .'

Brennan frowned, and as they reached the ginnel that Jaggery must have gone down in his futile effort to catch the mysterious eavesdropper, he stopped walking. He turned to the young widow and said, 'I don't understand, Alice. You sit there in your house with a paying customer and you say you get in touch with your husband, yet here you are telling me that the smell of rose petals is too upsetting. I would have thought it would bring you comfort.'

He was surprised when tears suddenly slid down her cheeks.

'I had no idea Aunty Doris was bringin' them rose petals. It was all I could do to stop meself from doin' what I'm doin' now.' She wiped away the tears, leaving a smear across her face.

He saw the lamplighter give them a funny look. Appearances can be deceptive, thought Brennan as he realised what the man was thinking. But, as was far too common, the man gave him a nod and went on his way. Interfering between man and woman, even when the woman was showing signs of distress, broke some unwritten code.

'So, the smell of rose petals upset you but Jack's spirit didn't?'

He saw her shoulders sag. She leaned back against the ginnel wall, her face now half hidden in shadow. Her voice was low, almost a whisper, as she said, 'Because the rose petals were real.'

'And the spiritualist stuff wasn't?'

He could sense rather than see her head shake slowly.

'It's all been made up. All of it.' There was a note of resignation in her voice, along with a powerful sense of relief.

He sighed. She wasn't telling him anything he didn't know. This was no grand revelation, no stunning confession. All this talk about communicating with the dead was arrant nonsense. And there were far too many gullible folk who swallowed it.

'So why start it all off?'

'Because it was a way of keepin' Jack with me. I woke up one mornin' and felt him beside me, in the bed. It was like I could feel his body lyin' there. His breath. An' I know it were just my imagination or the last bits of a dream but it *did* feel real. Then I fancied I could see him in the mirror. I told Aunty Doris an' she said it might well be real. An' there were folk out there who'd pay to hear me say stuff like that.'

'And the things you told these people?'

She gave a small laugh. 'Only bits I'd been told. Old Peggy Clayforth's husband told my Jack he kept his pipe hidden 'cos she were after slingin' it out.'

'And Jack told you.'

'Aye. An' I thought that would be it, but old Peggy went an' told others. An' then I found I were enjoyin' it. Givin' 'em hope when they'd lost it.'

'Len and Ettie Yates?'

'That were Aunty Doris. She told me about doin' what she did to that poor girl, gettin' rid. She said if I were to tell 'em they'd a grandson wantin' to make contact . . .'

'It would be a good source of income. They'd keep coming back.'

'I didn't like doin' that. It weren't right, that.'

'And the others? Betty Bennet? Lucas Wesley?'

'I told 'em what they wanted to hear. Gave 'em some sort of comfort. I knew Betty's lass when I was a little girl. She was older than me, and . . . It was before she went funny.'

'Before she was attacked?'

'Aye.' She took a deep breath and added, 'But when that happened to Aunty Doris . . . it frightened me.'

'And yet you were going to do another sitting for Hazel and her mother-in-law?'

'Only because Mabel begged me. An' I was goin' to say that their Bert was wantin' to be on 'is way now an' wished them all the best an' look after each other . . . an' the baby of course.'

'Ah yes,' said Brennan. 'The baby. How did you know about that? Hazel swears she told no one.'

Before she could answer, they both heard something from the darkness of the ginnel. It sounded like footsteps, and at first Brennan expected to see someone emerge into the street. But then he realised that the footsteps weren't approaching, they were receding. No one had passed them to enter the ginnel, which meant . . .

'Has somebody been listenin'?' Alice Goodway asked, a tremor in her voice now.

But Brennan remained silent. Following the footsteps would mean leaving the young widow alone on the street.

Suddenly, she launched herself forward into his chest and it was all he could do to catch her before she fell to the ground. He felt her body shaking, tiny tremors underscored by the way her arms now clung to his neck. He realised just how terrified she had been. The sound they'd heard only served to intensify her sense of horror.

'I'm so frightened!' she said in barely a whisper. 'I can't stand this much longer.'

He realised then how much she had been keeping the terror hidden, concealed behind a mask of confidence. It was like holding a child terrified by the monsters of the dark.

Quickly he escorted her back to the house, cursing to himself as he did so. Once she had been safely deposited in Hazel Aspinall's house, Brennan and Jaggery gave their apologies and left hastily. Brennan explained to his constable what he'd heard in the ginnel.

'Which might mean the one you thought you'd seen at the back gate was still around. Or it could just be someone hanging around the ginnel for an entirely innocent reason.'

'There's no bugger hangs around a ginnel when it's freezin' cold, Sergeant.'

'Well, we'll scour the entire alleyway from beginning to end. You go back down the street and walk back up the alley. I'll do the same at the other end. And keep your eye out for nooks and crannies, Constable.'

They went their separate ways, but after half an hour's search of the area they found nothing. No one was spotted in the alleyway – it was teatime, after all, and the temperature was dropping by the hour – and every nook and every cranny was empty of suspicious characters. Eventually they met in the middle of the alley.

'Anything?' Brennan asked.

'Not even a whistlin' budgie, Sergeant,' Jaggery said morosely.

Brennan didn't reply. As they emerged back onto Mason Street, he ordered Jaggery to spend half an hour patrolling the area, just in case, while he would walk back to the station and arrange for a regular watch to be kept on the property overnight. Surprisingly, Jaggery didn't utter a word of complaint. Again, Brennan suspected that his constable had a soft spot for the young widow. Somehow he felt touched by the big man's protective regard for Alice Goodway: perhaps she was the sister he never had.

He walked off, leaving Jaggery to his duties and smiled at the thought of someone trying to harm her with her protector around. Constable Jaggery would tear such a villain to shreds.

*

Ten minutes later, Jaggery was at the far end of Mason Street, where a small stretch of spare land marks the approach to Pennyhurst Mill. Although most of the work-force, including the mill girls who made up the vast majority, had left the place, lights were still burning in many of the rooms. He imagined the little ones scurrying on all fours in an effort to clear the floorspace of all manner of rubbish and discarded material before the next day's shift.

He gave thanks that his own son, Mark, would never have to take on such difficult labour. *No pit no mill* had been Freddie Jaggery's simple prediction for his son. Anything else, yes, but coal or cotton . . .

As he turned round to make his way back towards the Aspinall home on Mason Street, he saw a dark figure standing outside the house. For a big man, he could move quickly on occasion, and he thundered down the dark street with all the force of a charging bull.

The one who had just knocked on the door turned to see the source of the noise. The sight of a uniformed constable hurtling towards her with his black cape billowing behind him like the wings of a giant bat made Ettie Yates drop her small basket and stand with her back against the front door. She was convinced he was in pursuit of some dastardly fiend, so it came as a great shock when he fetched up against her, one arm pressed against the wall and muttering in a pantingly hoarse voice:

'And what do you think you're doin', woman?'

She quickly regained her composure. 'I'm knocking on a door. That all right?'

Before he could reply, the door opened and Hazel Aspinall stood there.

'Mrs Yates?'

'Aye, love. I just thought I'd call, bring you an' Mrs Goodway a bit o' summat. I heard she were stayin' here.' She raised the basket as evidence.

Hazel looked confused but stepped to one side to let

her in. Jaggery was about to follow when she said, 'We've 'ad enough police here for one night.' Then she shut the door, leaving him open-mouthed.

Still, he told himself as he breathed hot air into his cupped hands, *it's not as though I've let meladdo in, is it?*

While he remained by the front door, his large presence casting a shadow against the drawn curtains, the three women stood in the kitchen while Ettie herself emptied the contents of the basket. A few potatoes, an onion, two sticks of rhubarb and a small bag of potato flour.

'There,' she said as if the meagre fare before them were a banquet.

'It's very good of you,' said Hazel with caution in her voice. 'But Alice isn't a prisoner here, y'know.'

Ettie gave a beaming smile and sat at the table. 'Well anyroad, there's a nice meal there for the two of you.'

'We've just eaten, Mrs Yates.'

'Well isn't anyone goin' to offer me a cup of tea? Tell you what, I'll make it, shall I? I've a favour to ask.'

*

It really was too much, thought Lucas Wesley. Too, too much. As soon as he turned the corner from Miry Lane into Mason Street he saw that lumbering oaf of a policeman standing outside what he presumed was the Aspinall house, and looking for all the world like a bloated Cerberus.

All afternoon at the bank, he had been at his cheerful best with the customers, confident in the knowledge that close of business would mean he could seek out Mrs Goodway. The bank had closed at three, and he had made one journey already along Wallgate and down to Mason Street in his working attire, only to find Sergeant Brennan and the oaf paying court to Mrs Goodway.

And yet, hours later, the police were still here, and he began to sense a growing feeling of frustration. After his earlier unsuccessful visit that day, he had sat at home staring at the walls of his living room, picking up Mrs Crowe's volume *The Night Side of Nature* for encouragement and inspiration. But instead of hope, reading her work served only to remind him that she had once been found wandering the streets of Edinburgh stark naked with only a pocket handkerchief and a visiting card to protect her modesty. She said later the spirits had told her that if she were to carry those strange objects then she would be rendered invisible.

Did that mean that everything she wrote about was the product of a fevered mind and had no basis in the reality of experience?

Was he mad, too?

Was the whole world simply a place where lying was commonplace and lunacy lay just beneath the skin, waiting to erupt into a pustular obscenity at any moment?

Such thoughts had gnawed at his brain as the darkness slowly filled his living room until he too became nothing but a shadow.

But now, seeing the policeman outside the house at a

time when he sought the answer to so many questions, filled him with a seething resentment. He retraced his steps and made his way back along Miry Lane, turning right until he came back once more to his home on Taylor Street.

He would sit in the darkness once more, he promised himself, and see what spirits his mind could conjure up.

*

After Brennan had despatched two constables to Mason Street, with orders to patrol the street itself and the rear alleyway, he made it abundantly clear to them both that the slightest dereliction of duty would meet with instant dismissal and, if he had his way, they would both be boiled in oil. He would be there at any time later tonight, so woe betide any slackers.

He had, of course, no intention of going back to Mason Street that night – he had handpicked the constables and knew they'd follow his instructions to the letter. Besides, Alice Goodway was safe enough with her closest friend for company. The houses in Mason Street were packed closely together, and if anything untoward happened, at the first sign of trouble, neighbours would be round in a flash.

Normally, he'd head straight for The Crofter's and his usual pint of bitter, but somehow tonight he felt like heading home. Whether it had been the sense of danger lurking around the Aspinall house, or the conversation he'd had with Alice where she admitted fakery and he'd sensed once more her vulnerability, he couldn't tell. He just wanted to get home to Ellen and Barry.

As he walked along King Street towards Wallgate, he thought about how Alice had fooled everyone – apart from her mercenary aunt, that is. Why had Alice done it? Was she being entirely truthful when she told him it made her feel good, helping others come to terms with the bereavements they'd suffered?

All this meddling with Death. It was an end to be respected, sure, but then put in its place. There was death, then mourning, a wake, a burial, then heaven, hell, or purgatory. And for the living, well, they just carried on, relying on shared tales. Respectful memories.

'You're a bloody hypocrite, Mickey!' he said aloud to himself as he turned left and passed the railway station.

A sudden memory, suppressed for a long time, flashed in his mind like a firework. He was ten years old, back in Cashel, and the family all dressed in black. His da's great-uncle, a dour old cuss, was laid out in an open coffin the night before the funeral and the people were standing around drinking and keening and saying all manner of great things about the sour old sod. And he, Mickey Brennan, along with his cousin Rory, eleven, was seated beneath the table where the coffin rested.

And Rory had dared him, and you never refused a dare, even at a wake.

While the adults' backs were turned, listening to an old lament being sung by the priest, he had tied a long piece of string around the dead old bugger's finger. Once the song had ended and they all turned round once more, hadn't he tugged as hard as he could on the string and hadn't the corpse's hand flown directly into the air?

Hadn't the women cried out *It's a miracle*! And hadn't his dad reached under the table and dragged him out in full view of the entire wake, priest and all?

All this meddling with Death . . .

He tried to suppress the smile that was forming on his lips, but it was impossible.

Oh, he'd had the tanning of his life that day, for sure.

So it was in such a mood of fond reminiscence that he arrived home. Ellen met him with her usual embrace and Barry with the usual yelp of glee at seeing his dad home once more. It was later, after tea and as they sat at the kitchen table having tested Barry on his learning words, that Ellen said, 'I thought about you this afternoon.'

'I think about you all the time.'

'No, silly. I mean with what was being said in Yates's. I was there, doin' a bit of shoppin'.'

'Go on.'

'The usual gossips were saying really bad things about Betty Bennet and that poor daughter of hers. Isn't Betty one of the people who went to see Alice Goodway?'

He nodded, alert now.

'Anyway, I told 'em to stop it.'

'Good for you.'

'But I'd say both Betty and Mrs Yates are still keen to

visit her again. Mrs Yates in particular seems convinced there's more Alice can tell her.'

She told him about the heated conversation she'd witnessed that afternoon in the grocer's shop. He sat there for a while then insisted they talk about something else. It irked him that these people were such gullible fools, but then he admitted to himself that they hadn't the information that he was privy to: Alice Goodway had confessed that she was a simple fraud. It was their grief, rather than their gullibility, that urged them on. They were clutching at straws, but as he watched little Barry now playing with his beloved soldiers who were mounting an attack on the table top, he wondered if he too would clutch at straws if something ever happened to his dear son?

Something Jaggery had said the other day came to him then.

Betty Bennet had asked him about his son.

You'd die for 'em, wouldn't you?

Aye. An' kill.

Betty had lost a daughter after years of madness, caused by an animal who'd never been caught.

Len and Ettie Yates had lost a daughter too, after she got pregnant by someone Len couldn't name, and Doris was called upon supposedly to help.

The two friends, Alice Goodway and Hazel Aspinall had a shared loss, their husbands victims of a pit blast.

And Mabel Aspinall had lost a son.

Even Lucas Wesley had lost someone dear to him.

Everything revolves around loss, he reflected.

'What?' he said, suddenly aware that Ellen had been talking to him.

'I said, it's time our little man went to bed. Honestly, Mick, you might be here in body but your mind's somewhere else!'

Later, when Barry lay in bed, Brennan read him a nursery rhyme. Not the stories of derring-do and men o' war and soldiers fighting the heathens that he normally read. Somehow, tonight, he wanted his son to hear only innocence:

> *'Blow, wind, blow, and go mill go!*
> *That the miller may grind his corn.*
> *That the baker may take it, and into rolls make it,*
> *And send us some hot in the morn!'*

During the night, Brennan was disturbed by the strangest of dreams. Jack Goodway, whom he had never met, was roaming the Brennan house in the dark, groaning in abject agony and saying over and over again something about the string being broken and nothing could fix it. He even woke in a sweat and, according to what Ellen told him later, he'd been mumbling about the bread being far too hot.

She was actually teasing him about it as they lay in bed the following morning, when they heard an urgent knocking on the front door.

With a sense of deep foreboding, he rushed downstairs, slid the bar above the door and threw it open. Constable Corns was standing there, his chest wheezing, his face flushed as if he'd been running very fast.

'Constable? What is it?'

'Constable Jaggery's sent me, Sergeant. Seems like summat's gone on in Mason Street durin' the night.'

'What's happened?'

Chapter Eleven

When he arrived at Hazel Aspinall's house, he was met by Constable Jaggery, who opened the door and invited him inside. Constable Corns had told him nothing of what had taken place here, only that Jaggery had told him to bring him to the house with all haste. Brennan looked round the front room quickly, expecting to see scattered bloodstains or smashed furniture or a combination of both.

Jaggery saw his superior's rapid survey of the room and said, 'Mrs Goodway's upstairs, Sergeant.'

From his constable's relatively calm demeanour he knew the young widow was safe, but that was all he knew.

'Tell me what's happened then,' said Brennan. 'And where's Mrs Aspinall? Upstairs too?'

'No, Sergeant. That's why I sent for you. Mrs Aspinall's been taken to the infirmary. Alice came out to one of the constables on duty an' seemed in a state. Said Hazel Aspinall was takin' bad ways.'

'What does that mean?'

'She were in pain, Sergeant. So one of 'em ran for a cab an' he helped the poor woman get in. Took her up to the infirmary. That's all as I know, Sergeant. Alice Goodway's lied in bed, weepin' fit to burst.'

Brennan took the stairs two at a time. When he reached the back bedroom he knocked and heard a feeble-voiced Alice call, 'Come in.'

He felt no compunction entering the young widow's bedroom. There were things he needed to know. She was sitting up in bed fully dressed, her face pale and drawn.

'Mrs Goodway,' he began, but she interrupted him.

'It's all my fault, Sergeant. I'm like a curse.'

'How did Hazel come to be ill?'

Alice sighed and clasped and unclasped her hands. He saw that once again she was shaking. 'She got that worked up . . . about Mabel, an' Bert, an' the baby, an' everythin', and then she went to bed an' seemed to calm down. I went up an' all. I felt poorly, to be honest. I felt a bit better after I'd been sick a few times. I heard Hazel talkin' in her sleep, and thought it were just, you know, a bad dream. Then in the middle of the night she started screamin' fit to wake the . . . I ran in an' she were on the floor doubled up. Said she were hurtin' bad. An' she were clutchin' her stomach, just like I did, only she seemed worse. That's when I saw the blood. That's when I knew.'

Brennan went cold.

Had the poor woman lost her unborn child?

Alice Goodway went on, 'An' I wanted to go with her to the infirmary only that constable wouldn't let me. An' when Constable Jaggery got here, he said the same. I'm nowt but a prisoner!'

'They were acting under my orders. How do you feel now?'

'Bit drained. But all I wanted to do was be with her. I couldn't come to any harm in a cab, could I? Or at the infirmary?'

'I can take you there myself, Mrs Goodway. If you feel up to it?'

'Of course I feel up to it!'

She quickly left the bed and pushed past him onto the narrow landing.

*

The Matron of Douglas Ward steadfastly refused to let either Brennan or Alice Goodway see the recently admitted patient.

'Her mother-in-law is with her and there are to be no more visitors today. She has lost a lot of blood and, needless to say, the foetus.'

'What caused this to happen?' asked Brennan.

The Matron pursed her lips, and gave him a look of distaste that implied she thought it no business of any man to make enquiries of such an intimately feminine nature.

'Might I remind you I'm a policeman, Matron? I really do need to know.'

She gave a cough of protestation but explained. 'Anything can bring on a miscarriage, Sergeant. Agitation of body or mind, sudden jerks, even riding in a shaking carriage. And then there is the use of strong purgatives or any type of quack medicine. Any of those can result in the womb rejecting the foetus like a blighted fruit.' She paused and went on. 'Once she is discharged – and that will take time, dependent on the circumstances which I need not go into – she will need great care.'

'She's got me,' said Alice forcefully.

'With the right kind of treatment – castor oil for the bowels, you understand, and Epsom salts . . . well I needn't go into that now. But if you are to be her nurse when she is discharged you must take great care. Do you understand?'

Alice nodded, somewhat daunted by the nurse's spare manner.

He turned to Alice. 'Did she take any medicine yesterday, Alice?'

Alice shook her head. 'Nothin'. We just 'ad some boiled potatoes mixed wi' a bit o' butter. And a cup of tea when Mrs Yates came.'

'Mrs Yates? When did she come?'

'Yesterday. Round teatime.'

'I left strict orders . . .' He left that sentence unfinished. Instead he said, 'And you. Do you feel all right?'

She looked at Matron and gave a small laugh. 'I'm a bit weak, that's all. I'll live.'

He made a silent promise to have strong words with Constable Jaggery once he'd decided what to do next. Meanwhile, he thanked the Matron and asked her to let him know when Hazel Aspinall was well enough to receive visitors. Matron muttered a non-committal, 'We'll see,' before opening the doors to Douglas Ward and disappearing inside.

When they stepped out into the bright, crisp morning air, Brennan saw Jaggery talking to the cabbie who had brought them. The big man said something to the cabbie and shuffled over.

'How is Mrs Aspinall, Sergeant?'

'She's alive, Constable.'

Jaggery touched the tip of his helmet to Alice Goodway and drew Brennan to one side, out of earshot. 'What do we do now, Sergeant?'

'Now?'

'Well, we can't take Mrs Goodway back to Hazel Aspinall's place, can we?'

Brennan cast a quick glance in her direction. As she stood on the lowest step by the infirmary entrance, she looked more and more like a lost lamb, the only sign of her nervousness the way her hands kept clasping and unclasping each other.

Jaggery went on. 'And we can't let her stay in her own house, can we?'

Before Brennan could respond, Alice moved towards them.

'You're talkin' about me, aren't you?' she asked.

Brennan saw a flash of defiance in her eyes.

'Yes, we are.'

'Well, I've made me mind up anyroad so you can stop talkin' about me.'

'And what have you decided?'

'I'm movin' back to me own house. There's nowt to keep me at Hazel's now, an' I won't feel comfortable wi' Mabel Aspinall bobbin' her head round every five minutes. Once they let Hazel out I can go back. Till then . . .'

It was Jaggery who spoke up. 'You can't stay at your house, Mrs Goodway.'

'Why not?'

''Cos we still have to keep an eye on you.'

'But nothin's happened, has it? Not since Aunty Doris was attacked?'

'You're forgetting the letters,' said Brennan quietly. He thought it prudent to keep his thoughts about this latest development to himself. It could simply be coincidental that Hazel suffered a miscarriage.

'No, I'm not. But whoever sent them . . . he might just be somebody upset. Not enough to do owt. Whoever did for Aunty Doris might have nowt at all to do wi' me. She weren't popular, was she?'

Jaggery was about to protest but Brennan silenced him. 'You're right, Mrs Goodway. There's no proof that the letter writer and the killer are one and the same. And we might well be exaggerating the threat to you. If you insist on staying in your own home, there's nothing I can do to stop you. Needless to say, we'll make sure you are well guarded. Constable Jaggery here will escort you to Mrs Aspinall's house and wait while you collect your things then take you to your own home.'

As the three of them clambered into the carriage which Jaggery whistled over, Brennan watched the young widow carefully. It seemed to him that she had made her mind up about something, that there was an expression almost of fatalism on her face. He'd seen that expression several times in the past.

It was indelibly impressed on the features of those condemned to hang.

*

Brennan ordered the cabbie to drive him to the station first before heading towards Mason Street. Again, in the cab, he was struck by the way Jaggery fussed about the young widow. He'd never seen the man so diligent in his duties. Once the cab dropped him on King Street, he stepped into the station and nodded to the desk sergeant, who beckoned him over.

'Mick. There's trouble brewin', I reckon.'

'Trouble? What sort of trouble?'

'Ding-Dong got called in. Council business. Got back half an hour ago lookin' like he'd just seen his own arse.'

'Thanks for the warning,' said Brennan and headed for his office.

He barely had time to sit down when his door burst open and Captain Bell stood there looking his most spectral.

'There's been a complaint, Sergeant.'

'Really, sir. About what?'

'About your attitude towards council officials.'

Brennan realised immediately the source of such a complaint. He'd spoken to only one such official in the last fortnight. He also recalled the chief constable's reaction when Brennan had failed to charge Mr Ralph Crankshaw, Inspector of Nuisances, with sending the first letter. Now, here he was repeating a complaint about his 'attitude'.

'Do you mean Mr Crankshaw, sir?' he asked innocently.

'You know very well whom I mean. The mayor himself – who is apparently a close friend of Crankshaw – has expressed his dissatisfaction. Questioning the man in his own home, Sergeant?'

'In Hindley, at the address you gave me, sir, if I remember correctly.'

'Yes well, there are ways and means, Sergeant Brennan. Ways and means.'

Brennan nodded, although he hadn't the foggiest what his superior meant.

'Still, you won't have to travel all that far.'

'For what, sir?'

'To apologise, Sergeant. I have been able to save you a

journey to Hindley. The Inspector of Nuisances is in conference with our esteemed mayor all morning. So grasp the nettle while it's hot and bite the bullet. There's a good fellow.'

Brennan could recognise not only a mixed metaphor but also an ulterior motive. Captain Bell had been left in no doubt that the Wigan Borough Police Force would be given a rough ride at Watch Committee if he didn't issue the necessary order. He immediately stood up and moved towards the open door.

'Where are you going, Sergeant?'

'Striking while the nettle is hot, sir. As you instructed.'

Unsure whether he was being ridiculed, the chief constable accepted his sergeant's intentions, if not his words, at face value and stood to one side.

Brennan marched along the corridor, past the curious desk sergeant and out into the street. There he turned left, then left again, and marched up the steps to where the mayor's office could be found. One advantage of sharing a building, Brennan reflected. It didn't allow him time to seethe and rebel.

He knocked on the mayor's door and heard a stentorian voice call out, 'Enter!'

The room was large, an oversize mahogany desk taking centre stage, with walls bearing an elaborately carved Wigan coat of arms with '*Ancient and Loyal*' scrolled along the bottom. Alongside this, oil portraits of former mayors were ranged in order of their years of service, and along one wall stood a huge bookcase containing a vast number of leather-bound volumes with gold-embossed lettering, each one indicating its year of publication, that seemed to record the minutiae of council business going back many years. Indeed, the whole place gave off the impression of weighty urban matters.

Seated at his desk was his worship the mayor, another weighty matter, Brennan reflected, as he took in the man's chain of office resting on his voluminous chest and almost touching the lowest of his several chins. Facing him, with his head now turned to observe the new arrival, was the Inspector of Nuisances himself. He wore an expression that was a blend of smugness and umbrage. Brennan wanted no more than to break the man's nose.

'Ah. Detective Sergeant Brennan,' said the mayor jovially enough.

Both men remained seated while his worship beckoned their visitor into the room.

'We'll get straight to the point, seeing as how you're knee-deep in a murder you've yet to solve, eh? Mr Crankshaw here has made a complaint against you.'

'Sir?'

'Mr Crankshaw feels – correct me if I'm wrong, Ralph – Mr Crankshaw feels you overstepped the mark. I mean, visiting the fellow on his day off. At his home. With his wife present?'

Before Brennan could construct any sort of reply that had a hint of apology sticking to it, Crankshaw spoke up.

'The world is hurtling its way towards hell, Sergeant. We are six years away from the twentieth century and the forces of Armageddon. People like me strive to keep such an enemy at bay. And if that means writing a letter admonishing the practices of evil – communicating with the devil and whatnot – then it is my duty to do so. Do you understand, Sergeant?'

'I understand your comments perfectly. Does that mean you admit to sending the letter of menace, Mr Crankshaw?'

'My short note was clear, unequivocal and quite within the law. There was no menace. Merely a statement of biblical fact.'

Brennan sighed. Crankshaw was openly admitting to authorship of the note, which meant either that he was a most brazen villain or that the note Alice Goodway received had nothing to do with the subsequent murder of her aunt.

'For the sake of clarity, Mr Crankshaw, are you saying that you wrote only the one letter?'

'Good grief, man!' said Crankshaw, his eyes now bulging. 'Do you suppose I was in regular communication with this vile woman?'

At that point, as if to forestall any further eruption, the mayor stood up. 'Well then, that settles the matter. Apologise, man, and let's hear no more about it.'

But before Brennan could bring himself to utter one syllable of apology, Crankshaw resumed speaking.

'And evil swirls around that house like a legion of hellish demons. Metaphorically speaking, of course.'

If Jaggery were here now, thought Brennan, he'd rattle the man's chin.

Brennan cleared his throat and said quietly, 'That's probably going a bit too far, if you don't mind my saying.'

'I beg your pardon?'

'I'm aware of Doris Goodway and all that she got up to,' he went on before the mayor himself could voice his outrage, 'and I agree that what the young widow Alice Goodway has been doing, with all this talking to the spirits and that, is to an extent deception. But demons from hell?'

Now it was Crankshaw's turn to stand up. He walked over to Brennan and stood facing him. Brennan could smell stale cigar smoke on the man's breath. He could also see the man's eyes burning with a righteous indignation. He was filled with a religious fervour that manifested itself in an immediate lowering of the voice.

'Doris Goodway was a practitioner of evil, was she not?'

'She was an abortionist, yes.'

'A vile trade and no mistake. But did you also know that she kept a house of ill repute?'

Brennan blinked. It was the first he'd heard of it.

Behind the Inspector of Nuisances, the mayor gave a small but deliberate cough.

'I think perhaps we shall have your apology, Sergeant, then you may go.'

But Ralph Crankshaw was now on a mission. 'You know nothing about it, of course.'

Brennan found himself speaking in the same whispered tones. 'If anyone is caught running a brothel then we'd be the first to know.'

'Ah,' said Crankshaw, 'but the police were never informed.'

'Why not?'

'I can assure you I had every intention of doing so, Sergeant. Every intention.'

The mayor came round his desk, his face flushed now. 'Ralph, Sergeant Brennan is a very busy man.'

Crankshaw took a deep breath and seemed to control his ardour now. 'Suffice to say, Sergeant, that Doris Goodway's house – her house, not the widow's – in that cesspit they call Canal Street, was reported to me by someone who shall remain unidentified. She was seen bringing women to the house – and men. I made it very clear to the Goodway woman that this had to stop. This was before her nephew was killed of course.'

Brennan, all thoughts of a milky apology forgotten, said, 'But she was never prosecuted?'

'No.'

'I'll ask again, then. Why weren't the police informed?'

But by now the mayor had moved past them and swung open his door.

'I think we can take for granted your apology, Sergeant. Now if you don't mind we have council business to attend to.'

Crankshaw looked as if he might object, but instead

250

he turned around and resumed his seat at the mayor's desk.

Brennan bade them both good day and left the room.

As he made his way back to the station, he wondered at the strange meeting he had just attended. He had been called in to make an apology and hadn't. He had discovered that Doris Goodway had another vile string to her bow. Not only an abortionist but a brothel-keeper. And he learned too that someone on the council – perhaps his worship the mayor himself – had become somehow linked with a house of ill repute. It had been obvious that the mayor was uncomfortable with any mention of a brothel in Canal Street. He realised now why the Inspector of Nuisances held such sway with the great and the good.

He knew where all the bodies were buried.

Metaphorically speaking.

*

Once Constable Jaggery had seen Alice Goodway safely inside her house, he was reluctant to leave. For one thing, the house was cold and had a musty smell, and he saw it as his duty to build up a fire so that at least the front room would acquire some kind of life. He also took his time checking every room, both upstairs and down, and the small backyard.

'You can never be too sure, Mrs Goodway,' he said sombrely.

Alice, having divested herself of her outdoor coat, went

into the kitchen and offered to make him a cup of tea as the least she could do.

'But it's daft thinkin' somebody's after me, anyroad,' she called out from the kitchen as he set to with the wood and paper in the grate.

'Best to be safe than sorry,' he replied.

'I know that, but don't you reckon whoever was threat-enin' me would've done summat by now? I mean, nobody's been seen around Hazel's, have they now? Me an' Sergeant Brennan thought we heard somebody but it were nobody.'

He shook his head. He wouldn't mention the search he and Sergeant Brennan had made in Mason Street and the alleyway at the back. No point scaring her with what might have been nothing but their imagination. He reached for the coal scuttle for the first layer of coal. It was empty, and he gave a sigh as he stood up. 'I'll get you some coal,' he said as he went through the kitchen and unbarred the back door. In the yard, he stooped to the coal bunker and scooped coal into the scuttle before returning and resuming his task.

As she came into the front room carrying two steaming cups, she happened to glance out through the front window. For a second she thought she saw someone across the street, looking towards the house. But the impression faded as she moved to stand at the window, more out of curiosity than anything else. When she looked along the street she saw several people standing in doorways or strolling past, pulling coat collars close or drawing neck cloths tightly in.

But of the one she thought she saw there was now no sign.

Perhaps she'd imagined it, she told herself, and turned to give the helpful constable his cup of tea.

*

The big policeman was still there! Not only had he brought her home in a hackney carriage but now he was helping her settle back. Did ever a woman receive such preferential treatment from the police?

She'd told the detective sergeant in the ginnel that she was nothing but a fraud, that she had cheated all her visitors out of their money. Why, that was worse than grave robbing, wasn't it? At least grave robbers take only the dead remains of those buried in the ground. But this woman had taken people's hopes and turned them into something to profit by, with no regard for the feelings of her victims. And that's what they were – victims.

It was unforgiveable!

And she would pay for it.

Chapter Twelve

Brennan wasted no time in making his way to Canal Street on the other side of the borough, where Doris Goodway had lived in what was beginning to sound very much like a makeshift brothel. As he sat in the tram, rattling along Woodhouse Lane, he wondered if he'd been barking up the wrong tree, following a false scent. He grimaced as he realised his thoughts made him sound like a dog – not a bloodhound firmly on the right trail, but a half-demented spaniel rushing from one tree to the next. The more he found out about Doris Goodway, the less he liked.

At Canal Street, he knocked on the first door. As he waited, he glanced down at the doorstep. *A clean step is a clean house*, was Ellen's refrain whenever he teased her for it. The front step he was now looking at was anything but clean and hadn't seen a scrubbing brush for months. As he surveyed the rest of the street, he saw only intermittent cleanliness. The majority of steps were filthy.

The man who came to the front door was sporting a grease-stained shirt and trousers frayed at the bottom, his lack of self-respect underlined by the stubble on his face and his red, watery eyes.

'What does thy want?' he asked in a gruff, hostile voice.

'Where did Doris Goodway live?' Brennan realised the usual introductions weren't necessary.

'Who wants to know?'

'Me,' said Brennan.

'Well tha can ask somewhere else. Now piss off.'

He was about to slam the door in his face when Brennan deftly placed his foot in the doorway.

'I just need an answer,' he said.

The man threw the door wide open and stepped into the street. 'Ask me again, pal,' the man said, clenching his fists and advancing towards him at an alarming rate.

This was only going to end one way. Brennan swung his right fist hard into the man's stomach, causing him to howl in pain and double up, then grabbed his bowed head and forced it down towards his legs so that the man had no option but to stumble forward into the gutter.

'Where did Doris Goodway live?' he said in a reasonable tone.

Before the man could answer, Brennan heard a woman's voice behind him.

'Next door but one. Number five.'

He turned round and saw who he presumed was the man's wife, hair drifting in all directions and wearing a filthy pinny whose colour was now faded and indistinguishable. He thought he saw a flicker of satisfaction in her eyes at the sight of the man she lived with groaning in the gutter and mumbling incoherent curses. It was probably a secret delight to her to see him, for once, on the receiving end of a good hiding.

Brennan thanked her and stooped to pick his victim up. As he did so, he said to the woman, 'What can you tell me about Mrs Goodway?'

She sniffed and cast a glance across the street, where several of her neighbours had suddenly appeared, standing in their doorways and idly observing the free show.

'You'd best come in,' she said.

The man, too winded to object, allowed Brennan to help him into his own house as his wife closed the door with a bang.

It was one of the filthiest places Brennan had ever seen.

The front room, which overlooked the pavement, was filled with all manner of clutter: a pile of clothing – whether washed or unwashed he had no way of telling from its faded colouring and crumpled state – lay in a tin bath that obviously served no other purpose; three or four tin plates with congealed fat lodged around their rims were resting on a small dresser, and even the fire, which was lit, seemed to flicker this way and that in an effort to escape the stench of human sweat and stale grease.

The woman sat her husband down on an armchair of indeterminate shade and wiped her hands along her pinny in at least an effort to present herself in a better light.

'We were just about to tidy up,' she said with a nervous laugh in the direction of the tin plates. 'Ben here's been ill.'

Brennan got straight to the point. 'I'm a police detective. What can you tell me about the late Mrs Goodway?'

The woman licked her lips. 'She were a bad 'un was Doris.'

The man, who seemed to be getting his breath back at last, gave a sneer.

'In what way?'

'This is a respectable street. Might not look it but there's some good folk live here.'

'Aye. An' some bad 'uns an' all,' the man chipped in.

'Tell me plainly,' Brennan said. He gave the man a venomous look. He had the sort of face you could cheerfully smash on a regular basis, he reflected.

The woman lifted her head in a sadly proud gesture. 'All sorts went on in that house,' she said. 'Men would call round. An' more often than not they'd 'ave a woman with 'em.'

'Some of 'em were bonny an' all,' her husband said with a leer.

Brennan's heart sank. If he had indeed been looking at this case from the wrong angle, and Doris Goodway had been the intended victim all along, the prospect of an investigation widening so far as to include the numerous visitors to the house, not to mention the possibility of some of them being official members of the town council, filled him with horror.

But the woman's next words changed everything.

'It were disgustin',' she said. 'You'd hear 'em gigglin' an' canoodlin' in the street. Waitin' for Doris to let 'em in. She'd no shame, that one. Not even when her own nephew come round with his fancy bit.'

Brennan's heart beat a little faster. 'You mean Jack Goodway?'

Her husband spoke next. 'Aye. It were me what recognised him. Went to school wi' that bugger.'

'Who was the woman he brought here?'

Both of them shrugged, but the man said, 'Didn't matter wi' Jack. He'd give any woman a good seein' to.'

'What do you mean?' said Brennan, wishing at once that he'd phrased the question differently.

'Shag a pigeon, he would. If there were nowt else.'

Brennan cast a quick glance at the woman. He wasn't used to such language being used in front of a female, and he wondered how Ellen would react if she ever heard such an expression. Not that she'd know what it meant, he reassured himself.

'But the woman he used to bring. Can you describe her?'

Both of them shook their heads.

'It were always dark,' said the woman. 'We just heard whisperin', an' gigglin'.'

Her husband, who seemed to have regained some of

his earlier truculence, said, 'I reckon we've told you enough. An' I'm gettin' 'ungry.'

Brennan's stomach turned as he caught sight of the greasy plates. Whatever this man would be eating, he'd have to wade his way through a mound of grease first. He thanked them both and bade them good day.

Once he was out in the fresh air, he breathed in deep gulps. The neighbours across the street muttered to themselves, a mood of disappointment drifting across. They'd hoped for fireworks. Or a smashed window at least.

*

Although Jaggery was reluctant to leave Alice Goodway to an empty house, he knew he'd no option. Sergeant Brennan had insisted he return to the station as soon as he'd seen her home safely and had assured him that he would make sure the house was kept an eye on by the constables on the beat. Even so, he felt a bit like a deserter when he finally bade her farewell. She looked pale and nervous, despite her parting words.

'I'll be perfectly safe now, Constable. I've got Mrs Brogan next door I can call on if I get too lonely.'

Once he got back to the station, Jaggery made straight for Brennan's office. He knocked on the door and waited for permission to enter.

As soon as he got inside, he knew he was in trouble. The frown on his superior's forehead, the steepled fingers on which his tightening lips rested, were evidence enough.

Brennan sat back in his chair and said, 'Do you make a habit of refusing to follow a simple instruction, Constable?'

'Sergeant?'

'Last night, for example, did I or did I not tell you that no one was to be allowed to visit Mrs Goodway?'

Jaggery's heart sank. Mrs Yates and her bloody basket.

'You did, Sergeant.'

'You let the grocer's wife in.'

'Yes, Sergeant.'

'And in the middle of the night Hazel Aspinall is taken ill.'

It was Jaggery's turn to frown.

'And she is rushed to the infirmary where she loses her unborn child.'

Jaggery swallowed. 'I don't see as 'ow me lettin' Mrs Yates visit 'as owt to do with . . .'

He felt his collar tighten around his thick neck. Surely the sergeant didn't think her coming round to pay a friendly visit . . . Then he remembered the basket.

'You sayin' she poisoned the poor lass?'

'I'm not saying anything of the sort. I'm saying that it's a possibility. Hazel Aspinall's miscarriage might well be nature's way. Then again, it might not. It also might be just a coincidence that Alice Goodway was similarly taken ill during the night.'

Jaggery lowered his head and mumbled, 'I'm sorry, Sergeant.'

Brennan pushed his chair back and stood up. 'Well then.

We'll say no more about it. Just do what I tell you next time.'

'Yes, Sergeant.'

'Now you're to come with me.'

'Where we off to?'

'The grocer's,' came the reply.

*

In spite of what she said to Constable Jaggery, Alice had decided that she needed some human company.

She'd gone upstairs, stood on the threshold of the front bedroom and had to make a conscious effort to go in. The bed was now stripped bare. But she could still see Aunty Doris's body lying there, the eyes open and bloodshot. She blinked, and then she could see herself and Jack in that selfsame bed. He was holding her close and whispering in her ear and she was smiling and nestling her head against his powerful shoulders and she was saying how it was so hard to think of herself as Mrs Goodway now and hadn't they had the most wonderful day?

Memories are supposed to help, she told herself with a sad smile. But the vision, the sensation, of her and Jack coupling together that first time and the room seeming to sway like a ship at sea as she gave herself to him so completely, that memory gave her an actual pain, and she could stand it no longer. She had loved him so much. She closed the door and crept downstairs, desperate to seek out a human voice that contained warmth and understanding.

And of course old Mrs Brogan provided both. Alice sat in her neighbour's front room with a cup of tea, a plate of biscuits and a litany of old tales to give her a comfort she hadn't felt for such a long time. There was something reassuring, being with the old woman like this, and she was reminded of the times her mother used to wrap the blankets around her to ward off the chill. Such a warm, tranquil presence. Perhaps it was her neighbour's benign company that filled her so much with guilt. For the lies she had told and the people she had fooled. And for what? She had gained nothing from the deception.

And as the coals shifted and settled and dropped their ash through the iron grille into the ash pan, she sighed heavily. She realised that she would have to face the house, with all its memories, sooner or later, and so she thanked the kindly old woman and made her way back home.

By now the day was fading, and when she closed the front door and drew the bolt across, she saw the shadows of familiar things – sideboard, armchair, clock – and gave a heavy sigh. She reached up to draw the curtains and glanced out at the darkening street. She could hear the raucous gaggle of a group of mill girls on their way home from the nearby mill and as always she felt an acute sense of ostracism, of being barred from sharing the smallest of intimacies with those of her own age. Marriage, she guessed, had done that – drawn her away from such friendship and friendliness – but she wondered if she had ever really felt that way, been part of such a sisterhood.

She had never felt such loneliness as she felt at this moment.

As she turned to go to the kitchen – it was approaching teatime and she knew she needed to eat – she thought she heard something. Not the giggling from outside but something else – something closer.

It was the sound of someone moving, slowly, with deliberate tread. It came from above her head.

There was someone upstairs, in the bedroom.

*

'No, Sergeant Brennan, I've no idea where she is.'

Len Yates, standing behind his shop counter, looked flustered. The shop was full, some of the women having decided to leave their shopping until they'd finished their shift at the mill, and hoping at the same time to catch a few bargains as the food and vegetables neared the end of their shelf life. He was busy weighing and bagging when the two policemen entered his shop, and their request to speak to his wife had brought a scowl to the grocer's face.

'Does she often go out at such a busy time, Mr Yates?'

Len gave a sneer. 'These days she does what the bloody hell she wants.'

Brennan approached the man behind the counter and, while he was busy with a customer, whispered in his ear, 'Last night she went to see Alice Goodway.'

Len's eyes widened. 'Don't you mean Peggy Clayforth?'

'No. I mean Alice Goodway. My constable let her in.'

Jaggery gave a miserable cough.

'She must've gone there after then. She told me she were goin' to see old Peggy. Like I said, she's a mind of her own these days.'

'Well, when you see her, tell her I wish to speak with her. It's important.'

He gave the grocer a friendly pat on the shoulder and felt his iron muscles through the shirt.

Once outside, Jaggery said, 'You don't seriously think Mrs Yates brought poison with her, Sergeant? An' if she did, why give it to Hazel Aspinall if it's young Alice she were angry with?'

Brennnan adopted a brisk pace and Jaggery had to run to keep up.

'We're going to ask a few questions along those lines.'

'Where we goin'?'

'The infirmary. And if that Matron tries to get in my way this time you can arrest her for obstructing the police in their duties. Do you understand, Constable?'

'I'll have her in handcuffs before she can say *enema*, Sergeant.'

*

Mrs Brogan was alarmed by the frantic knocking, and she hobbled as fast as her legs would carry her to the front door. When she opened it, Alice Goodway rushed inside and slammed the door shut behind her.

'Goodness me!' said Mrs Brogan. 'What on earth's the matter?'

'There's somebody in my house! I 'eard 'em!'

Alice's voice was filled with panic, and the old woman brought her to the same armchair where she'd sat only a few minutes earlier.

'There now, lass. Just take a few deep breaths.'

'But there's somebody in there, Mrs Brogan. They're upstairs!'

From the panic and the fear evident in Alice's voice, Mrs Brogan gave a sharp nod and moved to the door.

'What're you doin'?' asked Alice.

'Don't worry, love. I'm not so daft as to go to a house where there's some devil hangin' about. I'm goin' to Orrells. Their Johnny'll be home from the pit. He'll not put up with any messin'.'

Before Alice could say anything, Mrs Brogan had donned her coat and shawl and left the house.

Alice moved to the wall adjoining her house and pressed her ear against it. She strained to hear, but there was nothing, no heavy footsteps on the stairs, no shifting of furniture or smashing of crockery or anything to indicate there was an alien presence in her home. Then she heard a door slam shut further along the street, saw a dark shadow from further up Vere Street pass the window, watched the unmistakeable shape of Mrs Brogan stand on the pavement, soon to be joined by another figure, one she recognised as Mrs Orrell, the young miner's mother.

She heard her own front door swing open – she recognised the squeak of hinges – and Johnny Orrell's presence made itself known as she heard him shout, 'Whoever's up yonder I'll give thee ten seconds. Then I'm comin' up. An' I'll brast thee!'

An interval, and she could imagine Johnny Orrell counting slowly to ten. Suddenly she heard his heavy clogged steps hammering on the wooden stairs and reaching the landing at the top. She waited with heart thumping, anticipating at any moment the sounds of a struggle and the yelps of pain and the thud of a body hurtling downstairs.

But she heard none of those things.

After a while she felt safe enough to go to the front door and pull it slowly open. Mrs Brogan was standing there, arms folded and talking quietly to her neighbour Mrs Orrell. Before either woman could say anything, Alice's front door opened and Johnny Orrell came out. In the glow of the streetlamp opposite, he looked quite a wild figure, with his thick shock of red hair and powerful arms glistening with coal black and sweat.

'See anybody, lad?' asked his mother.

Johnny gave a smile and shook his head. 'Couple o' ghosts an' a goblin,' he said cheerfully. 'But nobody livin', anyroad. Reckon you've been seein' them spirits again, Alice!'

'Go on, you cheeky bugger!' scolded his mother as she reached up to ruffle his hair. 'That pig's trotter'll be gettin' cold. Off with you.' She turned to Alice and said, 'You can go back in, Alice. If my Johnny says there's nobody there then there's nobody there.'

Johnny suddenly turned and yelled out, 'Might be an idea to keep your back door locked from now on though.'

Mrs Brogan gave Alice's arm a gentle squeeze and said, 'You're welcome to stay a bit, lass.'

But Alice shook her head. She glanced up at her own bedroom window and saw nothing but the reflection of the lamp across the street. 'I'll be all right,' she said. 'Happen it were my imagination after all.'

She gave Mrs Orrell a nod of gratitude and moved to her front door. She knew there was no one inside now, yet she had heard something. She *had*. But whether what she heard was made by the living or the dead, she couldn't say. Perhaps meddling with the spirits and claiming to be something she wasn't had stirred up things best left alone.

It could be Aunty Doris's restless spirit roaming the house and stuck between this world and the next.

Or the sounds might have been caused by neither the living nor the dead, existing only in her mind, badly affected by everything that had happened, and it was at last beginning to wander. She might end up like Frances Bennet, roaming the streets with a line of children following on behind giggling and calling her names.

Daft, Alice. Daft.

When she closed the door behind her and drew the bolt across, she moved to the lamp on the wall and reached on the small table beneath for a match. The gentle *puff* sound as the gas was lit gave her a slight reassurance, for it was the sound she heard every day and it was normal. Mrs Brogan was normal, and so were Mrs Orrell and her son Johnny.

Suddenly she remembered what Johnny had said about the back door, and quickly she entered the kitchen and noticed the door was indeed unbolted.

She began once more to panic. Was this how the intruder – if indeed she had heard an intruder – had gained entry to her house? She remembered Constable Jaggery opening the back door to get the coal from the bunker. Had he locked it behind him? Had she? God. She pressed a hand to her forehead and felt the cold dampness there.

She reached up and slid the bolt into place.

When she sat down and rested her head against the back of the armchair, she gazed into the embers of the fire that Jaggery had made earlier.

Was she losing her mind?

Again, she thought of Frances Bennet. She had lost her mind after being attacked. Would the same happen to her if she were attacked?

Penny Gawp.

Wasn't that what they'd called the girl after she'd been interfered with?

She had a clear image of Frances. Before the attack, she had seemed so grown-up to Alice and the other children in the neighbourhood. So friendly. But afterwards, it was as if a different person had crawled into her skin. That was when Alice felt guilty.

She closed her eyes and tried not to let such thoughts overwhelm her.

Betty Bennet . . . Ettie and Len Yates . . . Lucas Wesley . . . Peggy Clayforth . . . and Mabel Aspinall and Hazel, her closest friend.

She had told such lies . . .

*

Outside, small flecks of snow began to drift against the glass of the gas lamp. A gentle frosting began to cover the cobbles and the uneven pavement. A dark figure stood beneath the lamp, a thick muffler covering the face. Only the eyes could be seen, wide and sparkling, the pupils catching the glimmer from the lamp and turning it into tiny pricks of light.

Before this night is through, Alice Goodway, you'll have the shock of your life!

There was the muffled sound of a gloating sneer, and then the figure moved away from the gas lamp, the flakes of snow beginning to swirl more frantically around its dark shape like flies round a fresh corpse.

Chapter Thirteen

The Matron was with Dr Monroe, who was finishing his rounds of the ward before visiting time, and the curmudgeonly Scot, upon whom Brennan had relied on more than one occasion to help him solve a case, seemed uncharacteristically pleased to see him, offering Constable Jaggery beside him a curt nod.

'Don't tell me, Sergeant Brennan: you have a nice juicy corpse for me to get my metaphorical teeth into.'

The Matron tutted at such frivolity but remained silent when Brennan explained the reason for his visit.

'Ah, Mrs Aspinall. Most unfortunate, losing a child in that way. First the husband . . .'

Brennan glanced down the ward and watched as a stream of visitors began to pour in. He spotted Mabel Aspinall, Hazel's mother-in-law, who was heading for Hazel's bed at the end of the ward.

'Is there any possibility that the miscarriage was suspicious?'

'How d'ye mean?'

'Brought on by something she'd taken?'

Dr Monroe looked at the Matron, who gave Brennan a steely glare before making her excuses to leave them and their 'morbid speculations'.

'It's not something I should really be discussing, is it? She's ma patient and . . .'

'I just need to know if there's anything suspicious.'

'Sometimes these women do take things that are given to them by criminal abortionists and when things take an ugly turn they end up here. But Mrs Aspinall seemed genuinely bereaved. I'd say she wanted this baby.'

Brennan nodded. It would be a daily reminder of her husband Bert, both for Hazel and her mother-in-law, who he saw were now engaged in an animated discussion.

'But it may be that she was given something without knowing.'

Monroe stroked his beard for a while. 'To bring on the miscarriage?'

'Possibly.'

'But who would do such a thing?'

'I don't know. Yet. But if I knew for certain that she had been given something . . .' He left the question hanging in the air for Monroe to catch.

The doctor frowned. 'Well, the woman seems to be recovering quite well, all things considered. She's very tired, and I suspect there might well be some damage to the liver. When I first examined her, she was breathing very rapidly. She settled down after a while and her bodily signs became stable. But she needs to take care, Sergeant.' He thought for a while. 'I've already ordered some tests, of course, though as to whether they would show anything after the treatment she's had, I'm not sure. I can tell you that the miscarriage was complete, I myself overseeing the separation of the ovum.'

Brennan sensed Constable Jaggery shift his weight from one foot to the other.

'Wait outside, Constable,' he said. He knew the big man had a distaste for the more vivid aspects of a doctor's work.

With Monroe's promise to 'see what he could do', Brennan made his way down the ward and reached Hazel Aspinall's bed just in time to hear Mabel say, 'Not even got that to cling onto now.'

He was surprised to see how much better Hazel appeared than the last time he saw her. She had her head resting on the pillow, and she was continually licking her lips, but he sensed that was more a reaction to her visitor than anything else.

Mabel Aspinall scowled when she saw Brennan approach. 'Do you have to badger the poor girl *here*?'

'Just seeing how she was doing. Hello, Hazel.'

The patient gave a weak smile.

'Can I ask you a few questions?'

'No, you bloody well can't!' her mother-in-law snapped, a little too loudly, for it evoked a chorus of tutting from the nearby beds.

Brennan leaned in so that only Mabel herself could hear. 'I'm going to ask her a few questions while you wait outside.'

'I've no bloody intention of waitin' outside!' she said but in a whisper now.

'Well, my constable outside will be only too happy to take you down to the station where we can continue our argument in the confines of a nice cold cell. And, oh dear me, look.' He pointed to the window, where they could see snow falling.

Mabel snorted and gave Hazel a venomous look before picking up her small bag and storming back down the ward.

Hazel gave him a smile of gratitude.

'Now then, Hazel. Just a few questions. Last night, you and Alice had a visitor.'

She thought for a while then nodded. 'Mrs Yates. Ever so good of her.'

'She brought you some groceries.'

Hazel gave a slow nod, confusion beginning to crease her brow.

'What did she bring you?'

After some seconds, she said, 'Just some spuds. Onions. Other stuff. Can't remember.'

'And did you eat anything she brought?'

Hazel shook her head. 'We'd already had summat to eat.'

'She didn't offer you or Alice anything special?'

'Only a cup of tea.'

'*She* made the tea? Ettie Yates?'

'Aye.' Hazel gave a sigh. 'Not 'ad that for a long time.'

'What? Tea?'

'Mint tea,' came the reply.

His heart lurched. The echo of a conversation came back to him now, in the voice of Len Yates:

She said me an' Ettie could stay, there'd be nowt gruesome about it, no blood or owt like that. All she gave her were a cup o' tea.

Tea?

Aye. Funny smell to it, though. Like mint tea it were. An' our Eve drank it an' Doris left, sayin' we was to give it time to work its road through. So we did.

He could see that Hazel was eyeing him curiously.

'Hazel. Tell me what happened when Mrs Yates came.'

She thought for a few seconds then said, 'She started on at Alice, askin' her to do a sittin' for her. Wanted to speak to her little grandson, she said. But it was the way she talked about him. Like she knew him, as if he were part of the family. It made me shiver, t'road she were talkin'. I half expected her to reach into her shoppin' bag an' pull out a little pair o' shoes.'

'And what did Alice say?'

'Told her she couldn't do it. Said she didn't feel up to it anymore. Mrs Yates went mad. Told Alice she were as good as keepin' her away from her grandson an' didn't the little chap need his grandma, specially wi' his mam dead an' no one else to look after him. It was like he were *real.*'

Another consequence of superstitious meddling, thought Brennan.

'Should've heard her stirrin' the tea! I thought she'd smash the cup she rattled the spoon that hard.'

'So she made both you and Alice a cup?'

'Aye. Then all of a sudden she were calm, just like when the wind drops after a storm. Said as how she didn't bear grudges – an' that were just after she'd ranted an' raved about Alice bein' selfish. It was all me an' Alice could do to stop ourselves laughin'.'

'Did Alice drink her tea?'

She stared at him, and he could see the way her mind was now piecing together what he was implying. 'What you sayin'?

'Did Alice drink her cup of tea?'

'Aye.'

He remembered how Alice told him she had been sick herself on the night of Ettie Yates's visit. Had the vomiting been a blessing in disguise? But if Ettie Yates had wished to poison Alice Goodway, why do the same to Hazel? Was it because it was too risky? Cups of tea can be swapped around. Perhaps the only way to make sure she got Alice was by putting whatever the poison was into both cups. Or perhaps she poisoned the two of them to get rid of witnesses.

'Are you sayin' . . . ?'

He smiled and patted her hand. 'I'm not saying anything, Hazel. Just want to get as full a picture as I can of what happened. I'm a detective, remember? And we're nosy beggars!'

He could see she wasn't convinced. Nevertheless, he made his farewells with the hope that she would soon be well enough to leave the infirmary. As he made his way back along the ward, past Mabel Aspinall who was waiting near the entrance with folded arms and a scowl, he knew he had to find Ettie Yates as soon as possible. But he was bothered by this case, by the confusion it brought with it.

If Ettie Yates was trying to kill Alice Goodway for refusing to contact the departed spirit of her daughter and her supposed grandson, was she the one who also killed Doris Goodway? After all, it had been Doris who gave Ettie's daughter Eve a concoction made in mint tea that was designed to bring about a miscarriage, yet it ended in death. Did she blame the abortionist, even though she herself had asked her to carry out the procedure?

Was the woman mad?

Constable Jaggery was waiting on the steps of the infirmary, his overcoat a feeble protection against the snow which was now falling more heavily.

'Where to now, Sergeant?' Jaggery asked in as chirpy a voice as he could muster. It would be stretching fate too far if he were to suggest his shift ended nearly an hour ago.

'Back to the grocer's, I'm afraid,' said Brennan. 'Mrs Yates must be home by this time.'

Mercifully, he waved to one of the waiting cabs. During the journey down Wigan Lane and through the centre of town towards Sharp Street, Brennan was at his uncommunicative worst. Whenever Jaggery tried to initiate conversation concerning the case, he was rewarded with nothing more than a grunt or a shake of the head. *Fair enough*, he told himself after several gambits had failed, *if you don't want my help, you can sod off*.

Once they arrived at the grocer's shop, Brennan paid the cabbie and dismissed him, which caused Jaggery some consternation. It would mean a walk back to the station in the swirling snow. Not a prospect he relished.

The shop was locked up for the night, of course, and Brennan knocked hard on the door. Eventually a shaft of light appeared and they both watched as Len Yates registered their presence and seemed to curse to himself before lifting the counter lid and unlocking the door.

'What now?' he asked.

'Is Mrs Yates back?' said Brennan without preamble.

'Aye. But she's not well.'

Brennan brushed past him, Jaggery following behind with a menacing glance at the grocer. Len Yates accepted the inevitable and relocked the door before moving in front of the two policemen to lead the way.

When they entered the living quarters, they saw Mrs Yates sitting before a roaring fire, a blanket across her legs. She was staring into the flames, and she seemed to be rocking back and forth and humming an indistinguishable tune.

'Ettie, love?' said her husband. 'Police are here.'

No response. No pause in the rocking, or the humming.

'She's been like this since she got back,' said Yates.

'Where has she been?' Brennan asked.

'She told me she'd been to see Eve.'

For a second, Jaggery's heart fluttered until he realised he meant the cemetery.

'In this weather?'

'Doesn't matter none to Ettie. She hums that same tune by the graveside an' all. It were a lullaby at one time. Used to send little Evie to sleep.'

Brennan moved nearer to the woman, standing now between her and the fire.

'Mrs Yates,' he began. 'I want to ask you about when you went to see Alice Goodway and her friend.'

For the first time, she looked up at her visitor.

She licked her lips and both the humming and the rocking stopped. 'Not like a tap,' she said.

'What?'

'Alice Goodway. Said as she couldn't turn the spirits on and off like a water tap. Said she weren't doin' it no more anyroad. Not for me, not for no bugger.'

'And then you made some tea. Is that right?'

'Aye.'

'Mint tea?'

'Tea's tea.'

'Did you take the tea with you? Along with the other bits of food?'

She looked puzzled by the question. 'Now why would I take tea to somebody's house? You don't take tea to nobody's house, do you? Folk always have tea ready.'

'Did you put anything in the tea then?'

Len Yates spoke up. 'What the bloody 'ell's all this shite about tea?'

Brennan ignored him and repeated his question.

Suddenly, Ettie Yates began to cry. 'She said our Eve had a little lad with her. Our grandson. An' now she's leavin' the poor mite out in limbo where he won't get to see us anymore an' all because Alice Goodway's taken it in her head to be selfish an' leave the rest of us snatchin' at smoke. That's all we can do now. Snatch at smoke.'

She then resumed her humming and her rocking while her husband placed a hand on her shoulder.

'Just leave her be now, eh?' he said with a pleading simplicity in his voice. 'Just leave her be.'

Brennan watched her for a few seconds and decided he'd get nothing more from her tonight – if indeed he'd get anything from this woman ever again. He knew the signs of incipient madness right enough.

As they once more stood outside the shop in what was fast becoming a blizzard, Brennan was again alone with his thoughts. If Ettie Yates wasn't the poisoner or the murderer of Doris Goodway, then she would be seen as a victim of something Alice Goodway put in motion all those weeks ago. She had laid claim to psychic powers for no other reason than to placate her mercenary aunt and, if he were being generous, to bring small comfort to those who, like her, had lost loved ones. But whether her motives had been mercenary or altruistic, the result was the same: silly, futile hopes dashed and people left scarred by the experience.

Alice Goodway's meddlesome folly had its own victims, just as the murderer's actions had.

*

The last thing Brennan did before he signed off for the night was to leave instructions once again for the area constables to keep a close eye on Mrs Goodway's house in Vere Street with the usual dire threats if they failed him.

It was possible, he'd reflected on the long walk back to the station alongside a surly and shivering Jaggery, that the poison might have been placed in the tea by anyone, not only Ettie Yates (who insisted she hadn't taken the mint tea with her), but also by Alice Goodway herself, or Hazel Aspinall, or her mother-in-law. The list of suspects didn't stop there, however – it wasn't difficult for anyone determined enough to wait for an opportunity to get inside the house and leave the poison there. Jaggery had thought he'd seen someone lurking at the back of the house and he himself had heard someone creeping around the ginnel nearby.

But that didn't make much sense. If you're aiming to poison someone, you don't slip poison into a tea caddy and hope it will reach its intended target. You could end up killing several people that way.

His mood was therefore sombre as he braved the snow on his way home. He knew that Ellen and Barry would give him the warmth and the sustenance he needed, and the image of normal domesticity brought him some comfort, at least, on the walk down Wallgate.

His spirits would have been decidedly darker if he had any inkling what was about to take place in Vere Street, at the home of Alice Goodway.

But it would be the next morning when he found out.

*

There was no point delaying things, thought Alice as she watched the last of the dying embers sift their way through to the ash pan below the grate. She'd have to sleep in that bedroom some time, despite all the memories it held. She had lit the oil lamp in the bedroom earlier though, as she made up the bed, and she'd left it lit, just to make sure there was some chill taken off the place before she came up. That was a lie, of course. No oil lamp would have a flame strong enough to take the chill off anything, and she smiled at herself for having such a silly thought.

As she made her way upstairs, having made sure the front and back doors were firmly locked and bolted, she did experience a flutter of apprehension. Her thoughts of earlier, guilty memories of those she had in a way cheated and lied to, might creep back to infest her dreams and bring her nightmares. She'd often noticed that nightmares took what had happened during the day and distorted them to such a horrific extent that the ordinary source of the dream was lost altogether. But she reassured herself that nightmares can do no harm, not really.

She entered the bedroom and, in the flickering dimness cast by the oil lamp by the bed, she moved across to draw the curtains. She saw the heavy snowfall beyond the window, and the pure whiteness of the street below, the dull gaslight almost smothered by the thick flakes of snow. Not a soul out there now. Not even the figure she'd seen earlier.

With a shiver, she closed the curtains and climbed into bed. She was about to extinguish the flame in the oil lamp when she heard the crunch of footsteps, slow, heavy ones, coming slowly down the street. With her heart beating rapidly, she moved from the bed and ran to the curtains, pulling them ever so slightly apart, and peered down to the street below.

A policeman, on his slow march along the street!

She breathed a huge sigh of relief and climbed hastily back into bed. She lay there on her back for a few seconds and watched her breath freeze in the night air. With a sigh, she leaned over, lowered the wick until the flame was at its weakest then cupped her hand at the top of the lamp's glass chimney and blew downwards. Immediately the light was extinguished, and she could smell the smoke and the burnt oil in the darkness.

She lay there, stretching her legs the length of the bed even though that was where the bed was coldest. Again she shivered as she turned on her side.

At that moment she gasped and clutched her throat, and terror coursed through her veins in a way she had never felt before.

What she saw was impossible.

Chapter Fourteen

The next morning, there was something otherworldly about the scene that greeted Brennan in Vere Street.

An urgent message had roused him from his warm bed earlier than usual. The constable had said only that he had been ordered by the duty sergeant to rouse Sergeant Brennan and get him round to Vere Street without delay. Now, as he turned the corner from York Street, he saw almost every front door open, with both women and men vying for the best vantage point, despite the freezing temperature and the thick snow that threatened to spill over their various thresholds.

Standing outside Alice Goodway's house was Constable Corns wearing his great coat and hugging himself to generate some modicum of warmth. When he saw Brennan and his escort approaching he gave a grateful wave.

'Constable Jaggery's inside,' he said, almost bringing his chattering teeth under control.

'And Mrs Goodway?' asked Brennan.

Corns nodded. 'Aye, Sergeant.'

Brennan ordered the other constable to relieve Constable Corns who, he said, looked as though he could do with a hot drink inside him. He opened the front door and stepped inside, ushering the constable in and pointing the way to the kitchen.

Constable Jaggery was standing with his back to a roaring fire and looked guiltily at his superior for such indulgence. In the armchair to his left, the neighbour, Mrs Brogan, sat with a faraway look in her eyes, and her stooped shoulders, skeletal frame and hollow cheekbones gave her the appearance of a melancholy bird of prey.

'Where is she?' Brennan asked.

Jaggery surprised him by nodding towards the armchair beside the hearth. There, Brennan saw Alice Goodway slumped low, with her head resting lifelessly on one hand, a blanket around her legs and her hair unkempt and almost wild. She was staring listlessly into the fire.

'So what's happened?' There was a note of irritation in his voice, as if whatever had taken place was the fault of his constable.

Jaggery cleared his throat then began. 'You'll not believe me, Sergeant.'

Brennan's glare was enough to induce greater clarity in his constable.

'Mrs Goodway here reckons she saw summat last night. In her bedroom.'

'What was that then?'

He'd directed his question to the young widow, but she gave no sign of having heard him.

Instead, it was the neighbour, Mrs Brogan, who answered. 'She saw a ghost. I was in bed meself an' I could hear her screamin' through the wall. Never heard owt like that in all me born days.' Her voice was low, and there was a sudden crackling of the coals that made Constable Jaggery jump.

Brennan tried to keep the disbelief from his tone. 'And what kind of ghost was it, Mrs Goodway?'

For the first time she showed signs of awareness and raised her head from her hand. She turned to him slowly, and he could see the flames reflected minutely in her eyes. For a second he had an uneasy sensation, as if she were possessed by demonic forces. Then he shook his head to cast away such fanciful thoughts.

'It sounds daft, Sergeant Brennan,' she said, her voice almost hoarse. 'But I'd no sooner put out the lamp when I saw her.'

'Who?'

Brennan couldn't keep the scepticism from his voice any longer. This was the same woman who had confessed to him that all this psychic mumbo jumbo was just that – fakery to hoodwink the gullible. Now here she was claiming to have seen a ghost.

Alice Goodway gave a tired shrug. 'I've no idea.'

'Happen it were one of your spirits, Mrs Goodway,' said Jaggery in soothing tones that were completely devoid of artifice. 'Come back wi' a message, like.'

When he saw the look Brennan gave him, he looked down at his boots.

'Can you describe this woman?'

She swallowed hard and lifted her chin as if to defy him to contradict what she was about to say. 'She was glowin'.'

'What?'

'Like I said, she were glowin'. With a sad expression on her face.'

Brennan shook his head as Mrs Brogan reached across to hold her neighbour's hand.

'Where exactly was this ghost-woman?'

'I've told you. In the bedroom.'

'I said where exactly, Mrs Goodway.'

She looked at him for several seconds before giving her reply. 'She seemed to be comin' out of the wall. Between me an' Mrs Brogan's.'

Mrs Brogan crossed herself.

'Show me,' said Brennan.

But Alice Goodway shook her head vigorously.

Jaggery coughed once more and said, 'She'd best not, Sergeant. She were shakin' like a leaf when I got here. Goin' back up yonder might . . .' He let the implied descent into madness linger unspoken in the air.

Brennan was on the verge of saying something when he saw the look of sheer terror on the young widow's face. Possibilities that he had considered were dwindling: at first, he imagined she had been lying for some reason. Yet the expression he had just seen on her face told him otherwise. No one could fabricate such fear.

Which left him with only three other explanations for what had taken place the previous night. One, that she had been dreaming and imagined the sighting of this ghostly glowing woman – a strong likelihood now that he had discounted his initial suspicion. Two, that she had indeed seen someone who had been hiding in her bedroom waiting to terrify her – but if that was the one who killed her aunt, sent the second letter and possibly gave both Alice and Hazel Aspinall poison, then why didn't he or she finish the job last night? Or three, it had indeed been a ghost she had seen – a suggestion he dismissed as ludicrous.

He climbed the stairs and entered the front bedroom. The curtains were now drawn back, and the daylight, enhanced by the reflected snow below, gave the room an eerie innocence. The crumpled bedsheets, half hanging on the floorboards beneath the bed, showed evidence of a hasty exit. There was a strange smell about the room, something which at first he couldn't place. A combination of mustiness and something else.

Of a ghostly spirit there was no sign.

He moved to the bed and sat down, staring at the wall

separating the two terraced houses. Then he stood up and moved over to the wall. Finally, he called downstairs for Jaggery.

One thing's for sure, he reflected as he listened to the heavy tread that heralded his constable's ascent, no one would mistake Jaggery for a spirit from the ether. He resumed his place on the bed.

'Sergeant?' Jaggery asked as he stood in the doorway.

From downstairs, Brennan could hear the gentle solicitations from Mrs Brogan. He gave a self-satisfied smile and pointed to the window. 'Be so good as to draw the curtains, Constable.'

Jaggery, who wondered if this were some belated sign of respect, did as he was told. The curtains were thick and blocked out most, if not all, of the daylight from beyond.

'Now come and sit beside me on the bed.'

A flurry of thoughts whirled through Jaggery's head, none of them doing his superior any credit. Still, he followed orders and the bed wheezed as he deposited his huge bulk beside Brennan. He was staring at the sergeant, wondering what on earth was about to happen, when Brennan said, 'Shall we play a game, Constable?'

Jaggery shifted towards the end of the bed.

'I'll begin, shall I? Well then. I spy with my little eye something beginning with, *F*.'

There was no response Jaggery could possibly think of, so he remained silent.

Then Brennan pointed to the wall facing the bed.

Jaggery turned to look and made an involuntary exclamation more at home on a pitman's lips.

'No, Constable. That's not the word at all.'

*

'A face?'

'A luminous face, sir.'

'And what in the name of all that's holy is a *luminous face*?'

They were seated in the chief constable's office. Beyond his window, Brennan could hear the laborious progress of a tram as it sliced its way through the slush caused by the heavy snowfall last night. There were occasional obscenities from those on the pavement who, he imagined, had been splashed with the resultant spray of blackening snow.

'I thought I could smell something strange as soon as I entered the bedroom,' he began, 'but it was only when I sat on the bed and faced the wall she'd been facing last night that I saw it. A faint outline of a woman's face. Once we drew the curtains shut the outline grew stronger. It had been painted on the wall. Luminous paint, sir. The sort that glows in the dark.'

'I am fully aware of the meaning of *luminous*, Sergeant. There's no need to speak like a dictionary.'

'No, sir.'

'Are you saying Mrs Goodway put it there herself?'

'No, sir. She seemed far too unnerved by its presence. I think her terror was genuine.'

'Then who put it there? And why?'

'I think the motive is obvious, sir,' Brennan said, then added quickly to take away the implied rebuke, 'to terrify the poor woman. As to who, I'm afraid I can't be certain.'

'But you suspect someone?'

'Oh yes, sir. I have a person in mind.'

'Who?'

'I'd rather not say at the moment, sir. I may be wrong.'

He wasn't wrong, he knew that, but he didn't want the chief constable overreacting either. He'd have the suspect chained to a damp wall if he could.

'Then what are you waiting for?'

'I need proof, sir, for one thing. And there's something about this whole thing that bothers me. Like an inaccessible itch, if you know what I mean.'

'In India we applied the common flowers of sulphur with four parts of lard.'

Brennan looked perplexed.

'For an itch, man. And if it were inaccessible, why, we had the natives to perform the necessary application.'

Several most unpleasant scenarios presented themselves to Brennan's imagination.

'And what is it that you cannot scratch?'

Brennan thought awhile before replying.

'First of all, Alice Goodway and her aunt received a menacing letter.'

'A nuisance sent by a nuisance.'

'Exactly. Then Doris Goodway was found suffocated which led us to believe the sender of the letter and the killer were one and the same. Only Mrs Crankshaw is adamant that her husband was at home with her on the night of the murder.'

'She may be lying?'

'A possibility. And at that point it might well have been Doris Goodway who was the intended victim.'

'You told me she had slept in the widow's bed because of its melancholy associations. That she wasn't the target.'

'Indeed, sir. That rare demonstration of decency may have cost her her life. But then Alice received a second letter, more abusive, and written by a different hand. That suggested that she was in danger.'

'Crankshaw is no fool. He could have disguised his handwriting.'

'Again, possible. But if he is our murderer, why admit freely to sending the first letter? In front of the mayor, too?'

'Bravado?'

'And why call her a *lying bitch*? As far as I know, Alice Goodway hasn't spoken to Mr Crankshaw, let alone introduced him to the spirits. Which leads me to think that the sender of the second letter is someone who had visited her, sat there while she supposedly contacted the dead. Whatever she told them, the sender of that letter didn't believe her. Or . . .'

'Or what?'

Brennan recalled the sounds he and Alice had heard from the ginnel, when she confessed her fakery to him.

'Or they'd overheard what she told me. But then again, that doesn't make any sense.'

'Why not? You told me you heard someone in the darkness. If they overheard her admit it was all lies . . .'

'No, sir. What I mean is, the letter accusing her of lying was sent *before* that. Whoever sent it knew that she was a liar and this whole psychic nonsense was a falsehood.'

Then Captain Bell had a rare moment of insight. 'Whoever sent that letter accusing her of lying may have *suspected* her of lying, Sergeant. But then to hear it confirmed from her own lips might well have sent them over the edge.'

Brennan thought about that and accepted the reasoning behind it.

'It could be any one of her visitors, Sergeant. She hoodwinked them all into thinking they were talking to their loved ones.'

'Mrs Clayforth's an old woman, sir. And the contact with her late husband seems to have soothed, not embittered her. Besides, she hasn't strength enough to suffocate anyone. The poor woman is close to meeting her maker.'

'It awaits us all, Sergeant,' he said and gave a respectful pause before continuing. 'The grocer, Yates. You brought him in, didn't you, for assaulting a priest? Surely he has the strength?'

'He does indeed, sir. More than enough. And he had reason enough to want Doris Goodway dead.'

'In her role as vile abortionist.'

'Quite. Yates's daughter died during the abortion.'

The chief constable stroked his chin. 'But what possible reason could he have for wanting to harm Alice Goodway?'

Brennan shrugged. 'Perhaps for convincing his wife that their beloved Eve had not only returned to this world but brought with her the baby she lost. Alice told both Yates and his wife that their grandson was with her.'

Captain Bell gave a heavy sigh. 'That was a wicked thing for the widow to do.'

'Or an attempt at soothing their grief. She herself told me she felt she was bringing her visitors comfort.'

'Not my idea of comfort, telling someone they have a ghostly grandson.'

'No, sir. And Mrs Yates isn't in any way comforted now. She seems on the verge of losing her mind.'

'Strong motive for the grocer then.'

Brennan decided not to add the detail of Mrs Yates paying Alice and Hazel Aspinall a visit and taking them various items of food, not to mention making both widows a cup of tea. He would inevitably want to know how the blazes the woman got past the police guard on the house, and he was reluctant to offer him Constable Jaggery's head on a plate.

'There's also Mrs Bennet, whose young daughter Frances, a mere child, was ravished by some fiend. It affected the poor girl's brain. It also prompted Mr Bennet to cast his paternal and marital responsibilities to the four winds and desert them both. The girl had cost him enough, he said by way of excuse.'

'That evil creature who defiled the girl had no thought for the consequences of his bestiality. My predecessor failed to bring him to justice, I gather.'

'It was before our time, sir. And the girl gave no inkling of her attacker's identity.'

'Your impression of the mother?'

'She is a strong woman, sir, in both senses of the word. To endure those hardships and heartbreaks must have been difficult to say the least. And she takes in washing for her neighbours; she is quite muscular.'

'Any motive for killing Doris Goodway? Or threatening the widow?'

'None that I have discovered so far, no. She may have overheard Alice admit to fakery. In which case the claim that her daughter had regained all of her senses in the next world might arouse her anger . . .' He let his words fade away as another possibility struck him. He decided to keep it to himself for the moment. It may be nothing.

'This bank clerk. Wesley, is it? What about him?'

Brennan joined both hands together and rested his chin on them. 'He interests me, sir. He has an abiding fascination with the supernatural world. He visited Alice Goodway to seek the whereabouts of a girl he once knew. He thought that if she were a genuine medium, she could help him find her.'

'This girl is still alive?'

'So he told me.'

'And the widow claimed she was speaking with the girl's spirit?'

'Yes, sir.'

'A lie then.'

Brennan cleared his throat. 'Everything Alice Goodway said during those visits was a lie, sir. She made things up. It's the grieving and the gullible who pay money for such drivel.' He took a breath, conscious that he was allowing his sense of frustration and anger at the absurdities of the psychic world to cloud his judgement.

'But if this clerk felt his search for some childhood sweetheart were being mocked, Sergeant . . .'

'It might give us a motive.'

'Hmm. And we now have Hazel Aspinall in the infirmary. You suspect poison?'

'The fact that Alice Goodway was violently ill during the night suggests they both took something noxious, sir. I'm waiting for Dr Monroe to give me results of her blood test.'

'If it turns out she was poisoned, it begs the question, how?'

'That's still under investigation, sir.'

'Obviously, no one could have gained access to Hazel Aspinall's house undetected, could they?'

'There have been occasions when both women have been out of the house. They visited Mabel Aspinall, for instance. During that time, the place would have been empty.'

'Any signs of someone breaking in?'

'No, sir.'

'So where to next, Sergeant?'

'Wigan Infirmary, sir, where I hope Dr Monroe has some information for me.'

*

Brennan was met at the infirmary with two pieces of ostensibly good news.

Hazel Aspinall seemed much stronger now and was sitting by her bed, dressed and ready to be discharged. Her mother-in-law was on her way to collect her, despite Hazel's insistence that she could manage perfectly well on her own. There was at least some colour to her cheeks and some life had returned to her features. She had lost her baby, of course, and it would be many months, if at all, that she would recover from such a shock – the only connection with her late husband Bert had been cruelly taken from her, and now that Alice Goodway had cast aside all that psychic nonsense, she had no crutch to rely on. He felt a deep sympathy for the woman as he uttered meaningless words of comfort.

When he finally managed to speak with Dr Monroe, the surgeon told him that he had indeed found traces of something in the blood sample he'd taken from Mrs Aspinall.

'It's pennyroyal, Sergeant. Oil made from a flower. Quite common, of course. It accounts for the taste of mint in the tea. It's had widespread usage over the centuries, from the treatment of gout when dried and burnt to easing the excesses of leprosy. But it is used – sadly and illegally – as an abortifacient. Abortions, Sergeant. And in Mrs Aspinall's case, that has been the unfortunate result.'

Brennan thanked the doctor and returned to Hazel's bedside, pondering the implications of what he'd just been told.

Abortions were Doris Goodway's stock-in-trade. She'd used some mint concoction with Eve Yates who didn't survive the treatment. And he recalled the small collection of bottles Alice had handed to him when he'd asked for Doris's 'special stuff'. There had been a bottle of pennyroyal there, along with the laudanum and other concoctions. Alice had had access to it. But why would Alice make any use of the poison? She herself had drunk the same brew as Hazel. Then again, anyone would have had access to the poison – if it had been stored at Alice's house – when Alice had gone to stay with Hazel. The house had been empty for a while, and there had been no reason to keep an eye on the place when the one targeted was gone. Someone could easily have got into the house and taken the pennyroyal.

But then, he told himself ruefully, pennyroyal, as Dr

Monroe had said, was common. Anyone wishing to make use of it could lay their hands on it. No need to risk being caught in Alice's house.

He found that Hazel had been crying, and when she registered his presence she turned away. He was about to leave when he heard her say, 'Do you believe God is kind?'

A strange question. Still, he gave an answer. 'I do, yes. Though sometimes it's hard to understand why some things happen.'

She turned her head towards him now. 'I'm not a Catholic, you know.'

He nodded.

'But it must give some folk a lot of comfort. Confession, I mean.'

'It's both a comfort and a punishment,' he said. 'We still have to pay for our sins. That's why we have to say a penance.'

'D'you reckon God's punished me?'

'Why would He do that?'

She gave a sad smile. ''Cos I must've done summat wrong, eh? First my Bert, now . . .' She glanced down at her own empty body.

He thought for a moment how hard it must be for a priest, not only to hear confessions – he'd heard enough confessions in his time but none of them were prompted by religion – but also to provide meaningful answers when someone questions the judgement or the mercy of God.

There were times, like now, when the two roles of police-man and confessor were confused, blurred.

'You've done nothing wrong,' he said and reached down to pat her hand gently.

'Haven't I?' she said, and then she closed her eyes. 'You don't lose a baby for nothin'. Happen I should've been nicer to Bert. I should've told him.'

He shook his head. 'You can't blame yourself.' He thought for a moment and felt a chill inside. 'You sure you didn't tell your husband about being in the family way?'

'I never said anythin' to him.'

So Bert couldn't have said anything then to Jack Goodway about being a prospective father.

'And you never told Alice?'

'No. I told you.'

Then how did Alice know? Was it possible that she had some sort of psychic power after all? But he discounted that idea as nonsense. Those things didn't exist. Anywhere. Even she herself had admitted it was all a fraud. Then he remembered something Ellen had said to him years ago, just after she'd told him she was pregnant.

Couldn't you guess, barmpot?

How could I guess something like that?

Me mother guessed. And I'd said nothin', Mick. Women know, you see? Who says men are cleverer, eh?

Had Alice seen some sign in Hazel, some first flush of pregnancy, and used that feminine observation to hazard a guess at her condition?

'Doctor says I took poison, Sergeant. I reckon he were hintin'.'

'Hinting? At what?'

'That I took it on purpose. To get rid.'

'I'm sure he doesn't think that.'

Hazel held his gaze for a while. 'If someone put poison in that tea, who do you think it were, eh?'

He shook his head.

'But it weren't meant for me, were it?'

'It may have been meant for Alice.'

'Aye. I worked that out all by meself.' She smiled to take away the sting from the sarcasm. 'But Alice has done nowt wrong. She's caused nobody any hurt.'

She stared intently at the window, where the snow was already turning to ice as the temperature dropped.

He stepped outside into the bitter chill of the afternoon. A blast of freezing cold air seemed to stop him in his tracks. An idea had been forming and now it began to take more shape. There was only one way he could bring an end to all of this and expose the guilty one. But Captain Bell wouldn't like it. He'd say his detective sergeant had gone mad.

*

'I've brought no flowers, lass. Wouldn't last two minutes wi' all this snow.'

Betty Bennet gazed down at her daughter Frances's grave and wondered if she too could feel the cold. But that was a silly thought, she told herself, stooping low to brush away some snow from the top of the headstone. Still, it did give her comfort to speak to her. She looked round the cemetery. If folk saw her talking to a grave, perhaps they might think that she was indeed going the way of her late daughter. But then she rebuked herself for her selfish thoughts.

'I were thinkin',' she said in a lower voice. 'I know they say Alice Goodway's stopped doin' all that. An' she's got police keepin' an eye on things all day an' all night, so's it's not possible to just knock on her door an' ask her. But I were wonderin', Frances, I were just wonderin' if you'd put a word in, like. You can talk proper now, I know that. An' if you could find your way to persuade her. I mean, I'm sure she's just stopped it 'cos of what happened to Doris. But Doris were no good, was she now? Not really. So, think on, eh, lass? Think on.'

She said a small prayer then and turned round. There were tiny flecks of snow falling as she made her way along the path back to the main road. She had a fleeting vision of Frances, ten years old, screaming with joy as she stuck out her tongue and felt the thick snowflakes tingle and melt. When she reached the cemetery gates, Betty Bennet wiped away the moisture from her face, though she wasn't sure if it were snowdrops or teardrops that had been there.

*

When Brennan got to Vere Street, the idea had begun to glow more brightly. But that's all it was – an idea. He might be on the right track, but then again, he might be heading in completely the wrong direction. He would share his thinking with no one. Constable Jaggery was, for the most part, reliable and a valuable weapon in his armoury; the chief constable had been known to make precipitate orders based on the flimsiest of evidence, despite his adamantine insistence on the essential nature of proof. He would therefore tell his superior afterwards, and not before. No, if this case were to be solved, he would need to keep his own counsel, until such a time as the guilty one made a mistake. Because what he needed more than anything was proof.

As he knocked on the door, Constable Jaggery was quick to respond.

'Have you been here all day, Constable?' Brennan asked on entering the house. The fire was roaring and a clothes maiden lay open before the hearth. Damp clothing was slowly drying, and the smell of soap, combined with something much more alluring, helped to create the homeliest of scenes.

'I have, Sergeant. An' I've been helpin', an' all.'

Alice Goodway stepped through to the front room from the kitchen. She was wiping her hands, which were covered in flour, on a damp cloth.

'Just in time for a cup of tea,' she declared and returned to the kitchen before he could reply. She seemed in far greater spirits than before.

Brennan glanced between the items of damp clothing draped on the maiden and saw the source of the tantalising aroma: a large earthenware bowl had a cloth covering its surface, and the gentle rise at its centre told him that the yeast was doing its job.

'Been baking bread too, I see, Constable.'

'Supervisin', Sergeant. An' a bit of kneadin' 'cos Mrs Goodway here reckons my mitts are more suited than hers.'

The thought of a domesticated Jaggery made him smile.

'She reckoned she'd go mad if she didn't do owt all day, so after she gave that bedroom wall a good scrubbin' to get that glowin' paint off, she spent the rest of the mornin' washin', spite of the snow. Maiden's doin' its job right enough.'

'So I see.'

Jaggery lowered his voice. 'What's he up to, Sergeant? I mean, paintin' a face on a wall? Doesn't make sense.'

'Whoever did it wanted to give Alice Goodway a shock, Constable. And he succeeded. She seems cheerful enough now, though.'

'Aye. But it's a bit like ice on a pond, if you ask me. Put any pressure on the lass an' she'll break, I reckon.'

Brennan nodded, impressed. He'd never heard his gruff, pugilistic constable wax poetical like that before.

A few minutes later, Alice Goodway came back with a steaming mug of tea.

'Constable Jaggery's been a great help today,' she said in the tones of a teacher praising a helpful child. Then, as Brennan sat down, her voice took on a more serious note. 'You've been to see Hazel?'

'I have. And she's doin' well. As well as can be expected, at any rate. She should be home any time now.'

She let out a huge sigh of relief. 'It should've been me in that infirmary. Or the mortuary, Sergeant.'

'Well it isn't, and Mrs Aspinall is still with us.'

'But not her baby.'

'No.'

The cheerful mood she had been in prior to his arrival seemed to have vanished. She put a hand to her forehead and pressed hard. When she removed it, grains of flour were embedded in her skin.

'This is a nightmare, Sergeant. It doesn't seem to end. Last night, when I saw that face . . . Who's doin' all this?'

'That's what I intend to find out. Which is why I need to ask you to do something for me. Something that will need courage.'

She blinked, and he could see there were tears in her eyes. It was almost as if she could read his mind. 'What do you want me to do?'

He took a deep breath and saw Jaggery frowning at him.

'I want you to conduct another séance, Alice. For several people. But this time I need you to do exactly as I say.'

Chapter Fifteen

Brennan visited each of them in turn. The arguments he used varied greatly, and he was forced to adopt a sterner attitude with some of them, backing up his request with the sinister suggestion that a refusal to cooperate in what was actually a police matter would be deemed as obstruction and as such they might well find themselves in front of a magistrate and faced with an indeterminate spell behind bars.

With Len Yates, for example, he parried the man's outrage at being coerced into taking part in another séance by suggesting that it might well be something his wife Ettie would need to stem the flow of madness she was in danger of being drowned by.

'Bloody nonsense!' the grocer had responded. 'It'd be like stickin' your hand back in a blazin' coal fire after gettin' burnt.'

'No, Mr Yates. It would be more like sticking that self-same hand into a bowl of ice-cold water and letting it soothe the pain, not inflame it. Besides, this isn't a request. And unless you want to see your poor wife sitting in a freezing cold police cell . . . The chief constable is adamant this must go on.'

The last sentence was an outrageous lie, but no one was to know that, were they?

They had considerable difficulty with Lucas Wesley. When Brennan had called at his house early that morning, Wesley had flatly refused to attend the gathering that evening.

'Why not?' Brennan had asked. 'I thought that would have been right up your street.'

'Well I'm sorry to disappoint you, Sergeant, but I have actually lost faith in the practice of mediumship.'

'Mediumship in general or one medium in particular?'

Wesley failed to give an answer.

'Well, in that case, I shall need to ask you a few further questions about your visit to Mrs Goodway. I was going to ask them tonight but, well, never mind. Monday morning around eleven will be fine. It is the Standishgate branch of Parr's, is it not?'

That had done the trick.

Betty Bennet seemed different when he called at her house to issue the invitation. Her eyes were heavy, and he had the impression she had been drinking. He caught sight of the half-empty gin bottle by the side of the couch, and no sooner had she admitted him into her house than she slumped back down.

He explained why he had come, and despite the fog of alcohol she was peering through, her eyes shone that little bit brighter.

'I heard she'd done wi' all that.'

'She had. But as a favour . . .'

'Aye,' she nodded, as if he was confirming something already on her mind. 'They're good at doin' favours, the Goodways. S'why they're called *Goodways*.' She giggled at her own joke.

Yet he could sense that behind the drunken humour lay something else. A bitterness. His da had often said that a drunken man speaks a sober mind. He wondered if what he'd suspected about young Frances, her madness after the attack, and her father's subsequent desertion, were true. He'd said his daughter had cost him enough. Still, drunk or sober, Betty Bennet agreed to attend the séance.

Hazel Aspinall, on the other hand, had proved the most stubborn. She had rejected his invitation out of hand, saying that she had no further interest in the supernatural, in contacting the dead or those suspended in some dreadful limbo.

'And I know Alice herself has done with it all. So, what's the good, eh?'

'Alice has agreed to do one more sitting,' he said calmly. 'One final sitting.'

'Well, she can do it without me.'

Even his by now common threat of a cold cell and an appearance before the bench cut no ice with the young widow. She merely shook her head with slow conviction and said, 'Don't matter now what happens to me. I've lost what I 'ad an' there's nothin' else you can take away, is there?'

'If you stay away, when all the others who went to see Alice are going, well, what do you think folk will say?'

'They can say what they like.'

'Your mother-in-law has willingly agreed to go.'

'Aye well, she would. She'd do anythin' to get another go at speakin' to her precious Bert.'

It was that final comment, more than anything she had said before, that confirmed what he'd suspected for a while. Which is why he said, 'You know, I was curious as to why you were one of the very few who had a good word to say about Doris Goodway.'

Within five minutes, she had changed her mind and agreed to attend.

*

The day had been one of prolonged sunshine, and even though the temperature was on the low side and there was a crispness in the air, the brightness of the day had lightened Brennan's mood considerably. Everyone had now agreed to come to Alice Goodway's house at seven that night. He hadn't bothered to invite Peggy Clayforth: the woman was physically incapable of suffocating Doris

Goodway, and her obvious illness suggested she wasn't long for this world. Brennan had spoken at length to Alice about what he expected from her, and despite her initial doubts about the evening, and her worries that she had nothing left to offer any of them other than vague generalities, she had been swayed by his enthusiasm for the venture. Besides, he'd given her a script to follow.

'It's the best way we have of finding out the truth,' he had explained. 'I'm convinced that one of the group is guilty of killing your aunt and possibly of trying to poison both yourself and Hazel.'

'I can't see any of 'em bein' that wicked,' she said. 'Happen I don't want to think that anythin' I've done might have led to it.'

'I think your aunt Doris had a lot to do with what happened, Alice. I reckon she was the start of it all.'

'All what though?'

'Let's just see what happens tonight, shall we? Just do exactly as I've asked you. They all need to be sure you're in touch with the dead. All but one, that is.'

With that, he left Constable Jaggery to stay with Alice until he returned later that evening.

Jaggery had been a problem though. The soft spot he had for the young widow had driven him to the verge of insubordination, especially when Brennan had first mooted the idea of a final séance.

'I thought you disagreed wi' stuff like that, Sergeant,' he had said with feeling.

'I do, Constable.'

'Well then.'

'Well then, what?'

'Well then, why rake over old coals?'

'To get some sort of fire going. Isn't that the usual reason?'

'Aye, but hasn't the poor lass been through enough? She's lost her 'usband an' her 'usband's aunty. She doesn't want to lose anythin' else.'

'You'd rather her be in constant danger from an unknown person? A murderer who's struck once and tried to strike again?'

'I'm not sayin' that. Only ain't there another way?'

'There is, as a matter of fact.'

'Well then. Let's do that, eh? Not all this séance stuff. What is this other way, Sergeant?' There was a note of optimism in the constable's voice, which was immediately dampened when the reply came.

'We'll get all of them into the station in turn, and torture them to within an inch of their lives. Do you know where I can get hold of a good old-fashioned rack?'

*

Alice Goodway's kitchen was almost too small to contain everyone.

Old Mrs Brogan from next door had allowed Constable Jaggery to take the few chairs that she possessed, so that now seated around the table alongside Alice were Hazel

Aspinall, Mabel Aspinall, Betty Bennet and Ettie Yates, while standing behind them were Lucas Wesley, Len Yates and Constable Jaggery. Detective Sergeant Brennan stood in the open doorway leading into the front room, which was now bathed in semi-darkness. The front curtains were drawn and the gas lamp across the way cast a feeble light into the room.

'It's a tight squeeze all right,' said Brennan. 'But I can assure you all it will be well worth the discomfort.'

'Better be,' Len Yates muttered.

Lucas Wesley, standing next to the grocer, shifted his stance. It was clear he felt most uncomfortable being in such close proximity with the rest of them. *He's used to a counter between him and the general public*, thought Brennan, and he wondered if this were the closest the bank clerk had ever been to his fellow man since he lost contact with the girl he had come to regard as an intrinsic part of himself.

'Get on with it then!' It was Mabel Aspinall whose voice seemed to cut through the air like a knife.

'Like waitin' for a tram,' said Betty Bennet, whose tone at least suggested she meant to lighten, not darken, the mood in the room. She seemed to have sobered up from earlier in the day, Brennan reflected.

He reached down for something to his left, and they all watched him with keen interest, as if he, and not Alice Goodway, were about to produce an ectoplasmic surprise. But, after carefully closing the kitchen door, he merely lifted a small bag and carried it to the table where he emptied out its contents.

'What the bloody 'ell's all this?' said Len Yates.

'It's dried rose petals, Len,' said Brennan calmly.

The dried petals were scattered across the table. Ettie Yates reached out and picked one up. 'My little Eve loves flowers,' she said in a dreamlike voice. 'There's always some on her grave. Loves 'em, she does.'

Brennan noticed that Alice was sobbing quietly, Hazel's hand on her shoulder. She was making soothing noises.

'Rose petals again!' said Mabel harshly. 'Why does she need rose petals to bring my Bert back?'

Brennan watched the others keenly. 'She didn't need any rose petals for the rest of you, did she?' He looked at each of them in turn.

Slowly, they all shook their heads.

'Still, they're a help, aren't they, Alice?'

Her sobbing now under control, she nodded.

'Now,' said Brennan. 'If Alice could begin? Do people join hands or bow their heads?'

'Not here they don't!' Mabel Aspinall said. 'Nothin' fancy here.'

At that moment, Alice did lower her head. It was a simple gesture, but immediately everyone fell silent. Brennan watched them. Everyone, with the exception of Lucas Wesley, was watching her closely and, it seemed, holding their breaths. By contrast, the bank clerk stood listlessly, an expression on his face that was a mixture of boredom and resentment. Len Yates reached down and held his wife's hand. It was a surprisingly gentle gesture from the grocer, and Brennan noticed how his huge hand completely swallowed hers. Hazel Aspinall was staring at the table, her focus fixed on the scattering of petals along its surface. She stretched forward and picked a handful up, smelling them and shaking her head until her mother-in-law snatched them from her, saying in a harsh whisper, 'Leave 'em be an' pay attention!' before squashing the delicate petals between her fingers. Betty Bennet was whispering something that Brennan couldn't quite catch. At first, he thought she was praying, then, when he stooped to listen, realised what she was saying.

'Tell us, Frances, love. Tell us. Just give us a name, eh, love?'

Suddenly Alice raised her head and spoke. 'He's here. My Jack. He's here.'

'Is our Bert wi' him?' Mabel asked.

'Not yet. Got somebody else wi' him first.'

'Who is it?' Betty Bennet asked.

'It's your Frances,' said Alice in a dull monotone.

Betty sat forward, an intense expression now on her face. 'Ask her to tell us.'

'Tell us what?' said Alice.

'*She* knows. Our Frances knows. I've already asked her an' she'll let us know now, won't you love?' She was looking up at the ceiling, a bright glimmer in her eyes. 'Who was it attacked you, love? Just tell us his name, now that you're able.'

Alice turned slightly to look at Brennan, who gave a shrug.

'Jack says she's got summat to tell you,' Alice went on, unperturbed.

'There!' Betty almost shouted the word. 'I told you! Just give us his name, Frances love. We've bobbies here an' they can do the rest. Just a name!'

Brennan knew what the washerwoman was asking for now.

The impossible.

Alice too must have sensed that what Betty was asking she was utterly unable to give. 'Jack says it's not that. Frances is sayin' she wants to go now. Wants to go to where it's nice an' warm an' she can be happy again. She says she doesn't like it in the dark, even though Jack's with her. She says will you let her go an' be happy?'

A flash of panic appeared on Betty's face.

'But we've only just got talkin'. We've only just got my Frances talkin' proper again!'

'She says she wants to be happy. Says she will be happy if you let her go now.'

'But I'll be on me own again!'

Alice went quiet and let her head droop onto her chest, her eyes now closed. Betty let out a huge sigh of defeat, and she sat there, lowering her eyes from the ceiling and staring into space.

There was a moment of total silence. The women

around the table looked at Betty Bennet, and Ettie Yates reached out to pat her on the hand. She then broke the heavy silence and spoke in a voice that Brennan found disturbing, and more indicative of her state of mind than anything else. It was the sing-song way one would speak to a small child, the infantile tones one used to create a bond between the years.

'Is my little Evie there? And my little grandson?'

Alice once more turned to Brennan. The movement was so slight that it went unnoticed. He gave the merest hint of a nod.

'Jack says your daughter is laughin'.'

'Laughin'?'

'Aye. She's tellin' him summat.'

There was a pause. More than one of the visitors looked at the ceiling, their ears straining to hear something that wasn't there. *Could never be there*, thought Brennan.

Then finally Alice said, 'She's laughin' 'cos she's happy. She says to tell you she loves you – both of you – but now she has to go. She says it's time.'

Ettie cleared her throat. 'But the lad? What about him? My grandson.'

'Oh, she says he's already gone. Couldn't wait. He was so excited to go where it's warm an' bright. Plenty of other little ones to play with. Eve's dyin' to go too.'

If she felt any sense of irony or embarrassment at her last utterance she didn't show it.

'Then she should go,' said Len. He gave his wife's hand

a squeeze when she tried to object. 'We're not doin' the lass any favours keepin' her here, are we now?'

Ettie stared hard at the ceiling. Her lips were moving but no sound was coming from them. From the window came the tap-tap-tap of hailstones. Jaggery turned to peer through the glass and saw small globes of hail bouncing on the flagged yard beyond.

It was Brennan who spoke next.

'Alice. Does Jack have Susan Corbett with him now?'

There was a snort of derision from Lucas Wesley.

Alice raised her head and closed her eyes. 'Yes. Yes, Susan's here now.'

'And does she have a message for Mr Wesley here?'

'Yes. She says he shouldn't have done it.'

Several pairs of eyes turned to the bank clerk, who shifted uneasily with his hands gripping the chair where Hazel Aspinall sat with her body twisted round to observe his reaction.

'Shouldn't have done what?' asked Brennan.

'She says you're to ask him.'

'Well, Mr Wesley?' Brennan said. 'What is the spirit of Susan Corbett talking about?'

Wesley said nothing.

'They see everything don't they, the spirits? I think you'd better do as Susan says, don't you?'

Alice said, 'She reckons you're . . .'

But before she could finish, Lucas Wesley lurched forward and made a grab for Alice's throat.

Chapter Sixteen

Luckily for Lucas Wesley, Brennan was closer to the attack than Constable Jaggery. The consequences of Jaggery getting his hands on the bank clerk were too horrific to contemplate. As it was, Brennan had been expecting the attack and took swift action to prevent it. There were screams from the women and curses from the men as he hurled Wesley down onto the table, his face flattened against the rose petals that lay there.

'Now then, Mr Wesley. Not in front of Susan, eh? What will she think?' said Brennan as the clerk lay slumped and defeated before them all.

Len Yates rasped, 'Has the world gone bloody mad altogether?'

Brennan said, 'Mr Wesley here is an artist. He draws portraits, don't you, Lucas? He has what you might call a glowing reputation.'

Alice gasped and uttered a small cry. Wesley remained silent. The only sound that could be heard now was his raucous breathing as he found it difficult to get air into his lungs. Brennan grabbed his hair and lifted him up before standing him against the closed kitchen door. The expression on Wesley's face was murderous.

'Before I have Constable Jaggery here escort you in his own inimitable way down to the station, do you wish to offer Mrs Goodway some sort of apology?'

'Apology?' said Mabel Aspinall. 'What the hellfire has he done?' Then she moved her hand to her mouth, as if the truth had finally struck home.

But Wesley remained silent.

'Well then. I'm sure we can find some way of loosening your tongue down at the station, Mr Wesley. Constable. He's all yours.'

As Jaggery was dragging the young man through the kitchen door, which Brennan had thoughtfully opened for them, his superior added, 'And I want him unbruised. Do you hear, Constable? Unbruised.'

'He'll be like a newborn baby, Sergeant. You watch.' Then he added with a nod towards the kitchen window, 'Mind you, them hailstones look big buggers to me.'

'Unbruised, Constable. That's an order.'

No sooner had the front door closed behind prisoner and escort than Brennan bent low and whispered something to Alice that none of the others could catch.

'Are you tellin' me that young bloke did for Doris?' Mabel Aspinall asked.

When Brennan gave no answer she simply said, 'Well, I'll be buggered. It just shows, don't it? You can put somebody in a suit and wrap a tie round his neck, but under all that . . .'

Her daughter-in-law Hazel then stood up.

'And what do you think you're doin', madam?' Mabel asked.

'I'm goin' home,' came the reply. 'Fun's all finished now, hasn't it?'

'Oh no it bloody well hasn't!' snapped Mabel. She waved a hand in the general direction of the people left in the room. 'This lot 'ave had some sort of contact with their loved ones. Now it's our turn.'

Hazel shook her head. 'But I've had enough, Mabel. I want to be off home.'

'You'll go when we're ready. When we've had satisfaction. Isn't that what you promised us, Sergeant Brennan?'

Brennan looked at Alice for confirmation that she was strong enough for this last encounter with the supposed wraiths from the ether. She gave a firm nod.

Mabel grabbed at Hazel's arm to try and force her to sit back down, but the younger woman remained stubbornly standing.

'I'm goin' home!' she said, her voice as hard as flint.

'You'll sit down!'

Brennan intervened. 'Hazel, I think it might be best

if you did as your mother-in-law tells you. This once, anyway.'

Hazel jutted her chin towards him. 'You can't make me!'

Betty Bennet, Len and Ettie Yates, stared at the scene before them. Even if they had wanted to leave, there was something in the air that kept them from moving. A mood of expectation. And a sense of horror, too. Outside, the hail came down with greater force now, and Ettie Yates cried out, 'That's the spirits! They're rapping on the window tryin' to get in!'

'It's nowt but bloody hailstones, woman,' said her husband, a sad resignation in his voice. 'For God's sake.'

Brennan gave a harsh cough, and suddenly Alice spoke, softly and quietly, in direct contrast to the raised voices of a moment ago. 'Hazel, it's one last time. I won't be doin' this again. Ever. I promise you that. An' you'll regret it for the rest of your days if you don't sit down an' let me speak wi' Bert. Through Jack. It'll be your last message to your husband.'

For a moment, it seemed that Hazel would defy even her closest friend and rush out through the back door. More than once she cast a glance in its direction. But then something yielded inside her and she sat down, holding both her hands in a tight grip in the semblance of a prayer, earnest and painful. Brennan noticed how she had grasped hold once more of some of the rose petals, squeezing them between her hands.

'Good!' said Mabel. 'Happen now we can get on.'

Alice closed her eyes and once more raised her head towards the ceiling. Brennan was once again dismayed by the respectful way each one of them – apart from Ettie Yates – watched her, kept their silence in a far more intense way than any he'd witnessed in church. Ettie's eyes were resolutely fixed on the window, and its rattle of hail on glass.

'Is he there? Our Bert?' asked Mabel.

'He is.'

'I knew it! He wouldn't let us down, would he?' She turned to give her daughter-in-law a look of triumph. 'Shall you tell him? Or shall I?'

'Tell him what?'

'How you've lost his child.'

The stark, emotionless way she'd phrased it made it sound for all the world that Hazel had been reckless and careless about her unborn baby in the way one might misplace a purse. Brennan felt like slapping the woman.

'He already knows,' said Alice.

'How?' Mabel's word was filled with shock.

'Because they see things, Mabel,' said Alice. 'You can't hide anythin' from the spirits.'

Again, a long pause while Mabel searched for something to say to the spirit of her dead son. Finally, she said, 'Well, it mightn't be a bad thing, eh, Bert? I know he weren't born an' all that, but you might keep an eye out for him, eh?'

Alice turned to look at her then at Hazel, whose head

was bowed low. Between her fingers, the petals were torn and disintegrating, tiny fragments dropping back onto the table's surface.

But it was Brennan who asked the next question. 'Ask him how he found out about the baby, Alice. How did Bert know that Hazel was expecting?'

For a moment, Alice blinked then turned to look at him with a questioning look in her eyes.

This wasn't part of the script.

Her eyes narrowed and held his gaze.

But Brennan merely repeated the question. Alice frowned, uncomfortable with the request. Then she put the question to the spirit world. The rest of them held their breaths, unaware of the significance of what was happening but drawn like bargemen to a bloated corpse.

Alice paused, as if waiting a long time for an answer. Finally, she said, 'Like I said, the spirits see everything.'

Brennan looked at them all before moving closer to her. 'I don't think Bert saw that, did he? In fact, Alice, I don't think Bert saw anything. We both know that, don't we?'

''Course he bloody well did,' said his mother.

Brennan stood up and said loudly, 'Nor did anyone else. Nobody in the spirit world, at any rate.' He took a deep breath and addressed them all. The hailstorm seemed to grow louder, slashing with a crescendo of violence against the kitchen window. 'And that's because there is no spirit world. Alice has been lying to you all.'

Betty Bennet said, 'She spoke to my Frances. You heard her yourself!'

Ettie Yates spoke next. 'My Eve. She brought her little lad. She can't have made that up. Alice?'

Alice pushed her chair back and stood up. Her voice was cracked and tears were forming in her eyes. 'I've done everythin' you asked me to do, Sergeant. Word for word. An' now you show me up in front of me friends!'

Mabel Aspinall slammed her hands down on the table. 'Alice is no fraud! She can't be. She's spoken to my Bert an' he told us about the baby! How did he know that, eh? How in God's name did he know that?' She almost spat out the words in defiance, but even in her role as unlikely defender of Alice Goodway, there was a lingering note of despair.

Brennan walked over to the window and gazed out. The yard was a square of white now, the hailstones bouncing and spinning off in all directions. But the layer of white wasn't the smooth natural beauty of snow, rather the stubbled fakery of hailstones that would soon turn to puddles, not slush.

'It's the baby,' he said in a quiet voice that demanded attention from his confused and angry audience. 'It all started with the baby.' He directed his next words to Hazel. 'You can't keep it hid. Even if you wanted to. She'll see to that.' He nodded in Alice's direction.

'Keep what hid?' asked Mabel.

Hazel swallowed hard. She opened her hands and let

the broken rose petals fall onto the table. Some of them clung to her palms. Now, all eyes were upon her, and she flushed beneath their steady gaze. Something flickered in her eyes – sadness, resignation, defeat – and she said simply, 'How did you know?'

He sighed. 'That the baby wasn't Bert's?'

Her mother-in-law gave a gasp. 'What did you say?'

Brennan ignored her and directed his words at Hazel. 'You swore you hadn't told Alice. She too swore, but I could take that with a pinch of salt. Yet you also swore that you hadn't told Bert either. If you had, it would have been the most natural thing in the world for Bert to tell his best friend as they toiled together down the pit. But you didn't tell him. And therefore Jack couldn't have found out that way and passed the news on to Alice as he lay dying. Yet Alice still knew.'

'Because the spirits told her!' said Mabel, almost with a scream. 'Tell him, Alice!'

But Alice wasn't communicating with anyone.

'So, Hazel,' Brennan went on, 'if *you* didn't tell Alice, and if the *spirits* didn't tell her, how did she find out? The only answer I could come up with was Jack Goodway.'

'Jack Goodway?' said Mabel. 'But you've just said . . . Anyway, what the hell has Jack Goodway to do with any of this?'

Brennan looked from Alice to Hazel and said, 'Everything.'

For a few moments there was silence again, but this

was a far different silence from anything that had gone before this evening. Mabel Aspinall was beginning to see.

'When Hazel found out she was expecting, she told the father. But she was right when she said she hadn't told Bert, *because Bert wasn't the father. Jack Goodway was.*'

Hazel began to cry.

'It was the only explanation that made any sense. Unless you believe all that nonsense about spirits.'

'Well, it doesn't make any bloody sense to me!' Mabel yelled. 'Why on earth would Jack Goodway tell his wife that he'd fathered a bastard?' The coarse expression, reinforced by the look she gave her daughter-in-law, suggested that she was already halfway to believing the awful, shameful truth.

Brennan held his breath for a moment. Granted, the woman had had a great shock, but there was something grossly unpleasant about her nonetheless. At last he said, 'I'm presuming he told her the truth as he lay dying in the infirmary.'

He looked to Alice for confirmation but she was cold, motionless, like a marble statue.

'He was a Catholic. And no matter what you've done, as a Catholic when you're faced with death you want forgiveness. You want to be unburdened of your sins and your crimes and go to meet your maker with a clean, shriven soul.'

'So?'

'So, I'm guessing that Jack Goodway didn't know what was happening in those last few days. I know he was visited by his priest, Father Clooney, and his wife. Perhaps he grew so confused that he lost track of who he was talking to. Who he was confessing to.'

At that moment, Alice turned to him. There was such torment in her eyes, but there were no tears, and no matching expression on her face, which remained as impassive and emotionless as before. There was silence, filled only by the rattle of hailstones against the window.

'Besides, it struck me as strange. Alice and Hazel were the closest of friends. They shared a common bond when both husbands died. But three months have passed since that time. Hazel tried to explain her silence towards Alice by claiming it would upset her to hear the news, that Alice wanted a child.'

'That part's true,' said Alice quietly.

'Surely, if the two women were so close, Hazel would have taken Alice into her confidence? After all she couldn't hide it forever. So I wondered if there was a reason why she hadn't. There was only one answer. She was carrying Jack's child.'

Then Alice started speaking in a low, flat voice that bore no trace of the horror she was describing.

'Jack told me what he'd done. Told me he'd got my closest friend pregnant. He was rambling, didn't know who he were talkin' to. Me, Father Clooney or Hazel. All I know is he kept ramblin' on about wild roses. Said as how he'd loved lyin' there in the woods an' smellin' them flowers an' how his Hazel – *his Hazel!* – told him they were her favourite. Loved the smell of 'em. In their special place. Started mumbling something about dragonflies chasin' midges. Said as how he were sorry he'd got Hazel that way, that he'd said she should get rid. He could ask his Aunty Doris, 'cos she knew about that sort of stuff. *Forgive me, Father*, he'd said. He were askin' his priest for forgiveness when he should've been askin' me. His own wife! But then he told me another time that it were his Aunty Doris who'd let him have a room in the first place at her house in Canal Street where they could . . . meet. His *Aunty Doris*. You all know what that bitch was capable of.'

She went quiet and looked at Ettie Yates, at Len Yates, at Betty Bennet.

'Oh, I know about all of you, 'cos she told me. Reckoned we'd get money out of you lot every time I dropped a hint that the spirits were comin'. She weren't bothered whatever I told you as long as I fooled you an' you coughed up. She'd no idea I were foolin' her more than any of you.' She stopped, looked at Brennan and pursed her lips.

'I told you, Sergeant, but you didn't listen, did you?'

'Told me what?'

She then stood up and walked slowly over to the dresser, to the framed photograph of her and Jack on their wedding day. She picked it up, and Brennan saw the reflection of her face in the glass, staring at the two of them from a year ago.

'You asked if anythin' valuable had been taken the night Doris breathed her last. I showed you this.'

Brennan recalled what she had said. 'You told me it was the only valuable thing you had. And it's worth nothing anyway. You weren't talking about money, were you?'

'No.'

Suddenly she raised it high above her head and brought it crashing down onto the table. Shards of glass spilled over onto the floor, and the photograph now lay torn in several places. She sat down again and stared defiantly at each of them in turn.

Hazel seemed to gasp, as if something had just struck her. 'Oh, my God!' she cried.

'Bit late to be speakin' to Him!' Mabel snorted.

Then Hazel raised a finger and stabbed it towards her one-time friend. '*You* put that stuff in the tea!'

Alice looked straight ahead, no reaction on her face.

'I lost the baby 'cos of you. You bitch!'

Before Brennan could stop her, she lifted the table and pushed it hard across the room, slamming its hard edge into Alice's stomach with such frenzied violence that she doubled up with a scream that tore through the air. Len Yates lunged towards Hazel and grabbed her arms. Betty Bennet pushed Ettie Yates out of the way and reached out towards Alice who by now was gripping her stomach and gasping for breath.

Brennan rushed from the kitchen window and saw that Hazel's arms were now firmly held. She could do no more damage. He nodded to Len Yates to thank him and gestured to the door leading to the front room.

'Keep her in there,' he said.

The grocer gave a grunt and escorted the now sobbing Hazel from the kitchen.

Betty Bennet was standing over Alice, but it was soon clear that she wasn't offering the widow any sort of comfort for her pain.

'You'll get what you deserve,' she was saying. 'An' I hope you rot in hell for what you've done. I've lost my daughter twice now.'

Brennan brushed her aside and placed an arm around Alice. He helped her stand and she breathed in deeply.

'Do you need to see a doctor?' he asked.

She shook her head. 'Just winded,' she said.

Once he was sure she could walk unaided, he took her to the front room where Hazel was sitting slumped in an armchair with Len Yates kneeling beside her. Brennan reached for a coat that was hanging from a hook on the back of the door, placed it around Alice's shoulders and swung the front door open, where Constable Corns was standing and looking like a dog just dragged from the canal. The hail was still falling, but it seemed to have lost some of its intensity.

'Take her to the station,' he said before turning back inside, 'and ask for a doctor to examine her. She's been injured. Then lock her up. We'll talk in the morning, Alice.'

Corns nodded and took hold of her arm.

There were still questions Brennan needed answering, but for now they would have to wait. He saw that the others had moved into the front room, as if the kitchen was somehow a place to avoid now.

'I don't need to keep you any longer,' he said, addressing his remarks to them all. 'I'll be getting in touch with all of you when the time's right. But for now, you'd best be making your way home. At least the hail's easing off. Best hurry before it starts up again. But remember. Everything Alice Goodway told you, every single communication from the spirits of the dead, was false. There are no spirits of the dead. The dead are dead and buried. As for their souls, well, they're in a different place now. But souls are not spirits. Forget that nonsense. Let it go.'

There were no objections, although three of them had confusion written across their faces. They had no idea what was happening, no idea that they had been used as witnesses without their knowledge, but he knew that in the coming weeks, when things became public and the trial began, they would find some comfort in the fact that they were a part of it all, and what tales they could regale their listeners with. It would be one way of rejoining the real world.

He watched them leave by the front door and then turned to the empty house. He moved through to the kitchen and made sure the back door was locked and barred, his shoes crunching on the shards of glass from the now broken wedding picture.

*

The following day, Brennan spent some time with Alice Goodway in the cells. She looked paler than last night, and her eyes had a listless look, an expression of defeat and misery on her face.

'I gather you refused to let the doctor examine you last night,' he said.

She gave no reply. Instead she glanced up at the barred window through which the sounds of the morning drifted: footsteps hurrying past, snatches of conversation, a young girl's giggle.

'Nothin' matters now,' she said sullenly. All the life had drained from her voice now. 'Nothin' mattered since that day Jack told me everythin'.'

'While he lay dying?'

'Aye.' She looked up at him, and he saw a kind of pleading in her eyes. 'We none of us know each other, do we? It's all put on, what we show to others.'

'I suppose you're right. We all keep something back, Alice. Sometimes it's just what we're thinking; other times it's what we've done. Especially if we've done something bad.'

She gave a harsh laugh. 'Well, he didn't keep anythin' back that day. Told me everythin'.'

'About Hazel Aspinall? And the baby?'

She stood and walked over to the barred window, where the topmost edge lay at pavement level. Dark shadows flitted past.

'Oh, that were the worst thing, I reckon, for me.'

It was the way she lay emphasis on the last two words that made him ask, 'What do you mean?'

She gazed upwards. There was no sign of a blue sky, or any sort of sky. Only the dark shapes moving quickly past, all of them oblivious of what lay at their feet.

'It weren't the only thing he confessed to me, Sergeant.'

'Go on, Alice.'

'He told me about other things he'd done. It were like he was openin' himself up for the first time, lettin' me see what was really there. You know, like when you see a big stone, a smooth one, like them steppin' stones you see in the woods. But when you lift one up, there's all sorts crawlin' about. None of 'em nice.'

'What else did he confess to?'

'He told me about the Yates girl.'

Brennan went cold. Eve Yates, who was made pregnant by a lover she flatly refused to name, knowing what her fearsome dad would do to him.

'He said he wanted forgiveness for that more than anythin'. More than what he'd done with Hazel. I reckon he thought he were talkin' to Father Clooney at that point, 'cos it were like he were askin' him to put in a good word wi' God. He said at least he'd given Hazel a new life growin' inside her and that had to count for summat. But then he said what he did to the Yates girl killed 'em both. He knew it were dangerous if she got pregnant – said she'd told him an' he'd promised to be careful, but he did it anyway. Said he'd begged his Aunty Doris to help him an' she'd been more than glad to, specially with Len Yates bein' a grocer an' not short of money. But all she did was kill the girl an' the one growin' inside her.' She turned back to him with fire flashing in her eyes now. 'She were an evil, lyin' bitch!'

He took a deep breath.

Jack Goodway was the one Len Yates was after.

And if the grocer had found out, if his daughter Eve had given him the name of the man responsible, it wasn't beyond the realms of possibility that Len would have choked the life out of the miner. And if he'd done that, why, he wouldn't have been around to seduce Hazel, to impregnate her . . . and Alice here wouldn't be facing a charge of murder and an appointment with the hangman.

But it would drive you mad, thinking that way.

'Is that why you allowed Len and Ettie Yates to visit you?'

She smiled. 'Aye. They were victims, weren't they? Just like me. Just like Hazel, I reckon. And I told 'em what they wanted to hear, didn't I? I just wanted to make up for what Jack did to that poor girl.'

He nodded. 'And Betty Bennet? Surely Jack wasn't the one who attacked her daughter?'

She shook her head. 'No. That were years ago. But when I was a child I used to be one of the gang who followed their Frances round, callin' her names an' mockin' the poor lass. I just wanted to give her mam some comfort 'cos of all the times I'd yelled out *Penny Gawp!* That were my guilt I was facin', not Jack's or Doris's.'

He spoke with her for over an hour, and when he was sure there was nothing more to be had from her, he left her with the advice to eat something to take the pallor from her face. Her plate of bread and butter and the mug of water lay untouched.

Now he sat facing the chief constable.

'And you say Constable Jaggery has seen fit not to turn up for his duties?'

'I think he may be ill, sir. I did order him to bring Mr Wesley down to the station while the weather was poor. He may have caught a chill.'

'Hmph!' It was clear what Captain Bell thought of that. Nevertheless, he didn't dwell on what he regarded as something between dereliction of duty and malingering. Instead, he launched into the real reason he'd called his detective sergeant into his presence. 'I was always rather dubious about that woman,' he said.

'Yes, sir,' Brennan replied, unable to bring to mind any occasion when his superior had voiced any suspicion about the young widow.

'You too had your misgivings about her spurious claims from the beginning?'

'Indeed I did, sir. Anyone claiming to have contact with the spirits of the departed should come under suspicion – of fakery, at the very least.'

Captain Bell coughed to clear his throat. 'While I accept everything you say, Sergeant – the woman was devious and fraudulent, of that there is no doubt – I cannot share your complete scepticism of the ethereal world. I have far more worldly experience than you, of course.'

'Of course, sir.'

'And having seen at first hand the mysteries of the East . . . Yes, well. Nevertheless, it was well done. As for the case against her, you will have sufficient evidence to proceed to trial?'

'I think so, sir.'

'Let's see, shall we? Tell me about your earliest suspicions. I shall be judge and jury and, on occasion, counsel for the defence.' He settled back in his chair and placed his hands together in an attitude of judicial contemplation.

'Well, sir. When I was called to the house to investigate the sending of the first letter, I immediately felt two things. One, that Alice Goodway was a fraud. Psychic mediums always are. And two, Doris Goodway, the aunt, was shamelessly taking advantage of her nephew's widow.'

'In what way?'

'Financially, sir. Taking a share of the payments deluded people made.'

'Go on.'

'Still, I was bound to investigate the letter, and I was directed to the most obvious sender, Mr Ralph Crankshaw, the local council's Inspector of Nuisances.'

Captain Bell raised a finger of objection, now in his role of defence counsel. 'It might be an idea, Sergeant, to omit this part of your testimony in court.'

'Why, sir?' Brennan asked in a show of innocence and

ignorance. He knew full well why any mention of Crankshaw and his involvement in the case might lead to revelations of a more scandalous and, as far as certain unnamed members of the town council were concerned, a more compromising nature. He thought back to what Alice had told him, about smooth stones and what lay beneath.

'Relevance, Sergeant. Mr Crankshaw, you tell me, admitted to sending the first letter but he had nothing whatsoever to do with any subsequent letter or involvement with the case. And the letter *per se* was not of a threatening nature. It isn't a crime to send relevant quotations from the Bible, now, is it?'

Brennan shrugged.

'You may move on to the second letter.'

'Yes, sir. The second letter was written by someone whose handwriting differed completely from the handwriting of the sender of the first letter.'

Captain Bell raised another finger of objection. 'It might be best if we refrain from any reference to the *first* or *second* letter. It will only confuse the jury if we haven't already mentioned the first letter, which of course we have agreed not to.'

Brennan frowned. 'So, I am not to refer to any letter?'

'Of course you are. Just don't call it the *second* letter. Call it *the letter*.'

'I see. Well, then. When Mrs Goodway received *the letter*, which was written in an untidy scrawl, it merely accused her of being a *lying bitch*. She has admitted to being the author of that letter.'

'A question here, Sergeant. Why on earth would Alice Goodway send herself another – I beg your pardon – why would she send herself a threatening letter if she had already despatched her aunt?'

'She saw it as an opportunity to divert any suspicion from herself. It sent us chasing after shadows.'

'Hmm. I'm still not clear how Alice managed to get rid of the aunt. I mean, you yourself examined the house the morning after the attack.'

Brennan acknowledged the implied criticism. 'I accept I was as fooled as anyone.'

'So how did she do it?'

'Simply by opening the kitchen window during the early hours of that morning *from the inside*, unlocking the back door so that it would appear that the killer got out that way, and then going back upstairs and taking a pillow from her own room. Then stealing into the front bedroom and suffocating her victim. There were no signs left on the pillow – I'm sure she checked for specks of blood and suchlike, but Dr Monroe tells me it's unlikely there would have been any. I myself examined the pillow in her room and found nothing untoward. The thing is, there seemed to be nothing else in the room that could have been used to carry out the suffocation. And while a murderer might bring a knife to the scene of his crime, it's daft to think he'd bring a pillow. So, the only other pillow was in the room where Alice slept. Again, I can't see a murderer sneaking into her room, sliding a pillow from beneath her head, suffocating Doris then calmly returning the pillow to a still-sleeping Alice.'

'Fair point. But why not leave it at that? Seeing off Doris Goodway should have satisfied her, should it not?'

Brennan shook his head. 'She hadn't finished what she had set out to do.'

'Which was?'

'She had already killed her aunt for allowing her husband Jack and Hazel Aspinall to have a number of secret rendez-vous at her home in Canal Street, which was being used for immoral purposes, according to information received from Mr Crank . . .'

'Ahem!'

'According to information received from Doris Goodway's neighbours, that is. But she still wished to punish Hazel, with whom Jack had been carrying on, and who was carrying Jack's child.'

'That's all well and good – in a manner of speaking – but none of this explains why Alice Goodway should begin the psychic deception in the first place. Why go through all of that if only to gain revenge on the aunt and Hazel Aspinall? Surely it would have been far easier to just, well, kill them without all the fuss?'

Brennan steepled his fingers.

'I agree, sir, but you must appreciate how devastating the news of her husband's infidelity was to her. She was a young bride, married barely a year, and according to what Hazel Aspinall told me, she desperately wanted to start a family of her own. But not only was she robbed of that by the explosion down the pit, she then discovered, from the lips of her dying and confused husband, that as a result of his affair with her best friend, he was to be a father, even though he would never live to see it. I think that tipped her over the edge of reason. She told me down in the cells when I interviewed her at greater length, that she did indeed have a dream after he had died, a dream so vivid, of her searching frantically for her husband deep underground and when she eventually found him she listened once more to his soothing words. When she awoke she stared at the bed, at the place where she had once lain with him unaware of what he was doing with another woman, and the anger she felt was so powerful she thought it would consume her. But then, as she dressed before the mirror, she had a fancy that she had seen a reflection of her dead husband. That's where the idea was born. She knew that there were those who believed in all the childish paraphernalia of the psychic world. And she knew of Mabel Aspinall's fascination with that sort of thing. She'd heard Hazel's mother-in-law talk about her visits to mediums of every description. Wouldn't it be so satisfying to make Hazel believe that she could communicate with the dead? Make her believe that there was a real danger that her husband Jack would confess his affair with Alice's best friend?

Wouldn't it be exquisite torture to tease her with the knowledge of a child as yet unborn?'

The chief constable raised his eyebrows, impressed by his sergeant's eloquence.

But Brennan hadn't finished. 'And the psychic deception also allowed her to do some good – or what she saw as good – into the bargain.'

'What possible good did she accomplish?'

'She knew her husband had done some bad things – he had brought about Eve Yates's death through his own animal lust. So when Len and Ettie Yates came to see her, Alice gave them what she thought was good news, *a message from beyond*, that she imagined would make them happy.'

'And did it?'

'Unfortunately, it only served to tip Ettie Yates over the edge. The woman is devastated now that Alice's deception has been exposed.'

'Whether she did any good or not, she is still a murderer.'

'Indeed, sir. And something else she's admitted to. Alice was very clear on who she would allow to visit her for a "sitting". Doris herself told me that she was forced to yield to Alice on this point. And, apart from Lucas Wesley, who I'll come to in a second, the ones she did choose were picked for a specific reason that trumped altruism.'

'And what was that?'

'To provide her with others who might want Doris Goodway dead. People who had had dealings with the aunt in the past. She was offering us a group of suspects who had all suffered in some way by the aunt's actions. Len and Ettie Yates had a daughter who had an abortion at Doris's hands and died as a result. Strong motive for seeking revenge, and Doris would have shared such details with Alice if only to strengthen her claims of psychic powers. Betty Bennet's daughter Frances, who was ravished when a mere child, was left not only mentally damaged by the attack. The monster also left her pregnant.'

'Good Lord!'

'In that instance, Doris's handiwork came as a blessing, I suppose. The girl was only thirteen.'

'A blessing! Nonsense! I feel sorry for the poor girl but there's absolutely no excuse for that vile practice the woman carried out. For money, Sergeant, don't forget. *She* doesn't seem to have had an altruistic bone in her body.'

'I agree, sir. The result was, of course, that Mrs Bennet's husband left the family home after having paid for Doris's services. Mrs Bennet let that slip herself. She told me he'd left because he wasn't *forkin' out any more for a backward wench.*'

Captain Bell shook his head sadly at the depth of the man's treachery, or cowardice. They were abominable vices to an ex-military man.

'You say Alice Goodway has admitted to setting these people up as potential suspects?'

'Yes, sir.'

'It's curious. A full confession. As if she's clearing all her accounts. She is of sound mind, isn't she?'

Brennan shrugged.

After a pause, the chief constable asked about Lucas Wesley.

Brennan smiled. 'A boy who hasn't grown up, sir. He harbours feelings for a girl who was his close friend when they were both children. Apparently, they lived in squalor and she was his shining light. Now grown into manhood – supposedly – he sought her out again, hoping to rekindle what he once shared with her.'

'The man sounds an obsessive.'

'That's the very word, sir. He's obsessed with Susan Corbett; he's obsessed with the supernatural. Put the two obsessions together and you have someone who much prefers the past to the present and who therefore can't form normal friendships. He was the only visitor over whom Alice Goodway had no control.'

'Then why did she agree to see him?'

'Doris Goodway. She saw him as a great source of income – string him along and he'll keep coming back for more. So when he called one evening to arrange a sitting, it was Doris who answered the door and saw a well-dressed member of the banking profession ripe and ready for fleecing. So she overruled Alice on this occasion. But he has enough experience of the psychic world to recognise a fraud when he sees one. Alice had no information about him and so his session with her was full of vague nonsense, which he saw through at once. He was, after all, looking for a girl who was alive, not dead. It angered him beyond measure when Alice told him she'd contacted her spirit.'

'So inadvertently she had garnered another suspect with a motive to kill her.'

'Precisely. But then he discovered, through an investigation agency, that Susan Corbett was indeed dead. He must then have thought, *what if Alice Goodway is genuine after all?* He tried to see her again, to persuade her to contact his beloved.'

'She refused?'

'He didn't get the chance to ask her. He has admitted he was lurking around her home and found out she was staying with Hazel. It was Wesley who was hiding in the ginnel when Alice confessed to me she was a fraud.'

'I see. He must have felt a gullible fool.'

Brennan nodded. 'When he heard what she said, it enraged him. He wanted revenge. So he gained access to Alice's house with a small pot of luminous paint and produced a portrait of Susan Corbett on Alice's bedroom wall. It terrified her, and I think it sent her a little mad. I recognised the portrait – I'd seen miniature representations of what he thought his beloved would look like in adulthood at his home.'

'Why didn't you arrest him then?'

'Because if he were the murderer, how would I prove it? He'd be charged with painting a woman's face in glowing paint. I don't even think that's a crime, is it, sir?'

'Breaking into someone's house is.'

Brennan let that one pass. According to what Alice had subsequently told him, Jaggery himself had left the back door unlocked after bringing her some coal. The chivalrous oaf.

Captain Bell stood up and went over to his window overlooking King Street. He stared down at the everyday scene below and thought for a moment. Then he said, 'Wasn't she taking a great risk? The night she gave Hazel Aspinall the poison? What was it?'

'Pennyroyal, sir. Used by her aunt to bring on a miscarriage. I suspect Alice brought the stuff with her when she moved in with her friend.'

He recalled how he had been duped into making the suggestion that she should stay with someone. All that Alice had had to do was express her fears of remaining in the house alone, and he, foolishly, had been manoeuvred into suggesting she stay with her closest friend. Where she would have ample opportunity to bring on the miscarriage.

'Last night, when everyone had left Alice's house, I looked in the kitchen dresser where Doris had kept her various concoctions. Her bag was still there, including the small bottles, with the exception of the one labelled *pennyroyal*. Alice had known I would insist on her leaving the house, so she had put the substance where she could get her hands on it without rousing our suspicions. She had already stored the stuff upstairs.'

'What a devious woman!'

'Indeed, sir.'

Had she been goading him that day when he asked her if she'd got everything she needed?

Everythin' I need. Except me crystal ball.

He looked at the chief constable's thin frame against the harsh sunlight from the window. His back was straight, his shoulders square, his bearing aloof. Then he saw his posture change as he spotted something on the street below.

'The fellow looks like a drugged elephant walking up those steps. Have you ever seen him move at *any* sort of speed, Sergeant?'

'Who's that, sir?'

'Constable Jaggery. At this time!' he said turning and indicating the clock on the far wall. 'I trust you will be issuing a reprimand?'

'Of course, sir.'

'Well. You haven't answered my question, Sergeant?'

'Which question was that, sir?'

Captain Bell shook his head. 'Wasn't Alice Goodway taking a great risk? Poisoning Mrs Aspinall and taking the poison herself?'

'She didn't take any of the poison, sir.'

'I thought you told me she had been violently sick that night?'

'That's what she told me, yes, sir. But she quite simply lied. It's impossible to disprove. Even though Mrs Yates made the tea, it was Alice who dropped the pennyroyal

346

into Hazel's cup. Nothing simpler. And it had the desired effect. It also strengthened Mrs Yates as a suspect with the opportunity to plant the poison in the tea. I suspect when the grocer's wife turned up that evening bearing gifts to persuade Alice to revisit the spirit world . . .'

The chief constable frowned. 'I am confused, Sergeant. You say Mrs Yates turned up at the house? Meaning that she was *admitted* to the house?'

'Yes, sir.' He could have bitten his tongue off. He knew what the man was implying.

'But you left a constable on duty with the strict instructions to allow no one in, did you not?'

'I did, sir.'

'Who was it?'

'Impossible to say, sir.'

'Why?'

'They did it in shifts, sir. One man on, one man off. It may well have been during a changeover. I never did get to the bottom of it. Thick as thieves, our constables.'

'An unfortunate simile, Sergeant. And an unsatisfactory reflection on your command. If this were the army . . .'

'I fully accept the blame, sir. Although I don't think Alice would have acted any differently even if she hadn't had Mrs Yates as a visitor. I reckon the whole thing was getting to her. And she wanted her revenge on Hazel. The best way was to cause her to lose the baby. It was the baby that represented not only her husband's unfaithfulness but also her friend's betrayal. Imagine if she'd seen the child born, grow up. I think Alice wanted to see her suffer. As to whether she would later have gone on to kill Hazel, I have my doubts. Her venom – her murderous venom – had largely been expended on that aunt of hers by marriage.'

'Yes, well. All things considered . . .'

He broke off. Outside, there seemed to be some sort of commotion. 'What the blazes is that?'

Brennan got up and went to the door. The racket was coming from the front desk.

'Probably one of your drunkards, Sergeant. At this time of the morning!'

'I'll see,' Brennan said, and moved quickly through the door.

He recognised the raised voices. One of them belonged to the desk sergeant. The other was Jaggery's. When he got to the station entrance, he saw several constables had rushed from the station canteen and were watching the formidable Freddie Jaggery lifting the desk sergeant with one hand, sliding him up the wall so that his legs were thrashing around to gain some invisible foothold.

'Constable Jaggery!' Brennan shouted above the din.

The constables all took a step back, torn between watching the spectacle and fearful of Brennan's wrath. When the chief constable himself appeared behind the detective sergeant they realised that a move back into the canteen might be the safer option.

'Put him down, you lumbering oaf!' Captain Bell's voice

belied his skeletal frame. It boomed along the corridor and caused an enraged Jaggery to drop the man he had been slowly throttling. 'What is the meaning of this brutality?'

If Constable Jaggery had felt cowed by the chief constable's outrage he didn't show it. Instead he turned his violent glare onto Detective Sergeant Brennan.

'I've just been down to the cells,' he said, his voice menacingly low now, and somehow melancholy, like the growl of a wounded beast. 'An' she's dead.'

'What?' Brennan was already moving towards the section of corridor that led down to the cells.

'Alice Goodway!' yelled Jaggery. 'Lying down there in her own blood.'

'Pull yourself together, man!' Captain Bell snapped.

'I've just been down yonder, see how she were doin'.' He jabbed an accusatory finger at the desk sergeant who was even now trying to recapture his breath. 'An' this fool should've had a man down there, but there was no bugger down there when I went down.'

Captain Bell set his face in stone and brushed past, following Sergeant Brennan down the steps leading to the cells. When he got there, he saw the cell door open and Brennan kneeling beside the lifeless body of Alice Goodway.

'Is she dead?' he asked.

Brennan nodded.

'How?'

His sergeant stood up and took a step back. Bell gave a short gasp as he saw a pool of blood beside the body.

'She's taken her own life?' he asked, scanning the woman's body for any signs of incisions.

'Yes, sir.'

Brennan pointed to the deep cuts across her wrists. By her side, he caught sight of something glinting in the half-light of the cell. He reached down and picked up a bloodstained shard of glass.

'What is it?' Captain Bell asked.

'I'd guess this is the result of something that happened last night.'

He told him of the way Hazel Aspinall had rammed the table into Alice's stomach.

'She must have hidden it on her person last night when Hazel Aspinall attacked her.'

'But what is it?'

'It's a piece of glass, sir. And if I'm not mistaken it's from the framed photograph of their wedding day.' He gazed down at the lifeless form. Perhaps the piece of glass was simply the first thing she could grab hold of, something to store away for later. Or maybe she saw the fitness, the symbolism, of such a weapon. Broken glass from a broken image.

He gently placed the shard of glass on a small table.

Bell suddenly became brisk and official, ordering them to leave the body in place and the cell door locked until the doctor could be brought round to confirm the death.

Back at the front desk he gave Jaggery, who was now sitting behind the desk leaning forward, a ferocious look and whispered something to Brennan. Brennan nodded and said, 'Leave it to me, sir.'

He approached the still-glowering Jaggery and said, 'Constable. You need some fresh air. Follow me.'

At first it seemed that Jaggery wouldn't budge, but he eventually sighed heavily and followed Brennan out of the station.

EPILOGUE

The Crofter's Arms was getting busy. It was market day and the farmers and their hands were calling in and sneaking a crafty pint before returning to their wagons on the market square. The whole of Market Street was louder than usual, what with the sounds of animals and the trundle of wagons and the raucous good humour that took little notice of the frost on the ground. The smells, too, were strong, reeking – the sweat of steaming cattle, the all-pervasive stench of manure, the damp earthiness of hay and straw and soil-caked potatoes – and Brennan breathed in as deeply as if he were standing on the pier at Blackpool. He said nothing as the two of them made their way into the pub.

'Why were you late into work this morning?' Brennan asked after they'd they settled in their usual corner. There was no hint of recrimination in his voice.

'I weren't goin' to come in at all,' said Jaggery. 'Not after last night, when I'd no sooner got Wesley into his cell when down comes Cornsy with Alice Goodway. Couldn't believe it when he told me what had happened.'

Brennan gave a small sigh. 'I knew I had to arrest Alice, and I didn't want you to be the one to escort her down to the station. You've had a soft spot for Alice Goodway since we first met her, haven't you, Constable?'

Jaggery gazed into his frothing pint. 'I felt sorry for the lass.'

'There's more to it than that.'

Jaggery took a long gulp and shook his head. 'She reminded me, that's all.'

'Of who?'

He took a deep breath and wiped his mouth of froth. 'Don't matter now though. Were a long time ago.'

'Tell me.'

A mistiness seemed to fill the big man's eyes. He looked up from his glass and fixed on something through the window opposite: a small cloud high in an otherwise clear blue sky. When he finally spoke, his voice was low, gentle, and sadder than anything Brennan had ever heard from the man's lips.

'Me an' the missus, we 'ad a wee girl once. Long time before our Mark came along.'

This was news to Brennan. He had known Jaggery quite a few years and had no idea he had once had a daughter.

'What happened?'

'Usual. Little lass died when she were three. Measles did for her. Bloody suffered an' all.'

'I'm sorry.'

'Aye. Thing is, when I saw Alice Goodway that first time, well, it were like seein' our Mary all growed up.'

Brennan recalled that first time they'd visited the house, the way Jaggery stared long and hard at the young widow.

'Hell of a feelin', Sergeant. Just like that dopplething Wesley told us about when you interviewed him. She had the same nose, the same eyes, everythin'.'

Brennan thought for a while then remembered what the bank clerk had said about, what was it? Doppelgangers. Doubles.

'I went home and told the missus. She reckoned I were bein' daft. *There's no tellin' how the lass would've turned out*, she said.

It explained a lot. Why his constable had become so protective of the young widow.

'An' I remember, that day she got the second letter, she put her hand on mine. Felt as thin as a twig. My little lass did t'same. Just before she . . .' He coughed loudly to clear his throat then added, 'Anyroad, I even thought of askin' Alice Goodway to . . .' Jaggery drained his glass to avoid embarrassment.

'Help you contact your daughter?'

'Daft, Sergeant, eh? Big bugger like me believin' stuff like that. But I reckon if I'd asked her, an' she'd done it

– you know, got in touch with the lass - well, I'd have been convinced.'

'Because it would have been a comfort, Freddie. And then your missus would've got involved. But it wouldn't have been real, would it? You know now what a fraud she was. So where would that have left you?'

But Jaggery said nothing, giving his attention instead to a couple of young farm labourers who were pushing each other, apparently unused to the beer they were drinking.

Brennan placed a hand on Jaggery's arm, felt the powerful muscles beneath the sleeve. He knew exactly what the big man had been thinking.

'But apart from that, I just thought, she's got nobody, Sergeant. Husband gone. Mam and dad gone. An' that bloody aunt!' He shook his head. 'I know she shouldn't have done what she did. But I got to wonderin', if that'd been my lass treated like that by a swine of a husband, well, I'd be havin' a word with meladdo. No bother.'

A group of farm-hands burst into laughter at the far end of the bar.

Jaggery turned to Brennan, the ghost of a smile on his face. 'I suppose you think I'm a big soft sod, Sergeant?'

But Brennan shook his head and stood up, nodding to Jaggery's empty glass. 'I think we've time for another, Constable. What do you think?'